PRIVILEGE 900

LYNLEE BURTON

authorHOUSE®

AuthorHouse™
1663 Liberty Drive
Bloomington, IN 47403
www.authorhouse.com
Phone: 1 (800) 839-8640

Published by AuthorHouse 07/31/2018

ISBN: 978-1-4969-2072-0 (sc)
ISBN: 978-1-4969-2071-3 (e)

Print information available on the last page.

Any people depicted in stock imagery provided by Thinkstock are models,
and such images are being used for illustrative purposes only.
Certain stock imagery © Thinkstock.

This book is printed on acid-free paper.

Because of the dynamic nature of the Internet, any web addresses or
links contained in this book may have changed since publication and
may no longer be valid. The views expressed in this work are solely those
of the author and do not necessarily reflect the views of the publisher,
and the publisher hereby disclaims any responsibility for them.

To Knuckles With Love

FOREWORD

Kathy St. John-Cocheran jostled a pizza carton topped with a day old newspaper and her current mail as she opened the door to her El Cerrito home. She slipped off her shoes and gently closed the door with her heel. She placed her bundles upon the table by the front door. Her feet and legs felt twice her forty-three years. Kathy triggered her answering machine and played the waiting messages. Among the host of calls, was one from her husband. Pete explained that he had been delayed in Buffalo and would not be home until late the next evening. Kathy smiled and shook her head. "How did I know!" she said to the empty air. She felt weary from her long day and considered how it would be to feel comfortable. She picked up her shoes and bid her fatigued body to travel the long hallway to the master bedroom. Kathy changed into her lounging pajamas and corralled her shoulder length blond hair into a banana clip.

The silky fabric of her pajamas caressed her body and rejuvenated her as she returned to the living room. She grabbed up her parcels and eased herself into a cross-legged position in her recliner. Kathy sifted through her mail, tossed aside the junk mail, and concentrated on the four remaining envelopes.

She spied the envelope from Associated Partner Group. A quick push of her letter opener sliced open the top of the envelope. The content was what she expected, her annual check for $25,000.00. Kathy had received this check for some twenty years. Each time she held this check in her hands, familiar feelings of guilt and culpability surfaced. She fanned her face with the check as she thought back to her days at Columns. A child's face formed in her mind's eye. It was the face of Zachary Pendrake.

Kathy remembered all too clearly the pain she felt at the separation between herself and the boy. Still, more than twenty years later the memories stabbed at her heart. She dropped her head and experienced the familiar anguish buried in her soul. The futility of feelings of grief did not matter to her. The events of that time in her life had affected her deeply.

Reminiscence of the little boy had stained her memory with sadness. She so very often wondered what had happened to Zachary. Kathy was aware that knowing what had become of him did not alter reality. Zachary Pendrake's fate was out of her hands. Once again, as she had become accustomed to doing, Kathy allowed reason to gain control. She took a deep breath to push aside the melancholy affecting her.

She set the mail aside and began to munch on a slice of now cold pizza. She folded flat the San Francisco Chronicle, Sunday edition. Front-page center grabbed her attention as she read the headline. "Chronicle prints the truth about Campo murder." The article was a damning criticism as the author cited the misleading information regarding the Campo murder case as reported by the Tribune. A familiar contributor, Steven

Morris, wrote the story. Morris, a well known journalist had a reputation for his caustic jabs at his competitor. His sources were always 'unnamed' and his scathing attacks were frequent.

The line-by-line description of the actual cause of death combined with new facts surrounding the death was editorialized in all of their gory glory. Kathy read the piece and began to recognize the similarities between events in her own memory and the depiction in the Chronicle. Dizziness washed over her. Kathy's hands trembled. She could feel her heart throbbing wildly in her chest. She laid the paper on her lap and rocked her head onto the headrest. She breathed deeply and attempted to slow her pounding heart. Slowly she regained her composure. She read the last part of the piece that discussed the investigation. The names of the detectives working the case were prominent throughout the article. Kathy picked up the telephone and began to dial the number for the police. The phone began to ring as she spied the check lying on the table. She hung up and paced the floor. Kathy wondered for years why the Pendrake's had been willing to pay her this stipend. It was a great deal of money solely for being quiet about what went on at Columns.

She pondered her options throughout an incredibly long sleepless night. In her mind, Kathy relived a culmination of past experiences with the Pendrake clan. She revisited tormenting events and memories two decades past. The familiar nagging questions once again rear their head. What Zachary's life may have been like, had she been allowed to raise him. These questions had plagued her for over two decades. Now the controversy uppermost in her mind was, what has Zachary become?

The new day's light was her only companion at the end of her hours of wavering. Kathy reasoned to herself, that should she call the police, she would have to identify herself. That would be her only option for attention to be paid to the information she had to offer. She re-read the heart wrenching account of the murder as diagrammed by the Chronicle. Kathy's years of wonderment regarding Zachary's fate had ended. She knew without a doubt, what had happened to Zachary Pendrake. Kathy St. John-Cocheran decided to make the call. The telephone was picked up on the third ring and a weary sounding voice answered, "Detective Hall."

Kathy cleared her throat and said, "Yes, I understand that you're working on the Campo murder." Hall's voice paused, "Yes, that's right."

Kathy took a sip of her coffee to chase the dryness from her throat and said, "I think I know who killed JoAnn Campo."

CHAPTER 1
Denise Haver

Allison Dean maneuvered her car into a narrow parking space on Windover Street. It was early enough that the sun's morning light had not yet brightened the horizon. Turning off the ignition, she sat quietly with her eyes closed, as disturbing visions of her husband Will raced through her mind. The time spent in reflection was all too brief as a police officer approached her vehicle. Allison rolled down the window and showed her press pass to the police officer. "Dean of the Sun Times," she said. He offered her a quick nod and re-joined the police-line controlling the crowds of people milling about the crime scene barrier.

Dismissing her body's need for sleep, Allison pushed her fatigue and bitter feelings aside. She rubbed her dry, stinging eyes with the palms of her hands and drew in a long breath of the cool pre-dawn air. Cradled in the bucket seat of her car, she craned her neck and took in all of the up-roar taking place on the street. Considering that it was just short of 4:30

1

in the morning, this street was a busy place. Police swarmed in protective patterns maintaining control of interested onlookers. With one last breath of fresh air, Allison pushed her weary body from her sports car. She pulled her camera case from the back seat and settled the shoulder strap firmly into position. She hooked the press pass to her lapel as she threaded her way through the emergency vehicles. Fire trucks, ambulances and other official vehicles were parked at skewed angles preventing non-essential cars from driving by the scene. The wavering blue lights on the police cars drew throngs of curious people, while at the same time warning them to stay back. Encircling the entry of a large brownstone was the telltale crime scene ribbon used to block entry. The words, gruesome and bloody were voiced by her editor during his initial call to her. His description rattled in her ears as she approached the heart of the scene. The everyday person would use such language to speak of murder scenes: however, these descriptions are not usually used by case hardened detectives working the case: nor were these words commonly used by her editor, John Hughes. For some reason, the nature of this particular crime seemed to carry a special weight and concern.

Allison began looking for Captain Sanders of Robbery-Homicide. "Allie, hey Allie. Over here!" The din of noise provided by both the constant chatter of the crowd and the reverberation of the radios, in the official cars, made it difficult for her to hear her name being called. When she did see her contact for the crime, she approached and said, "Hi Sandy, what's the story?" The large, balding man cocked an eye toward her and admonished, "It's Captain Sanders, please, Allie."

The long-standing fight-play banter they normally engaged in had begun. Allison returned a feigned angry expression and responded, "Captain Sanders, please, it's Allison, not Allie."

Allison noticed that Sandy's demeanor had suddenly and dramatically changed. He looked at her curiously and said, "You look tired Allie. "Bad night?"

Allison waved his concern off with both hands. "Nothing new, S. O. S. D. D. He looked at her curiously and said, "Same old shit, different day, means more problems with Will, I'd guess."

"No comment," she said as she looked around the crowd. "Ms Dean," he countered, "that's supposed to be my line." After his last comment, he looked at her and his facial coloring turned pallid. He took a deep breath and said, "Business time Allie."

She peered at her friend's sudden darkness. He guided her by the elbow saying, "Let's talk where it isn't so noisy."

All at once, an expression of dread shrouded his face. "Sandy, are you all right? I've never seen you like this." As she tried to continue, he stopped her in mid-sentence by holding out a hand that was almost as large as Allison's head. "Allie kid, have you had your breakfast?"

Befuddled by the question, Allison responded, "No, Sandy, why?"

He motioned for her to sit down on the steps of a neighboring building. He rubbed his hands together nervously. "This is going to be a tough one kiddo! I wouldn't have called you in on this murder, but the district attorney insisted we need your eye on this job. After all, this is an election year."

"But Sandy, I", Allison objected.

Sandy once again cut her short with an open-palmed halt signal. "Just hear me out before you go up there Allie. There is some, um, what most people would call kinky stuff in this place. First, we know you can keep your mouth shut, secondly, you and your camera seem to bring out the small details. You see the hidden stuff that others, who aren't as sharp as you, seem to miss. But I'm afraid that we have a real sicko running around this town. We're going to need the best crime scene photos we can get."

Allison looked as Sandy with searching eyes. "I've seen bloody crime scenes before, Sandy. Why are you so concerned about this one?"

Sandy's expression was a testimonial to his misery. It was an expression which Allison had a difficult time understanding. The case-hardened detective seemed squeamish about this homicide. Captain Sanders took a deep breath and began. "Well, first of all, the victim has been up there for at least a few days, so the scene isn't exactly fresh. We couldn't open a window because of the possibility of contaminating the scene. But, that's only part of the problem. To be straight up with you, Allie, I don't know how to prepare you for what you're about to see." Sanders hesitated and drew in another long slow breath before speaking. "Believe me Allie, I want you to take your time. But if you need to take a break, you just go for it girl!"

Allison opened her camera bag and searched through the bottles, film canisters and other supplies for her oil of winter green. Tapping on her shoulder, Sandy said, "Looking for some of this stuff? She looked up to see him holding out a jar of the odor-guarding gel. "Thank you, Sandy; I have a jar in here somewhere. I don't want to take yours." Sandy smiled weakly and said, "I have more and you may need an extra jar!" She gave an exaggerated eyeball roll to communicate that she understood the comment and plucked the jar from his hand.

Following Sandy, Allison made her way through the crowd. They walked up the stairs of the brownstone. He lifted the crime scene ribbon for Allison to slide under. "Case information for the file," he began. "Address, 921 Windover Street. Apartment number, 217. Victim, Denise Haver. Age, twenty- three. The case number will be: CPD-1994-H992."

Prior to the duo reaching the door of Ms. Haver's domain, the thick and sweetly putrid odor of decay assailed their nostrils. Allison opened her jar and applied a generous amount of the wintergreen to her nose and upper lip. "Whew! This smell is so hot and heavy. And yet it just seems to hang in the air," she said as a shiver jolted through her. "I don't know how any human being could get used to it."

"Yeah," Sandy replied. "It takes a damned morbid person to be a medical examiner or mortician!"

Allison nodded in mock amusement. Levity or not levity, the humor did nothing to lessen the smell. She snapped her light bar into place and returned the joke, "Or a crime scene photographer, right?" Sandy gave her his familiar, "I agree with you nodding wink."

Criss-crossing the door to apartment 217, was the same barrier tape. No admittance and crime scene it read, in bold black on yellow. Allison opened her bag and loaded her camera with fresh film. She peeked around the doorway to visualize the light quality in the darkened room. The full impact of the odor slapped her in the face, she wrinkled her nose and her squinted eyes began to water. She turned and looked directly at Sandy. She felt her stomach turn as she applied more gel to her upper lip. As she collected herself, Allison dabbed at her eyes with a tissue and gave Sandy a look of complete agreement. This was indeed, going to be a tough job.

Her light bar fully illuminated, Allison moved into the doorway and began taking pictures of the surroundings. With each step, she snapped one frame after another. She followed a precise pattern, a practiced method that would provide not simply pictures, but a sense of being on the scene. This strategy seemed to provide more clues for detectives. District Attorney's swore by Allison's method: the results worked to gain the desired hostility from juries. Allison was a prosecutor's delight and a defense attorney's terror.

Allison had a habit of talking either to herself or to others in the room during these shoots. The conversations, no, matter how mindless, helped to keep her mind off of her grizzly task. Somehow, she felt she could distance herself as long as there was dialogue taking place. The furnishings in the living room were a mish-mash of what Allison referred to as early garage sale style. The disheveled living room clearly showed that a violent struggle had taken place. She looked at Sandy and said, "Looks like she really fought her attacker. Any ideas?"

Sandy pulled his eyes up from the pattern on his oxblood wing- tip shoes and said, "You mean the perp?" No, but we'll find him. It may take some time, but sooner or later, we'll get him." Sandy had never seemed so concerned for Allison before.

She was a bit surprised to see him stay within a few steps of her. Every nook and cranny in the apartment was captured on the film in her camera. She focused on broken furniture and papers scattered liberally about the floor.

"How'd you find her?" asked Allison.

"Neighbors called in about the smell," replied Sandy. "Said they hadn't seen Ms. Haver for a while"

"Witnesses," asked Allison as she clicked another frame.

"None that are talking. You know how people are about involvement," he replied as he scratched at a spot on his tie.

Allison lowered the camera to her waist and delivered a sideways look at Sandy. "With all this should struggled, there had to be some noise! Didn't anyone complain or become concerned about it?"

He returned her look with a knowing gaze. "The neighbors that we've talked to have told us that they were used to a lot of noise coming from this apartment."

Confused, Allison said, "But, but just look around. She must have screamed or something."

Sandy drew in a long breath as he rotated his chin upward. "You'll understand by the time you're finished with this job."

Allison moved from room to room. She expended as much film, as necessary to catalog the scene. So far, although the rooms were torn asunder, there were no visible bloodstains. Allison moved into the hallway and focused tightly upon scratch marks on the white walls. There were three gouges that were deep in the beginning and lessened close to the bedroom.

Allison spied a discoloration in the middle of the center scratch and moved the section into the center of the frame. As she snapped the photo, she realized that the groove held prisoner within its borders, a fragment of red fingernail.

The sheet rocked walls showed signs of denting and scraping. The damage was undoubtedly caused by the struggle the victim put up to save her life. Allison turned off her light bar. "Sandy, I've gotta' get some air. Just give me a few minutes. Sanders offered a quick nod toward the door."

Allison emerged on to the stoop of the building and struggled to clear her head from, the disgusting odors. The team from the lab stood impatiently outside waiting for the shoot to be completed. Officials from the various departments were walking by her. They turned their heads in the direction of the smell, directly at her. The ominous fragrance had penetrated her clothing and that combined with the glare of those waiting made it difficult for her to relax. She sat on the steps and leaned back against the stairs with her elbows supporting the weight of her upper torso. Shortly, her aspirations of gathering herself failed. She gave up on her short-lived break and returned to apartment 217.

Allison moved her equipment into the bathroom. She followed her full coverage pattern of shots. As he stood behind her, Sandy reached into his pocket and pulled out a ballpoint pen. He inserted the pen into the curtain ring and slid back the partially closed vivid red drape. He exposed the entire bathtub and surrounding walls without touching the curtain. She snapped frame after frame of blood-spatters and cast off blood drops on the tub surround. Encircling the tub drain was what appeared to be dried watery blood mixed with a few what appeared to be pubic hairs. The black tiled floor revealed evaporated wipe marks. The killer had cleaned a telling trail that led form the next room into the shower.

Allison took great pains not to disturb any of the accessories in the bathroom. She focused tightly upon the dried lather marks on the soap bar. A neatly folded facecloth lay on the corner of the tub. The cloth was pleated in a unique triple fold pleating fashion; it too was photographed from all angles possible. When satisfied that the entire room had been documented, she turned to Sandy, swallowed hard and said, "Next."

The grimace on Captain Sander's face, told her what was forthcoming. Her next task would be to photograph the victim. This was always, the foul part of the job. Allison knew that she had to capture Denise Haver's body where life had left her. Catching the nature of this crime meant covering all of the specific detail she could amplify. Taking a deep breath against the winter green gel, Allison turned into the doorway of the bedroom. She began, once again, to release her frames. The instant she was in the room her eyes fixated upon writing on the wall. Above Denise Haver's bed, were the words scripted in blood. The letters were strangely proportionate. The exacting handwriting read, "I AM MY MIDDLE NAME"

Allison talked not only to Sandy, but also into her tape recorder. She was surprised at the dramatic decorating reversals from the living area to the bedroom. The sleeping quarters of Ms. Haver were lavishly decorated in bright orange-reds, deepest blacks and vivid white. The stark white walls were liberally adorned with depictions of sadistic sexual encounters. Each illustration was bordered in broad and ornate frames coated in black lacquer. The shiny black, of the picture frames matched the room's furnishings. A metal bar, tightly attached to the headboard held mute testimony to the disciplines witnessed by the walls of the chamber. Above the headboard, was a large print depicting a mass group of individuals midst the practice of bestiality.

Allison re-loaded her camera and looked at Sandy as he stood resting his shoulder against the doorframe. "I thought you said the killer was a real weirdo!" sputtered Allison.

"Nobody deserves to die like this Allie. No matter what their choice of life style," he sullenly responded.

Feeling contemplative and a bit small for her comment, Allison waited while her camera cycled in fresh film and said, "True Sandy, very true."

Any absence of bodily fluids in the other rooms of the apartment was made up for in the bedroom. It was obvious that the violence that had taken place in the other rooms, had reached a deadly climax in the bedroom. Dried blood spatters and sprays were everywhere on the chalk white walls. The black carpeting was rigid with timed hardened plasma. Bright red satin sheets were partially pulled from the king sized bed. "The furniture stood as spattered dark sentinels, unable to speak their saga. The only telling evidence of the location of the body was a lifeless gray hand seemingly suspended in mid air. The hand, intertwined in a tangled blood sodden satin sheet, seemed to beckon the onlookers to her air. The ripped and torn red polished fingernails had dry tracings of blood that had run down her slender fingers and pooled onto the bed. Among the blood splatters, sprays, and pools sheltered on shredded linen, were a mixture of sex toys. Whips and other pain-pleasuring devices were liberally scattered throughout the room Allison moved around the bed, carefully placing her steps to avoid disturbing anything that could be construed as evidence. Sandy's voice blurted out startling Allison. She snapped her head upward to see Sandy waving his hands gesturing for her to stop. He then turned and shouted into the living room, "Franklin, get Mack in here to put the blanket back the way he found it."

Allison took the time to once again recover her composure. She understood that the initial pictures needed to be just as the investigating officer had found the scene. She watched as the officer carefully picked up a full size black satin comforter from the foot of the bed. He carefully placed it over the remains of Denise Haver. His duty met, Mack hastily made an exit covering his nostrils and mouth saying, "It's all yours."

At the far corner of the bed, Allison turned and focused upon the black cover. Only fragments of the hidden body were available for view. When every possible angle had been photographed, Sandy carefully removed the covering and exposed Denise Haver. A sudden wave of familiarity struck Allison instantly. She shook her head to clear her spiraling mind.

The full view of the butchery caught Allison by surprise. Sickened, Allison whirled away from the sight of the body and retreated to her camera case to get a plastic bag. She opened the bag and vomited, then gasped for breath. Sandy had watched her hasty exit and in rapid steps, stood next to her. He braced her trembling body and attempted to reassure her.

"I know kid, it's a bad one. I tried to prepare you." Sandy cupped Allison's chin and gently directed her face upwards. "Allie, I really need you on this one. " He then looked in the direction of the corpse and said, "She needs you too! Do you think you can keep it together long enough to finish?"

Allison nodded as she wiped her mouth and said, "Yeah Sandy, just give me a few minutes to get it back together. There's just something about her. Something I can't put my finger on. Allison paused for a moment and reflected upon the earlier conversation and said, "Sandy, you're so right, this is the worst that I have ever seen."

"Remember," he intoned, "I'm right here with you."

Allison settled herself by taking even breaths and closing her eyes to settle her heartbeat. The two walked back into the bedroom and the shoot continued. It was difficult for her not to rush her way through the procedures. This time Allison was quiet. She gulped air through clenched teeth for fear of retching again.

Denise Haver was lying face up on the floor. Her remains filled the space between the bed and the wall just below the bloody words. Her legs were bent at the knees. The wall and bed were supporting each joint. The white marble-like skin on her knees was contrasted by the purple lividity in her feet and ankles. Her right hand lay close to her side by her hip. A large smudge of blood colored her abdominal area. On her wrist was one locked cylinder of a pair of handcuffs. The other cylinder was hidden by her body. Her breasts were carved in circular incisions, which rotated clockwise to the nipples. Her left nipple had been completely removed. There were dried discharges of blood that had emanated from her nose, mouth and ears. Massive bruising around her neck was patterned in one large handprint. Denise's sky blue, dilated eyes appeared owlish. They stared flatly upward as if to watch the path her soul had taken. The left side of her skull was misshapen and crushed. Shocks of long platinum hair lay in chaos, mired with dried blood. The torso of the body had been cut in the lower abdomen from hipbone to hipbone. The invasion of the body cavity had permitted the victim's entrails an avenue of exit from her body. The escaped organs girdled the pubic area and provided a ghoulish cover to the sexual outer structure of her body.

Allison attached her macro lens to focus tightly upon each area of Denise Haver's remains. The head to toe macro shots would document the actual size of the victim. It was then that she realized that the large blood smear on her stomach was actually a footprint. She felt another twinge of nausea as she realized the killer had stood on the body to write the bloody words on the wall.

At long last, she pressed the button on her last frame. She turned and immediately headed for the hallway. Her face felt cold and clammy to the touch and she was sure that she looked ashen. Once outside, Allison allowed her body to slump with the fatigue she felt. "Okay Sandy, that'll be it. You can let the lab crew in now."

The coroner's officials brushed past as Sandy escorted Allison to her car. The imposing detective held out a halting signal to the masses of news hounds pushing in toward Allison. Questions flew at her from every direction. Questions she knew she couldn't answer, even if she had the strength and wanted to answer them.

Sandy opened her door and watched as Allison slid into the driver's seat and closed the door. Sandy gently knocked on the window. "Allie, how long will it be till we get the prints back?" She lowered the window and looked thoughtful for a moment before answering. Allison shook her head slowly trying to shake off the vision of the slaughter she had just witnessed. "I'll have them processed as soon as I get back; I should have them for you by 2:00 this afternoon. Sandy, when you get them and you see which enlargements you will need, just give me a call. I'll get them to you as soon as I can."

Captain Sanders peered down into her face, with an expression of concern. "Thanks kiddo, I'll let them know," then added, "you gonna' be okay?"

Allison's eyes hurt from the strain she had just endured. She turned her head up to look back into Sandy's piercing green eyes. "I hope you get this guy, really quick!" She patted Sandy's hand and said, "I'm okay, just really tired. Don't worry about me, guy."

Allison pushed herself back into the bucket seat and stretched her arms out before starting her car. Regardless of what she'd said to Sandy, she felt weak and ill. She watched him vanish into the maze of people, she tried to get the nausea to leave her before she drove back to the Sun Times.

14

She was just starting to pull out of the parking place when the sounds of sobbing caught her attention. She turned her head in the direction of the crying. A note-taking detective was talking to a young woman. Allison noted her appearance. The wailing woman was dressed provocatively. The short black leather skirt, matching halter-top and studded leather collar struck Allison as being in keeping with Denise Haver's apparent life style. The woman's feet wobbled in spiked heels as she wept uncontrollably into her hands. Flaming curls of red hair fell across her shoulders and face. Just as Allison pulled clear of the parking spot she heard the red head say to the plain-clothes officer, "Vixen, yes that's right. But I called her Vicki."

Allison left the scene on Windover Street. She was more than relieved that this part of the job was done. The light of day seemed to diminish the dark feelings pressing upon her. The infirmity she felt in the pit of her stomach was waning. The glittering Chicago morning seemed to be the messenger of spring. Surely, she thought to herself, cataloguing the stills would be an easier task than what she had just endured.

Upon her arrival to the Times, Allison turned in her film to the lab for development. She found herself pacing the floors as a remedy for the waking nightmares. Each time she tried to rest, her mind filled with visions of Denise Haver's body. Feelings of familiarity pressed upon her. Her heart felt like a grape being crushed by a boulder. The victims' eyes with their empty gaze seemed to permeate deeply to the under surface of Allison's soul. She paced in circles until the first batch was delivered to her desk. The workers in the lab knew their business well. Each roll was developed in the order taken. The process of labeling and arranging them into chronological order was a simple, almost mindless task. As Allison filtered through the photos, the inter officer courier wheeled his cart by her desk. He dropped a file into her basket. "Haver obit," he said as he moved on.

Allison opened the file and read the vital statistics data regarding the crime article which awaited writing. Suddenly the reasons for the nagging feelings of familiarity made sense. Denise Haver was Denise Park and known as DeeCee to Allison as well as other friends. However, the dead woman was so far removed from the DeeCee of memory that she was virtually unrecognizable. Allison dropped into her chair and rested her forehead on crossed arms as grief surfaced and enveloped her. "Oh my God DeeCee," she said out loud, "what happened to you?" As the initial shock ebbed, anger grew within her. An anger and a resolve engulfed her body to the depths of her soul. "I'll find out. I'll find out who did this to you, I promise," declared Allison.

The normally simple work took on ominous undercurrents. Preparing the photographs for the murder book presentation exacted a toll upon her. She cried openly as she placed each picture into the record. As hard as she tried, it wasn't possible for her to maintain the objectivity as she had always had in the past. To Allison, the photos did not contain sights of a nameless, voiceless victim. This woman lived and breathed, felt joy and sorrow. She had been a human being. She was Denise Haver; she was DeeCee and not simply a number on a homicide report. Viewing what was left of her caused Allison to empathize with the agony she must have endured in her last few hours of life on this earth. Allison's rage and indignation grew.

Placing the final macro shots into the album of horrors, Allison noticed some peculiarities she had not seen at the time of the shoot. The first macro of the abdominal wound showed tracings of pencil type lines. They were surrounded by red markings that ended just outside of the point of disembowelment. The second oddity was discovered in the photo of Denise's feet. Allison's attention was drawn to the inner left ankle of the corpse. She pulled her desk lamp close over her magnifying lens. The enlarged area was difficult to decipher. However, with close scrutiny she could see a tattoo. The design was almost obliterated by the purple lividity. Allison concentrated and traced the outline of each letter and when completed she saw the word, 'VIXEN' adorned upon Denise Haver's ankle.

CHAPTER 2
The birth of infamy

Throughout her childhood, Adelle Coolige had been delicate in both body and mind. The tirades and violent tantrums over the most insignificant pain or discomfort engendered anger and frustration on the part of her mother. Nell, the matriarch of the family, surrounded herself with women whom she considered women of substance. She busied herself with social functions and civic duties. Nell viewed her daughter with scorn and frequently described to Adelle, the dismal future awaiting her.

Nell sought the marriage of Adelle to virtually any man. Thus, the only correct decision Adelle had made in the eyes of her mother, was to marry a wealthy businessman named Norman Pendrake. The fact that he was twenty years Adelle's senior, held no concern on the part of Nell. The whispers and controversy surrounding the powerful prospect never made their way to the ears of Adelle. Nell the socialite desired very much to be shed of the stigma of having a child whose frailties landed her into hospital after psychiatric hospital. Likewise,

Adelle was convinced that joining with Norman would provide a conduit to leave her oppressed up bringing far behind.

The ceremony was brief and in the privacy of a judges chamber. Absent was the pomp and circumstance, which customarily accompany such events, surrounding the wealthy and elite. Adelle envisioned her life way from, the hounding of Nell and found the arrangement acceptable.

Adelle married and retired from life. She left behind any obstacles that accompany a beating heart, seeing eyes and a lust for even the slightest of attainment. She exchanged everything she could have become or any dream she may have dreamt. Her perceived reward was financial security and the protection of the large secluded home, aptly named Columns Manor. It all seemed so perfect and away to find a safe haven from Nell.

Her wedding night was filled with pain and anguish as her new husband took possession of her body. The torture of her first sexual encounter was so intense that Adelle faded into her secret universe. A realm where any form of punishment was nonexistent, let alone the brutality of his assault on her.

Adelle spent the majority of her time sequestered in her two-room domicile. She prayed that her monster of a husband would never return. Sleepless nights were spent, agonizing at every noise she heard. She remained wide-eyed most of each night until exhaustion finally closed her eyes to sleep. Adelle thought it was the constant feelings of fear that caused her to be ill as the morning's light reached her bedroom. She could barely focus on Molly, the cook the day that the server said, "Ms. Pendrake, I do believe you're gonna' have a baby." Confused and frightened, Adelle didn't know what to think or do. "Have a baby," she muttered to herself. Fear gripped her instantly as her mother's voice thundered through her mind. Adelle remembered all too well her mother leaning over her and screaming, "You weren't worth the pain I had to go through to bring you into this world. Just look at what you have done to me!"

The distant and vacant expression on Adelle's face evoked a worried comment from Molly, "You should be very happy Mrs. Pendrake." She watched as Molly gathered the breakfast trays and tried to assimilate the happiness part of Molly's remark. "I'm sure Mr. Pendrake will be happy with the news." Adelle stopped her as she was leaving the room, "Yes," said Adelle, "Mr. Pendrake should know. Can you tell him for me?" The servant seemed stunned by the request and offered, "But Mrs. you should be the one to tell the Mr. about this. He will be very happy. I will, however, let Mr. Geyher know of your request to see the Mr." With that statement, she vanished through the double doors. A mixture of fear and nervousness coursed through her body.

Adelle's precarious levels of self-esteem withered to its deepest point when she informed her husband of two months of her pregnancy. Norman's feelings on the matter were communicated by an open-handed slap across the face of Adelle. The power of the blow spun her completely around and landed her onto the plush carpeting. Rage distorted his face as he stood with legs wide apart and feet firmly planted. He strained the muscles of his face. His voice was clear and menacing. "You can't do anything right, you bitch," he spewed.

He turned and stormed from the room before Adelle could catch her breath. She flinched as he slammed the door closed behind him. "This couldn't be," she said to herself, "I thought he would be happy. Even Molly thought he would be pleased." Though her face burned and the ringing persisted in her ears, Adelle could hear the noise of people bustling about. Though she felt weak, Adelle needed to know what was happening. Fragmented determination bid her to leave the security of her bedroom. She descended the stairs quietly, bracing herself on the handrail to keep from fainting.

She recognized the voices emanating from the library as those of Norman and Karl Jacobs, his administrative assistant. Adelle paused at the end of the stairs and quietly listened to the conversation.

"Take it easy Norman," said Karl. "I'll get a doctor in here to take care of the situation. I hate to see you in this state."

"Damn it Karl, I didn't want to marry the stupid little bitch in the first place! Good for business my ass!" thundered Pendrake. "She has been one headache after another. I tell you Karl I bought and paid for a decoration! Something to quell the rumors and I've been rooked. I'd divorce the whore if it wouldn't create even more talk around this town."

Karl's voice sounded soothing and calm. "I know Norman, I know." Adelle could see slivers of movement between the cracks in the partially open door. "I never would have touched the wretched bitch in the first place had it not been for that fucking lawyer telling me to consummate the marriage." Norman's voice was filled with a searing rage that seemed to overwhelm him.

"I know how you feel Norman!" said Karl. "But, in all honesty, the attorneys were giving you advice to stop possible annulment claims against our assets and us."

A slamming noise startled Adelle as she began to feel her vision dim from the revelations filtering through the library doors. The conversation continued with Norman spitting, "The stupid little ass doesn't even know how disgusting she is, the only amusing part of this whole fucking deal is that I consummated our marriage, I sure as hell wasn't easy on the broad. I hurt her! The more I hurt her the more aggressively I took her. I made good God damn sure she wouldn't want me to ever return." Norman's voice dropped to a more even pitch as he said, "You know Karl, consummating the marriage may have protected our business assets, but it sure didn't do a thing for my stomach."

"You know, some good can come out of this Norman," consoled Karl.

Suddenly Norman moved into Adelle's view. She could see a limited area in the crack of the door where he stood. "Oh yeah and just why would you think that," questioned Norman.

"To the world you will be a married man and a father. A family man," explained Karl. "There will be no more questions about our private life. I know that screwing that cunt was no picnic. I would have had a difficult time myself, but we do as we must."

Adelle's gaze was diverted to Karl, she watched as he moved gracefully toward Norman. He looked ardently into Norman's eyes and began stroking his hand. His voice was satin smooth. "We both know the type that I'm attracted to. A woman's body does nothing for me either. Moreover, I appreciate the fact that you sacrificed yourself for us, to protect us. I know you understand that if the truth came out, our business ties would evaporate. All of these, holier than thou, businessmen would pull away from you and we would be bankrupt."

Adelle made her way quietly back up to her haven. She closed the door and stood at the mirror. She dropped her dressing gown. She examined herself in the reflection. Her five foot one inch frame was covered with all of the shapes and curves that she had seen in other women and nothing was remarkably ugly or attractive. She recalled her trials of her wedding night remembering her clothes being torn from her body and being flung upon the bed like a rag doll. The view in her memory sent a ripple of shivers down her spine. The man she had just promised to love and obey was biting her nipples like an enraged animal. The pain seemed still to be within her. She still felt his hand plunging into the soft pink flesh between her legs. All the while, he screamed obscenities at her. He drove his penis into her 103-pound body with a power unimagined by Adelle. He called her names she had never heard before and Adelle could not distinguish the vast difference between love and violence nor ardor and anger.

The horrible remembrance of the taking of her virginity, rippled through her entire body like sheet lightning. Adelle's screams of suffering during the attack were met with ever-increasing furor and aggressiveness. She finally endured by escaping into her nether world and allowed the assault to belong to another being. She simply couldn't prevail over the pain and torment required to satisfy his sexual intentions. Through her reflection in the mirror, she noticed a slight outward curvature in her lower belly. She rotated her hips and touched her stomach with her fingertips. She traced the outline of the curvature. Adelle begrudged the life of the fetus that grew within her. A special bond was being created, one of hatred and fear. She looked at herself and remarked aloud, "you wrecked it why do you have to be there?" She slowly pulled up her robes, sat on her bed, and wept.

A short time later, a new series of sounds jolted Adelle back into reality. Servants running and yelling orders to each other drew her to the door of her room. Adelle peeked through the cracked door.

She watched Harold Geyher, the butler as he walked briskly down the corridor toward the stairs. He was carrying as many suitcases as he could handle. After he passed from view, Adelle slipped out to the landing to see what was going on. Through the open door of the main entry, she could see the chauffeur quickly loading the trunk of the limousine.

Adelle hid herself behind a pillar and watched the goings on as she heard Norman and Karl as they emerged from the downstairs guestroom. The men walked in cadence, their dark mood was evident by the length and the pounding footfalls of their matched stride upon the marble foyer. Norman turned abruptly to Harold. "I will let you where to send the rest. Otherwise you have your orders."

Harold offered a respectful and well-trained nod and replied, "Yes, Mr. Pendrake." The seemingly perfectly matched men entered the waiting limousine and vanished down the drive.

Adelle mustered enough courage at this point to step out from behind the pillar and call out to Harold. She questioned, "Where is he going?" The manservant, seemingly careful to keep in character replied, "I'm not at liberty to say, Madame." Adelle was trying to balance out the confusion of panic and relief she felt at the fact of Norman had left. "When will he be back?" The manservant kept careful to keep in character and replied, "I don't know, Madame, maybe never." He then turned and walked out of sight.

Adelle retreated to her bed for the remainder of her pregnancy. She refused any visitors, even from doctors. The growing circumference of her belly was only out-sized bye the acceleration of her loneliness. Anger festered within her psyche as she placed blame upon the unseen child, for the predicament in which she found herself. The movement of the child she was about to bear only served to provide additional turmoil to her world. A world that was all too bereft of anything except for vacant existence.

The seasons passed unnoticed by Adelle, as she remained month after month hidden in her room. The drapes, like the door remained closed. Only Molly and Harold were allowed inside of her sanctum. Moreover, that was only for the delivery of food and cleaning needs. Adelle consumed only enough to keep herself alive.

As gestation neared its end, her dread became even more pervasive. Perhaps she should have let the doctors with their shiny butcher's tools do their work. They had wanted to remove the growth that was distorting her body. Nevertheless, the fear of the pain, which she would have to endure, forced her to reject the procedure all together. She didn't believe the doctors when they told her that the pain of childbirth was much more intense than their task as ordered by Mr. Pendrake. She sensed betrayal from the man who had cast such injury upon her. Adelle could not permit their trespassing upon her or her private world.

*   *   *

Adelle awoke before dawn to an incredible feeling of nausea and cramping. Her swollen stomach provided her with a distress that she had never felt before. The periodic misery seemed to encircle her lower stomach and meet in the middle of her spine. She called for Harold to bring her medication tray. In moments, he stood by her watching as she screamed in terror. "Help me!" screamed Adelle. "Find someone to help me. I'm going to die!"

Harold was a gentlemen's, gentleman. He was ill prepared to act in any manner of assistance to the flailing and out of control mistress of the house.

Harold struggled to keep his composure. "Relax Madame, it's just your time. I'll go get Molly to assist you." He extricated himself leaving the cook to attend to Mrs. Pendrake.

Molly had been in the employment of the Pendrake family for almost twenty years. Her accomplishments as an outstanding cook were vastly outweighed at the time by the fact that she also was the mother of five children. Molly was well versed in the matter of bringing forth new life. She adopted the roll of midwife and labor coach and did all she could to re-assure and comfort Adelle. Molly was visibly relieved when the ambulance finally arrived to transport Adelle to the hospital where the professionals could handle her.

*   *   *

The staff of the obstetrics department were flurrying about due to the unexpected arrival of Mrs. Norman Pendrake. The head nurse sized up the situation the moment she laid eyes upon the wide-eyed attendants. The screaming and incoherent woman who was strapped ever so firmly to the gurney was totally out of control.

Adelle was placed hurriedly into an isolation ward located in the Pendrake wing where she was far away from the other patients. The staff was confounded by the events unfolding. There was no prenatal care history regarding Mrs. Pendrake. Therefore, the health of both the mother and child were in question. Adelle didn't care if her behavior was unruly. All that mattered to Adelle is that someone put an end to her agony. Following a quickly called meeting with doctors and nursing staff, the decision was made to perform a cesarean section and bring the histrionics to an end. Thus while Adelle rested in a drug induced, limbo baby boy Pendrake was put upon this earth. In order to keep Adelle manageable, she was regularly provided with painkillers. The obliviousness, which accompanied the injections, seemed to be more than comfortable for her.

The young Pendrake was seriously under weight and dehydrated upon birth. Every effort was provided for his survival by the medical staff. It was many days later when he was at last presented to his mother for the first time. Adelle stared for an extended length of time at the infant. She exhaled a long sigh and in a monotone voice said, "A boy. Well I won't be alone anymore. He will love me, in every way.

The pediatric nurse waited while the new mother became acquainted with her child. She asked, "Have you and Mr. Pendrake decided upon a name for your son?" Adelle's odd expression didn't change as she said, "Yes, Zachary, Zachary Payne Pendrake." The ever so delicate balance of Adelle's ability to cope had been compromised and the scale now tipped to the side of insanity.

CHAPTER 3

Emotional Poison

Soon after the vital statistics department of the hospital reported the birth of the Pendrake heir, journalists began calling for details. Harold informed Norman Pendrake of the inquiries. Having fatherhood foisted upon him infuriated Norman. However, Karl put the complication into perspective. He slyly explained, "Norman, you can have the name and not play the game." We can end the speculation about your sexual orientation with a single press release." After the reality of what Karl had said penetrated him, Norman dictated the information for release.

Zachary Payne Pendrake never understood the symbolism that his middle name represented. The first few years of his life were not spent in Austria, as was indicated in the press release. His young life was spent in the confines of Adelle's private and personally designed asylum. She had become completely addicted to the painkillers and sedatives freely provided for her. Her weak mind thickened from the blurring of the drugs. She beheld the narcotics as her savior during what she considered her arduous labor. Adelle preferred the zombie-like state that they provided for her.

Columns Manor's staff, Harold Geyher and Kathy St. John, the new cook and Betty Johnson, the housekeeper were the only people allowed into the suite of Adelle. Then admittance was only permitted for the purposes of delivery of food or changes of diapers. Adelle would not permit anyone to touch the infant unless she decided it was absolutely necessary. The newborn's need for maternal bonding and imprinting remained unheeded.

Harold, abandoning his usual detachment, wrote letters to Mr. Pendrake informing him of the situation. He, however received no reply and at long last, deserted his letter writing campaign. Betty quit her job. Her resignation reflected that she could not stand by and watch as the poor child suffered. Betty claimed that the young Pendrake starved, he hungered not from a poor diet, but from lack of emotional sustenance needed by all human beings. The duties of Betty fell upon Kathy St. John, the cook.

A turning point in Zachary's young life occurred when Kathy sat down in the kitchen determined to talk with Harold. She leaned forward resting her body weight on her elbows. "I can't deal with this anymore," began Kathy. "Two months of watching this neglect is too much for me." Kathy sat back in her chair and picked at her fingernails. "Betty was right to leave. It was the only decision that she could have made. I've thought about quitting myself but then I think of Zachary." She looked off into space, focused on nothing, yet showing pain she held in her heart for the baby. She continued, "That poor baby. He has a lunatic for a mother and a father who obviously doesn't care a bit about his son."

As Kathy rambled on, Harold sat quietly, his hands folded on the table. He seemed to keep his emotions in check, not allowing any feelings in the matter to be evident to her. She leaned forward leveling an intense look at Harold. "After all Harold, if I just quit and leave too, who would take the time to give that baby any semblance of love or attention? But," she continued, "I have a plan!"

Finally, Harold scrunched his nose and adjusted his glasses. He looked as if he were trying to guess where Kathy was headed with this idea of hers. Kathy took a deep breath, held it momentarily and then said, "I thought about calling the welfare department or child protective services."

"Whoa there!" Harold threw his hands forward as if to push her away. He jumped to his feet, then turned quickly and faced Kathy. His former detachment seemed to have vanished as he said, "If you did something like that, we'd both be fired! Believe me Kathy," Harold continued, "the Pendrakes and their billions of dollars wield a vast and powerful sword. A sword fully capable of buying off any social agency. I don't know about you, but I'm not ready to face the loaded guns of the family legal arsenal. Not now. Not ever."

Kathy was stunned by the out of character and forceful reaction from Harold. "No, no, no," Kathy said as she tried to calm Harold. "Please, just listen to me for a minute. Hear me out and then you can decide, okay?"

Harold tugged at his vest and sat back into the chairs. He took off his glasses and placed them onto the table, then folded his arms across his chest. "All right, I'll listen, but then I'll forget we had this conversation." His glare was so concentrated that Kathy had to swallow hard to continue. "This is what we do," she began. "First we will talk to her doctor. He, more than anyone, knows how strange that woman up there is. I think he will go along with us for the sake of the boy. Anyway, Madame likes her morphine and prefers to be zoned out. So, we give her what she wants. And we'll keep her out of the way."

Harold furrowed his brow and squinted his eyes, "What," he burst in. "Keep her that way?" Kathy held out a lowering hand and said, "Look at the situation Harold. When she is drugged she doesn't know or care what is happening to that baby or anyone else for that matter." Kathy watched as Harold leaned forward. He began rubbing his eyes and the bridge of his nose. He appeared to be deep in thought. Harold replaced his glasses and stroked his chin slowly with his index finger and his thumb. His eyes popped up over the rim of his glasses, "but what if the doctor won't go along? He will!" Kathy jutted forward on her elbows and said, "He will! He's in the pocket of Pendrake isn't he? This way," Kathy pressed on, "there won't be any scandal. And," Kathy slyly confided, Mr. Pendrake would be more than just a little bit indebted to us. Kathy searched Harold's face for his reaction. "Well, what do you think?"

Harold continued to rub his face thoughtfully. Kathy waited, picking at her fingernails while he considered the plan that had just been laid out to him. Finally, she slammed her hands into her lap. "Oh come on Harold! You and I both know that he doesn't care about that baby in the first place. But, you sure as hell can believe that he doesn't want the public knowing what is going on up there, right?"

Kathy's flush of anticipation mounted as Harold once again sat and weighed the positives and negatives. At times, he would look up momentarily and seem to want to say something. But then he'd retreat back into his thoughts. Until at long last he spoke. "We would," he stated "have to know what amount to give her. We'd have to know all of the particulars. But you know," he looked at Kathy with a softer glance, "I think it would work. However, this situation needs to be handled just right. Mr. Pendrake would have to agree to all of this and be totally informed at all times."

"Informed," said Kathy. "Does he even know what has been happening here?" Harold gave her a sideways look and said, "He knows it all." The realization that Pendrake had known and was kept abreast of the things happening to his child and still didn't intercede on the boys behalf, stunned her.

Kathy shook off the feelings that were attempting to overwhelm her. She knew that this wasn't the time to be emotional or lead by them. Harold continued, "As I said, Mr. Pendrake would have to be informed of everything that is done." Kathy jumped into the conversation again and said, "I'll call him about this if you want me to." He shook his head and said, "No, that wouldn't work. Mr. Pendrake wouldn't listen to you. He doesn't know who you are." Harold pivoted in his chair and turned his head upward and stared seemingly at the light fixture.

Kathy sat, although impatiently. Her first order of business of convincing Harold to go along with her plan was under control.

She allowed him the time to consider. His concentration came to an end when he turned back to Kathy. "One thing I know for certain "began Harold, "is that the Mr. despises people running to him, with problems, especially when they don't have a clue as to the solution. He expects those around him to do their homework enough to offer a path to resolution. We at least have that in our court. The last thing we need to do is to upset him."

"But we do have a solution," replied Kathy.

"Right, but the problem goes deeper than just the Mrs. up there," said Harold. "I can tell you that Mr. Pendrake is a very busy man. He is also a very private man. If we go through with this the child will be our responsibility."

"Yes," said Kathy, "I know."

Harold gave her a stern look and repeated, "our responsibility,' then added, 'our sole responsibility. Are you sure you want that on your shoulders?"

Kathy supplied an enormous grin. "Oh yes, Harold, I could take care of Zachary."

"Fine, as long as you understand that I may be making the call, but you are the one who will take care of the child. I don't know anything about children. I purposely avoided working in homes that had them."

"Really Harold, I'd love to see that baby well cared for. I'll accept full responsibility."

"Alright then, I'll go into the library and call Mr. Pendrake." Harold stood up from the table and started to leave the room, Kathy held out a hand and held onto his arm. "Don't you want me to go in there with you?"

"No," he replied," I know what I'm doing. You just wait here in the kitchen. As soon as I have finished my talk with Mr. Pendrake, I'll let you know, thumbs up or down."

Kathy waited as the first half an hour passed. The tension was causing her stomach to ache. She resorted to pacing back and forth in front of the library door. Listening through the thick wood was futile. Finally, after another forty-five minutes, Harold emerged. In an instant, Kathy stood in front of him. He looked directly at her.

"Well, what did he say?"

Harold paused long enough for Kathy to double up and shake her fists. She uttered his name through clenched teeth. He smiled at her and gave her the thumbs up signal. "Remember," he said, "Zachary might as well be your own child."

"I'll remember." Kathy's joy was temporarily halted as she asked, "What about the medications, what did he say about that?"

"The doctor will be arriving sometime today. He will go over the procedures with you. Mr. Pendrake should be talking with him about now. In addition, understand Kathy, I am going to turn over all of this stuff to you. I'm not comfortable working with a baby and a mad woman."

*   *   *

Thus for the first time in his young life, Zachary was being held in comforting arms, bathed in warm water and fed properly. Month after month of caring for Zachary secured a bond between caregiver and child. Kathy's affection for the baby grew. Kathy had given Zachary the nickname of Zatch. She indeed treated him as if he were her own child. She truly loved the child. Somehow, through it all, Kathy and Harold did not understand that the vital time for imprinting had passed. They had no way of comprehending the reasons behind the vacant stares of the child.

However absent of the bonding, his life was, every luxury was provided for him.

Adelle in turn inhabited a drug-induced exile. For months on end, she vegetated as the caregivers continued with their tasks.

Adelle's tolerance of the narcotics grew until perilous amounts of the drug were required to keep her sedated. The Pendrake family physicians insisted upon slowly reducing her intake of medication. The goal was to bring her around without serious withdrawal. Zachary was a year old and walking as the process was begun. In that time, Harold and Kathy were the only genuine source of humanity available to Zachary.

* * *

Adelle slowly became more coherent. Her newfound rationality presented unique complications to the relationship between Zatch and Kathy. Adelle had been accustomed to the drugged limbo existence. She pushed reality away and founded her own twisted style of coping. Bathing herself for the first time in months, Adelle paid particular attention to the seven-inch scar on her lower abdomen. She repeatedly washed the telling mark of her suffering. She acted as if cleansing the area would remove the traces of the pain she had endured. She would trace the path of the scar, feeling the varied texture of her skin along the seam. To Adelle, the blemish became illustrative of her life and her wounded self-image.

Inevitably, she was allowed to interact with her son. Kathy resented the wedge drawn between herself and Zatch. It was difficult for her to simply back off and leave the child to anyone else, especially someone the likes of Adelle Pendrake. Kathy spent hours agonizing over the contact. Her sensibilities told her that Zachary was not her son, but her heart told her he was. Kathy was confused and hurt. She never, however, allowed her emotions to betray themselves in front of Adelle. She worried that Zachary would be confused as well. Neither Kathy nor Harold had any idea how this contact with his mother would color the future of Zachary Payne Pendrake.

*   *   *

A day came when Adelle was in particularly good spirits. She indicated to Kathy that she wanted to help bathe her son. Kathy reluctantly submitted to the mother's request. Kathy was trying hard to realign herself with her role of caregiver and not that of a parent. The misery she endured was masked to everyone's eyes. Only in the confines of her room did she cry herself to sleep night after night.

Zachary was eighteen months old and Adelle wanted to help give him his bath. His body was decisively male, with all of the typical male body parts. Seemingly disarmed, Adelle couldn't abide seeing Zachary's maleness. She insisted that the boy's genitals be covered. Until her orders were met, Adelle stood transfixed staring at her child. She appeared simultaneously fascinated and ultimately repulsed by the nudity of her son. Kathy didn't know what to think about Adelle's response. When Adelle excused herself, Kathy said nothing. The visage of Zachary's body began a series of convoluted and distorted thoughts in the mind of Adelle. She would make absolutely certain that he would never hurt any woman. He would never torture a woman as Norman had done to her. Adelle began insisting upon more and more time with her son. She suspected that Kathy and Harold were pipelines to Norman. She became secretive about her dealings with Zachary.

Whenever Zachary was in her care, she would show him her scar. She would force him to touch, caress and rub the affliction. All the while Adelle would utter to her son, "Just look what you have done to me. She would induce an erection from Zachary, and then viciously assault the protrusion, all the while speaking the obscenities and language she'd heard on her wedding night. She repeated over and over, the same vicious words she had heard from Norman. As Adelle's obsession grew in enormity, her endeavors to teach Zachary kept pace.

* * *

Zachary was four years old when Harold had received orders from Norman to have pictures taken of his son. Kathy and Harold had no doubts that these photos were to be flashed at opportunistic times to opportune people. Kathy prepared Zachary for his portrait which included an unscheduled bath.

As she removed his clothing, she noticed a stain around the band of the youngster's underwear. Kathy examined Zach and found that he had been marked with what appeared to be a combination of pencil drawings and a red greasy smear. The design of the smudged marking took on the appearance of stitches, which were encircled with what looked like eyeliner pencil and the vivid red lipstick worn by Adelle. The shape and the location resembled a lurid simulation of the caesarian scar on Adelle.

Kathy attempted to clean the markings. Zachary achieved an erection. He rapidly pushed Kathy's hands anyway as he covered his swollen genitals. He slid across to the far side of the bathtub. His eyes took on the appearance of a wounded animal. His face contorted and filled with expressions of fear and loathing. Kathy tried to reassure the boy and only succeeded in frightening him more. He protected his groin and whined while he pressed himself against the tub walls.

"Harold," Kathy gently called through the intercom. "Can you come in here for a minute?"

A few moments later, Harold walked into the room. He was surprised to see Zachary still in the bathtub. "Aren't you finished yet? The photographer will be here any time."

"Look at this," said Kathy. "What has been happening to this child?" Harold's eyes widened as he looked at the markings that had been drawn on the boy's body. "I'll call Mr. Pendrake at once," he said as he walked briskly from the room.

Kathy finished dressing Zachary for the photographer who was just arriving. Harold was gone for what seemed to be forever. When he finally walked into the room, he instantly saw the contractor setting up his cameras and lights. Kathy watched in amazement as the stoic butler stood by until the pictures were taken. He never once betrayed to the innocent eye that anything was amiss.

Once the door was closed behind the photographer, Harold looked at Zachary with agonized eyes and said, "I didn't get a hold of Mr. Pendrake, but I did talk with Karl Jacobs." Kathy was surprised and a bit pleased that Harold was actually showing some affection for Zatch. It was the first time Kathy had ever seen him break character. It warmed her heart to know that he really had one of his own. Harold paused and looked at Zachary and then continued, "There are plans in the works. We are to keep him from Adelle at all costs. Even if we have to drug her, she is not to see him again."

Kathy interrupted him, "But what plans? What's going to become of Zachary?" Kathy flung her hand up pointing toward the upper level of the massive home and said, "And that vicious bitch up there, is she going to get what she deserves?"

"I'm not sure Kathy, but Karl assured me that this matter would be dealt with right away. So, I guess we wait and follow the orders that we do have."

*   *   *

Within two hours, a messenger came to the door. He delivered a manila envelope. Inside was a packet of white powder. Sealed inside another envelope were instructions from the doctor, the message directed Harold to mix the concoction in Adelle's evening tea at 9:00 p.m. sharp.

* * *

Harold and the rest of the household were awakened at 1:15 a.m. by the clanging of the door chimes. Harold wrapped himself hurriedly in his robe and slid his feet into his slippers. On his way to the door, Kathy called out to him, "Harold, who is it?" Harold gave her an annoyed look and shrugged his shoulders. He went to the window where he could ascertain the identity of the caller. From his vantage point, he could see two limousines, parked in the drive. The chauffeur was on the porch and once again pressing the door chimed. Harold opened the intercom and said, "Yes may I help you?"

The caller at the door replied, "We're here to pick up Mrs. Pendrake, on the orders from Karl Jacobs. Please open the door."

Harold complied with the request. The chauffeur stood holding the doors wide open as three men emerged from the first car. Harold recognized Adelle's doctor, but the others were strangers. Dr. Hughes offered Harold a quick nod of recognition. "Mr. Geyher, was Mrs. Pendrake medicated as directed?"

"Yes sir, exactly as ordered." Hughes turned to face the waiting limousine and motioned toward the men waiting by the car. The tallest of the three men opened the trunk of the car and pulled out a strapped jacket and a medical bag. "Mrs. Pendrake, please," requested Dr. Hughes.

Harold motioned to the upper floor and replied, "Upstairs, in her room. If you will follow me."

The four men climbed the stairs to Adelle's waiting unconsciousness. They wrapped her in the jacket and carried her down stairs. Adelle was placed into the waiting limousine. As soon as the doors closed, the limo drove away. As the first Cadillac containing Adelle pulled out, yet another vehicle took its place, behind the second black limo. The driver of the third car remained sheltered inside the confines of the Mercedes. The tinted glass windows concealed their identity. The doors to the second car opened and another three people appeared. There were two men and one woman. They walked in matching rhythm toward Harold. The woman appeared to be at least forty-five years old. As she neared Harold, she stated in no nonsense terms, "Where is the child?"

Speechless and stunned Harold simply pointed toward the house. A moment later he cleared his throat and found his voice, "He's with Kathy, the cook. I'll show you."

Zachary had been awakened by the commotion. Kathy was sitting on her bed, holding Zachary in her arms as they entered the room. Zachary began to cry and cling to Kathy's neck. The uniformed woman tried to take him from Kathy's arms. Knowing she was out numbered, Kathy tried to calm Zatch. The woman quite literally had to pry the child away from Kathy. He held on for all he was worth and dug his nails into Kathy's neck. She winced in pain when the child's grasp was finally broken. Kathy followed on the heels of the retreating woman. She lunged at the uniformed woman who was taking Zatch away from her. The two men, in matching green uniform acted as a barrier between Zachary's captor and Kathy. When she would try to move around them, they would block her path. When she tried to reach for Zachary through them, they pulled her arms away. Kathy fought with every ounce of strength she possessed. She felt her heart was going to burst. She begged for information about where he was going. Nevertheless, the silent fast moving uniformed female was non-responsive.

"Where is he going? What are you going to do with him?" Kathy repeatedly called to Zatch as she tried to keep pace. Tears were streaming down her face. Her head throbbed in agony as her pleas went unanswered. "Please," begged Kathy, "At least let me hug him goodbye. While keeping the brisk pace the woman simply said, "He'll be in good hands, Miss."

Zachary was in full panic as he was carried away from the mansion. Kathy called out to him, "Zatch, I love you."

The woman stepped into the back seat of the limo, leaving Kathy with tears stinging her eyes and her heart feeling as if it had been knifed. The two men climbed into the front seat and they immediately drove away.

Harold was considerably less emotional than Kathy. He stood in the drive watching until the vehicle faded from sight. The closing of a car door averted the attention of Harold and Kathy. The focus changed from who was leaving, to whom was now arriving.

Standing bedside the limo, stood a tall imposing figure, as he stepped from the shadows into the light, Harold blurted, "Mr. Pendrake, sir, I didn't realize that you were here."

Kathy had never seen her employer before and caught herself staring through her teardrops. A strong glare from

Pendrake brought her evaluation to a halt. Harold introduced Kathy as the two men walked into the house. Kathy waited outside for a short period of time to try to collect herself and her aching heart. A few minutes later, she joined Harold and Mr. Pendrake. Upon reaching, the door to the library Norman stopped short and looked directly at Kathy. "We won't need you any more tonight, Ms. St. John. Goodnight." Without another word, he closed the heavy wooden doors to the library with only himself and Harold inside.

Kathy stood outside the doors feeling the agony of separation and the bewilderment regarding the coldness of Norman Pendrake. Her employer didn't seem to care even the slightest bit about his son. The confusion finally gave way to irritation. She completed her mental assessment that had begun earlier outside the house. She declared aloud that her employer was an ass hole and an unfeeling idiot. That critique being settled, Kathy returned to her quarters and cried herself to an erratic sleep.

She was awakened the next morning at 7:30 a.m. by the clamor of people moving about in the house. She flew out of bed and wrapped herself in her robe. She opened the door only to be met by Harold.

"Kathy," he began, "can you please dress and meet me in the library?" "Sure," she replied. Kathy swiveled her head in every direction and wondered what was happening. Countless men and women dressed in coveralls scurried around the house. Some carried boxes while others packed them. Still, more boxes and wrapping paper was strewn throughout the rooms. Stacks of furniture drapes were lying by the doors of each room.

Minutes later, Kathy stood in front of Harold with a quizzical expression on her face. She had a headache from crying herself to sleep the night before. Inside of herself, she was hoping that she would be able to find out where Zachary had gone and when she could be united with him.

Harold motioned for her to sit with him in the chair directly in front of the massive mahogany desk. He pulled a file from the drawer and placed it in front of him on the desk. He began, "Mr. Pendrake has had Adelle committed."

"And Zatch?" asked Kathy.

He gave her an aggravated look for her impatience. "I'll get to him in a minute Kathy, but first things first. Mrs. Pendrake is now in a setting where she will be looked after for the rest of her life." He shook his head as he looked down at the desk. "The retched creature doesn't even know what is happening to her. But over a bit of time she'll adjust."

Kathy looked at Harold with eyes that were everything except patient. "Harold, please, what about Zachary?" She watched as Harold stiffened his posture. He seemed like he was preparing to deliver the worst news he'd ever had to give.

"Zachary is on his way to be enrolled in a very exclusive boarding school," he said.

Kathy flew to her feet and with all of the power she could muster shouted, "A military school, isn't it Harold!" That, that storm trooper who came in here last night. She's Zach's new guardian, isn't she!" Kathy reeled on her heels and raved, "That son of a bitch. Why couldn't he give even the smallest piece of himself to that baby?" Kathy's tears streamed down her face and her entire body shook both from rage and renewed heartache.

I know how you feel Kathy, but it is simply not our decision to make. It's entirely out of our hands. Mr. Pendrake," Harold forged on, "would not make an ideal parent. He never wanted the child in the first place. He definitely does not want any controversy surrounding him. Not about this! Not about anything. As I have said before he is a very private person."

Kathy looked at Harold with eyes that showed nothing but hatred for even the mention of Pendrake. "Yeah, right a very private ass hole." Kathy understood what Harold was telling her. Still, it didn't make much difference in the pain she was feeling. The fact that Pendrake was a private man didn't lessen the void she now felt in her heart. Zatch was gone from her life. Kathy felt both hopeless and helpless.

Harold opened the file folder that rested on the desk before him. He set aside some documents and then placed another envelope back into the file. He sighed deeply as he handed her the first stack of papers.

The papers contained a reference letter. It was a fine recommendation providing a glowing recount of services provided during Kathy's tenure with Pendrake the estate. "Just like that, huh? Just like that!" Kathy mumbled.

Harold narrowed his eyes in a rare exchange of strong emotion. He glowered at Kathy and explained. "Well, no, it's not quite that simple. I have a contract for you to sign."

Kathy felt suspicious and said, "What kind of contract?"

Harold rolled his eyeballs and raised his left brow. "The contract is an agreement not to ever divulge any of the things you have seen at Columns Manor. Mr. Pendrake is closing this house down. He sees no reason to keep this place going with no one living here. Columns holds a lot of bad memories for him and I can understand his wanting to put it behind him." Kathy dropped her head and looked at the legal document lying in her lap. "So this is his way of keeping a lid on it huh?" And what if I decide not to sign this contract? What then?"

Harold shook his head slowly. His intent gaze upon her made her feel a bit uncomfortable. "Kathy, hear me out and then make your decision. There's more to this situation than meets the eye. Try to understand that Mr. Pendrake had nothing to do with the maltreatment of the boy. In addition, when he was made abreast of the situation he instantly took steps for the good of both mother and child. Try to view the situation this way you have an opportunity to come out of this with a win in your column. Or, you can risk the reprisals of someone against whom you wouldn't stand a chance. "Believe me Kathy, this is the better way. Harold pulled the envelope from the file. "In exchange for your agreement, I have been authorized to offer you this." Harold handed her a piece of paper.

Kathy could hardly believe her eyes. She had never seen so many zeros in her life on a check. She looked up at Harold, amazement painted on her expression. "Fifty thousand dollars," she sputtered.

"Yes, Kathy and all for leaving what happened in this house behind you. As you move forward with your life the Pendrake family will be secure that the illness of Mrs. Pendrake is not common knowledge. But, there is more," he continued, "You'll notice that according to the covenant that Mr. Pendrake warrants you'll be issued an annual check for twenty-five thousand dollars each year, as long as."

"As long as I keep my mouth shut," quipped Kathy, "right Harold?"

Kathy jumped as Harold slammed his hands upon the desk. Startled by his exasperation, she gave him her full attention. "Look Kathy, you need to use your head. Think, Kathy, think. Call it an insurance policy for the family. Abruptly Harold stood and circled the desk to stand at Kathy's side. He touched her shoulder and took a deep breath. The pause seemed to aid Harold in calming his wrath. "Look Kathy you have an opportunity here for financial security throughout your life. It demonstrates that Mr. Pendrake appreciated your work and all that you did. Personally, I think the offer is very generous. It's an offer he doesn't have to make at all."

Harold returned to his seat and allowed Kathy to think for quite some time. She was overwhelmed by even the thought of having this much money. At last, Harold interrupted her thoughts and said, "So what do you say? Will you sign the contract?"

Kathy reasoned that there was little or nothing she was able to do about the situation surrounding Zachary. She persuaded herself that this indeed was the better solution. Her heart still tugged a war with her mind regarding Zatch. Still in the final analysis, Kathy resolved there was little she could do. Kathy signed the contract. As she dropped the pen onto the desk, she crumbled into tears once again. She dabbed at her eyes with a tissue from her pocket. "I'm sorry Harold, I just feel so guilty about Zatch."

"I know."However, we can only do what we can. There's nothing we can do about this situation." Kathy watched as

Harold placed the signed contract into an envelope. The envelope had been addressed to the Pendrake attorney's office. He stood and shook hands with Kathy. "This will be the last day we spend together, and I must admit that I will think of you often and hope that you are doing well. So I will say farewell and good luck to you Kathy. I know you will do well."

* * *

Adelle awoke to a drowsiness that she had never before experienced. She opened her eyes upon very different surroundings. She realized that her arms and legs had restraints firmly holding her limbs immobile. Waves of panic coursed through her as she attempted to focus her drug-laden eyes. At last, she saw a nurse standing at the foot of her bed.

"Where am I?" Adelle asked weakly.

The attendant turned away from her chart. "You're here in Avery Center, Retreat and Sanitarium, Ms. Reynolds."

Adelle struggled to think clearly. "Who is Ms Reynolds?" And who are you?"

The medic offered a caring, yet appraising gaze and said, "Why you're Ms. Reynolds, don't you remember who you are? I'm Tere Case your aide during your stay with us."

"My name isn't Amanda Reynolds, there has been a huge mistake, and I'm Adelle Pendrake." Responding to the comments the nurse moved to her right and loosened one of the restraints. She held up Adelle's arm, just high enough for her to see an identification bracelet. Tere Case read the band to Adelle.

"See here, it says Amanda D. Reynolds. Unity commerce Bank 071-0030-967. And just under that is your doctor's name.

"I've told you, my name is not Amanda Reynolds," protested Adelle. "It's Adelle. Adelle Pendrake, why won't you listen to me?" Terror began to set in to Adelle and she struggled to break free of the straps that kept her bound.

When all attempts to calm her patient failed, Tere Case retrieved a syringe from the medication table. She injected her patient with its contents. While the nothingness began to envelop Adelle, Nurse Case's words echoed through her mind.

"It's going to be alright Amanda. You will feel better shortly. In time you'll become accustomed and even be happy with your life her at Avery Center.

The relenting of her senses to the medication heralded the commencement of Adelle's acceptance of a challenge free existence. Indeed Adelle was quite retired and contented.

CHAPTER 4
Lanchester Academy

Norman Pendrake left the care of his son to his business managers and advisors. He wanted nothing to do with the child. Viewpoints of the professionals varied greatly as the business of caring for Zachary was at issue. They did however accept that Zachary was totally their responsibility. It was made their obligation to secure the proper educational format for the young heir.

That, in the perception of the Pendrake managers, was the reasoning behind Karl's choice of schooling. He sent Zachary to Lanchester Gentlemen's Academy. A scant twenty-five young men were inducted into the prestigious facility each year. Only the 'cream of the crop', so to speak were enrolled.

The fact that Zachary was many years younger than any of the other cadets held neither weight nor concern to the administration. This was particularly true when the Pendrake's power along with the sizeable amount of money became involved. The abettors outlined their needs to be met. And so, in the company of those with rigid spines and unbending knees, the task of rearing the youngest Pendrake was undertaken.

Heading the old guard was Commander Higgins. His six-foot frame seemed ever so much taller by virtue of his erect mannerisms. "The Hig," as most cadets clandestinely dubbed him, possessed eyes of blue steel and a full head of graying sandy blond hair. It was said that 'The Hig' would never go bald, as he would never tolerate deserters in any form. The square set to his jaw denoted his matter of fact and unyielding attitudes. He held out his own idea as to what a man's man, truly was. Commander Higgins had his own methods to go about creating his determination of what goes into the quintessential man. The Hig, with a flash of a steely glance could virtually control any situation. He successfully quelled the often spiteful behavior of the outrageous rich. He and his staff boasted of their control and took pride in their ability to build the leaders of the up-coming generation. Senators, Congressmen and four Presidents of the United States were among the alumni. Accordingly, a very high percentage of the power brokers of the business world had attended Lanchester. The Hig and his support personnel felt satisfaction in what they considered their achievements, therefore failure in the case of Zachary Pendrake was not an option.

To the personnel at the Academy, there was no such thing as a boy. Children of the male gender were only small men with budding egos. Subliminal selves to be manipulated into fully functioning, success oriented gentlemen, Lanchester style. The

Hig tolerated no child-like fantasies or problems. He would consistently shame away any tears and fears.

Zachary's assimilation into the lifestyle of Lanchester Academy was at first fraught with complex emotions. He couldn't understand where Kathy and Harold had gone. He couldn't understand what he had done to be removed from his home. The sterility of Zachary's new environment for most any other four-year-old child would have been much too cold. Zachary however, had learned early on in his young life to adapt. He soon fell in line and acclimated for the sake of survival. To him this was simply another place in which he needed to learn to cope. It was yet another atmosphere devoid of the family nurturing. Vacant were any of the close bonds that made up normal family life. He was once again held at arm's length, once again empty.

Zachary was disciplined in the militaristic fashion and referred to as Mr. Pendrake instead of the familiarity of his first name. Commander Higgins became his role model and championed Zachary's understanding of the true meaning of manhood. The stern officer took over the education and rearing of his youngest student. Higgins epitomized the stalwart and conventional attitudes that were a normal part of life, Lanchester style.

*   *   *

By the age of six, Zachary had the mannerisms down to a science. He exuded conformity in the regimented style of Academy life. Zachary's quarters as well as his growing body were immaculate. He carried a straight 4.0 in all of his classes. He possessed virtually no social skills and seldom interacted with the other cadets. During his younger years he relied upon Commander Higgins for direction with most any course of action. Although cold, the protective wing of the Hig was at least safe. Once he realized that he could instill fear in his classmates, without the aid of Higgins, a separation of dependence began. The fact that the name Pendrake carried its own weight in any situation hadn't yet completely settled into Zachary's mind.

The graces of social propriety were part of his schooling and Zachary knew how to display the appearance of refinement. He inwardly despised the roles required of him during most social functions. He consistently and successfully begged off attending any that he could. The Hig never concerned himself or his charge with such commonplace societal pressures. As the years passed, small cracks in the metal that made up Higgins the man, were being seen by the magnifying eye of young Pendrake. As he grew in age and experience, he began seeing the once less subtle chinks in the armored cloak, which was put forth by the Commander. The reality check began when Zachary was ordered to give Higgins a small sum of money to cover a cab ride in the city. The Hig's shortfall in cash was kindling to the fiery thought that perhaps Higgins was less than he appeared to be. As Zachary grew in sophistication, he began to view even his relationship with Lanchester as parasitical and truly felt that the Hig was a paid servant and nothing more.

* * *

Zachary had just turned 15 when he was summoned to the offices of Commander Higgins. Standing directly in front of the door, he soundly rapped three times. He waited for a response from inside. The strong voice of Commander Higgins rang out. "Yes, enter."

Zachary entered the room, closing the doors behind him. Then he turned and took two paces forward in a strong striding motion, instantly stood at attention. He clicked his heels and saluted Commander Higgins. "Cadet Pendrake, reporting as ordered, sir."

Higgins returned the salute. "Pendrake at ease."

Zachary spread his feet and cupped his hands behind his back. He looked directly at Higgins. He didn't acknowledge the other man in the room with him.

"Mr. Pendrake," Higgins began, "I have someone here to talk with you. This is Mr. Weymour. He's your father's banking consultant. He has some matters that are quite urgent. "Higgins stepped aside as if to be out of the conversational loop.

"Yes sir," said Zachary. He abruptly shifted his gaze to Weymour. Although it didn't show in his outward demeanor, Zachary was perplexed at the arrival of this stranger. The mention of his father after all the years had surprised him. Zachary nodded his head in a well-trained and deferential manner. "Mr. Weymour, sir."

The tall, gray haired man was wearing a three-piece suit that indicated great care in choosing his wardrobe. Zachary noticed that his tie was off center and there was a small piece of lint showing in the cuff of his trousers. In deference to Commander Higgins, he bit back the urge to point out the inadequacies of the visitor. He listened intently as Weymour began to explain why he was seeking an audience with him.

"Your father has been killed in an automobile accident. I'm sorry to be the one who brings this dreadful news. But Karl Jacobs, your father's administrative assistance is out of the country and requested us to make this notification."

Zachary sat without flinching or diverting his attention from Weymour's speech. No emotion crossed his face whatsoever. His attitude seemed to baffle the banker. "I have some papers here for you to sign." Weymour stammered.

"Papers," said Zachary in a matter of fact tone. "What papers do you need for me to sign and why?" Zachary barely blinked as he peered into the eyes of the obviously nervous banker.

"Well," began Weymour as he dug into his briefcase. "One of the documents is a power of attorney. Signing this will allow your fathers businesses to continue to operate in his absence." He handed Zachary a thick document. "There is another, which is a validation letter. You see Mr. Pendrake, you were your father's only heir."

Commander Higgins stepped forward and halted the conversation. He questioned Weymour. "Who is the designated executor for the estate? And who is acting as young Pendrake's counsel?"

Zachary watched as Higgins fired questions at the banker. Without voicing a single word, the anger within him began to grow. He felt that Higgins was seeking a way to feather his own nest and make certain that the academy interests were covered. He wasn't so sure that Higgins had his best interest at heart.

The banker said, "Karl Jacobs is the executor of the estate. He was your father's right hand man for almost two decades." Weymour nodded toward Zachary and said, "Your father trusted him implicitly. He has full knowledge of your father, and now your assets and holdings."

Zachary waited for a lull in the conversation and interjected. "This accident, tell me about it. What sort of car was my father driving? What happened?"

"Well Master Pendrake, the fact of the matter is that he was not driving. His chauffeur was at the wheel. The limousine was struck full force in the passenger side, directly where your father was seated. He, I'm sorry to say died instantly." Weymour dropped his eyes to the floor, trying to convey a sense of grief. "The truck that hit your father's car had run a red light. The results of a field sobriety test indicated the driver was under the influence of alcohol. The truck driver has been cited for driving while intoxicated."

Zachary questioned, "Are there any other charges pending against the driver of the other car?"

"Yes," said Weymour. "Beside vehicular homicide, being pursued by the district attorney, the Pendrake counsel has filed suit against the man's family for wrongful death. Those papers are here for you to sign In order to move the case forward. He handed them to Zachary, who without comment signed the papers. Silence followed as he and Commander Higgins read the legal paperwork. Weymour stood quietly clinging to the back of a chair. Zachary's cold voice rang out once more. Without taking his eyes off the papers in front of him, he asked. "And in what condition is the chauffeur?"

Weymour drew in a deep breath in an expression of apparent relief. "You'll be happy to know that he suffered only minor injuries. He is out of the hospital and back with his family."

Higgins once again took control of the conversation, "Getting back to the reason for your visit here today. After viewing these papers, I feel Mr. Pendrake should have his own legal counsel prior to signing anything more. He has an immense measure of interest in what transpires from these documents."

"Very well Commander, would you like for me to contact an attorney for you?"

"No!" retorted Higgins. "I feel we have the ability to secure our own counsel. You will hear from Mr. Pendrake's representatives very soon."

Weymour opened his briefcase and placed the signed documents inside and closed it with a sound clip. He indicated that he would wait to hear from young Pendrake's solicitors. He turned and began walking to the door. Zachary stopped him short. "The chauffeur, Mr. Weymour, have him fired immediately. Good day Mr. Weymour."

The stunned banker looked at Zachary with eyes that expressed disbelief. A chill coursed through Weymour's body and translated itself as a visible shiver. "Yes, Mr. Pendrake, at once." The sudden fearfulness that showed so obviously on Weymour's face, supplied Zachary with the first real taste of power. He savored the control as if it were an appetizer. He knew that much more was coming his way.

Through short intense, negotiations between Zachary's legal counsel and those of the Pendrake Industries, a deal was struck. Zachary's trust accounts paid him an enormous annuity. He agreed that he had no intention of becoming involved with the business dealings of the company. However, Zachary did hold out for a codicil which allowed him to step in should any of the management team become less than desirable. Karl Jacobs allowed this codicil to remain as long as Zachary signed an agreement in favor of the corporation. The agreement stated that should Zachary ever be adjudged mentally incompetent, the existing management would handle all control of the Pendrake holdings. All annuities and monies would still be paid. He then, in name only, would still own all of the holdings and its enormous wealth. With all in agreement the documents were signed and put into force.

*   *   *

Time and distance held no mercy for Zachary. His developmental years had been devoted to a brand of fulfillment without the cost of emotional input. Not present as well, were the consequences that are a normal part of learning and emotional growth. The sentiments upon which most people gauge and measure their humanity were non-existent for young Pendrake. For Zachary, the void of emotional structure was to have a profound effect upon his future.

*   *   *

Soon after turning 16, Zachary accompanied Raymond Tiergren on a trip to town. Their mission was to purchase a new set of dress uniforms. Raymond, a lower classman clung to Zachary for what he felt was safety's sake. He was much smaller than Zachary was and had a pinched, bookish appearance. He found himself to be the target of hazing until his alliance with the incredibly imposing Zachary. The mere presence of his protector tended to dissuade those who may have chosen to harass the nerd. Raymond had much in common with his counterpart on an intellectual basis. They both scored over 165 in Intelligence Quotient testing.

Zachary guided the academy van down the winding roads toward Lanchester. The warm summer evening's twilight had faded into a half moon night as the duo traveled on. A car pulled up behind the van. The driver forgot to dim his lights. Zachary became annoyed with the inconsiderate driver. The longer the episode continued the more his anger grew. Zachary was familiar with the road. He watched for landmarks that would pinpoint his location. A plan was forming in his mind. Arriving at the graveyard would be his signal to put the plan into action. Zachary traveled the two-lane road until he spied the section where the hills leveled off. The road's soft shoulder gave way to wide ditches. The shadows reflected by the moonlight provided the timing for this opportunity.

The time was right and Zachary pressed the gas pedal to the floor of the van. He sped the vehicle a short distance from the trailing car. He then slammed on the brakes and turned the wheel to the left. The van promptly swerved to a stop, resting sideways in the roadway. The van blocked the highway. The approaching driver reacted to avoid a collision. Panic braking his car, the compact swerved until coming to a halt next to the van.

Zachary's maneuver shocked and frightened Tiergren. He grasped the dashboard with his hands and drew in a fearful gasp. "Pendrake, what the hell are you doing?" Zachary flung the van door open and leapt out toward the offender.

Cadet Tiergren watched as Zachary vaulted from the van. Raymond shouted after him. "You're crazy Pendrake! You're fucking nuts!"

The stunned man driving the other car tried to clear his head. He looked up to see a visibly angry man striding toward him. Zachary's face was contorted with a sinister smile. The target of Zachary's rage tried in vain to lock his doors and roll up his window.

Zachary in quick wide steps covered the short distance. He reached into the car and grabbed the frenzied stranger by his throat. The strength of Zachary's grip forced the driver's head backward onto the headrest. Zachary's left hand pinioned his opponent as he opened the car door with his right. He jerked the man from his seat with such ferocity that fear overtook the victim. He lost control of his bladder as he begged his assailant not to hurt him.

The headlights illuminated Zachary as he dragged his captive through the ditch into the graveyard. The beams of light highlighted a tall memorial grave marker. An angel carved in stone dwarfed the other headstones. The statue seemed ready to ascend to the heavens on wings spread wide. Her lifeless stone arms were open and extended as if to bid all to follow her.

61

Zachary braced the pleading man against the beckoning headstone. He began pummeling his victim with fists powered by a lifetime's outlay of rage. The captive dropped to the ground with the third crushing blow from hate and anger filled knuckles.

Tiergren scrambled out of the van as he watched Zachary's prey fall to the ground. He ran toward the two shadows shouting, "Pendrake, stop it! You're killing him! Pendrake cut it out now!" Tiergren wedged himself between the two as Zachary was kicking the unconscious man in the head. "That's enough Pendrake," begged Tiergren. "Let him go! Let's get out of here!" Crippled with fear as Raymond was, he could not just stand by and let the thrashing continue. He grabbed Zachary's arms at the biceps and with an all or nothing shove, pushed Zachary backwards. Zachary gave way and stepped back from the bloodied man. Tiergren stood between Zachary and his prey. Tiergren tried to divert his attention. "Pendrake, all right Pendrake, he's learned his lesson. Now let's get out of here before anyone sees us."

Zachary peered at Tiergren with green eyes that seemed to reveal an extraordinary calm. In fact, for the first time in Zachary's life he felt a rush of relief and satisfaction in his conquest. Indeed, his breathing was unhurried and normal. The spotlight effect of the van's headlights seemed to provide Tiergren with an awesome look into the emotional condition of Zachary. Raymond Tiergren shuddered with the realization that he had just looked into the eyes of a monster. He had an up close and personal glimpse into the eyes of the most dangerous man he had ever or would ever know.

The chilling effect upon Raymond was genuine. Once he had Zachary's attention, he couldn't back off. He acted as a barrier to the comatose man and urged Zachary to leave the scene. Zachary finally turned away and confidently began walking to the van. As Tiergren walked close to Zachary's side, he turned to take a quick look at the man lying motionless at the feet of the stone angel. They climbed into the van and closed the door and quietly drove away. Tiergren studied the remarkable composure of his fellow cadet. "Christ Zachary," said Tiergren. "You look like you just had sex or something; what the fuck is with you!"

Zachary stopped the van in the middle of the roadway. He pivoted his body and glared at Tiergren. The intensity of his stare made Tiergren visibly shutter. Zachary once again enjoyed the reaction. He smiled in satisfaction and in a voice spoken more somberly than Tiergren could fathom said, "Never, ever call me crazy again. That jerk was asking for it and I simply obliged him." Zachary turned the van back into the traffic lane heading toward Lanchester and ended the conversation by saying, "Stupid people always get what they deserve."

*   *   *

Zachary noted the distance being placed between himself and Tiergren from that point on. No impact or consequences were in the offering. Zachary truly felt he didn't need the simpleton around him at any rate. He reasoned that Tiergren was a nonessential. Raymond's decision to disassociate himself from Pendrake was validated when he watched the 11:00 p.m. news. It was reported that the man in the graveyard would remain there forever more. The single difference is that he would be six feet deeper.

The incident in the graveyard awakened feelings in Zachary. The beating excited him to a depth he could hardly grasp. All he really knew was the power that had been granted him during his release of rage was incredibly arousing! Only he knew that during the meting out of his retribution, he'd ejaculated and felt ecstasy as never before. Afterward during the remaining drive, he felt level, serene and gratified. He liked the relaxed sensation that he felt after the conquest. He didn't view the eroticism of the event as perverse in any way. He wanted to attain that sensation again and began to feel the urgency of desire. Zachary had learned to lust for the sexual release supplied by the terror in the faces of others.

Zachary's appetite for fear developed. He began challenging his classmates and with each new assault, his rush grew. He gained expertise in the ways of achieving his gratification. His physical elation bloomed until the euphoria became an addiction. It was an obsession that took root in his very soul. He, as other predators, became adept at choosing the weakest individuals to victimize. He knew who would never have the courage to turn him into the Hig. Most cadets considered the closeness of Zachary and the Hig and thought of them as one. They therefore, feared reprisals from the commandant should his favored be maligned in any way. His feet were firmly planted upon his life's path and his physical needs were now fully appreciated, if only by himself.

* * *

During the course of his 14 years at Lanchester, Zachary had grown to an imposing height of six foot five inches. He stood much taller than his classmates and the indomitable Hig. His lean yet muscled body bespoke the consistent health and exercise regimens that were standard and maintained by his instructors. His brilliance in his schoolwork as well as his known deportment connoted a fine officer candidate. These attributes, in the minds of the schools leadership, made up for the lack luster relationships with other cadets. The academy's philosophy was to be a *man*; one must stand alone in the winds of challenge. Zachary Payne Pendrake was alone and now by his own choice.

Those in his peer group seldom challenged Zachary. Doing so would incur consequences for which few of his classmates were prepared. Whenever he was annoyed, his physical reaction alone was awesome. He would lift his chin high, augmenting his height. Zachary would then tilt his head slightly to the left and provide the recipient of his wrath a sharp glare. It was said that Zachary could clear a room with a glance and on more than one occasion that was proven to be fact.

* * *

Nearing the end of his time at Lanchester talk about a 'secret' was rampant with the cadets. On several occasions, he overheard conversations about this *secret*. The whispers were met with eyes that were wide and filled with mischievousness. The intrigue surrounding the closely held prattle was too tantalizing for Zachary to ignore.

Zachary cornered Brad Tylman, one of his favored playmates. He pulled Tylman by the coat collar into the auditorium. Tylman was rigid with fear as Zachary pulled him under the bleachers. "You have some information I want," sneered Zachary. Tylman shook visibly as Zachery towered over him. "I'll offer you a trade. You tell me what is going on with this "*Secrets'* business and I will let you go. If you don't," Zachary put his face down to the face of Tylman and continued, "Well, I guess you know what it will cost you."

Tylman's hand trembled so hard that he could barely push it into his pocket. "I'm waiting," hissed Zachary.

Finally, Tylman recovered a slip of paper. He handed the note to his captor. Zachary studied the numbers scrawled upon the paper. The inscription read 900-732-7387. Confused, Zachary spat, "What the hell is this?"

Tylman could barely speak. His voice stuttered as his body trembled. "It's a sex line. You call that number and you'll see. Everybody's doing it," Tylman meekly explained.

Zachary scrunched up his face and said, "This is what everyone is whispering about?"

"Yeah," Tylman stammered. "Anything goes on this line. They don't even check for your age. You hear some really weird stuff from the weirdo's that call in." Zachary let go of the collar of Tylman's coat and dismissed his captive. Tylman scurried from the auditorium.

*   *   *

Later that evening Zachary took out the paper and dialed the number. There were at least a dozen people talking. The discussion of the evening was sexual pleasuring techniques and games. Zachary found the conversation physically stimulating beyond his wildest imaginings. He was ultimately fascinated by the desires described by the uninhibited participants of the Secrets line. Zachary had found a new outlet to fulfill his deviant sexual needs. He was hooked.

*   *   *

Upon the dawning of his graduation day, Zachary shaved with all the precise firm strokes as commander Higgins had taught him. He peered into the mirror rubbing his strong angular jawbone up to his high prominent cheekbones. He ensured that there were no missed whiskers. When at last satisfied that the shave was close. He stepped back in order to view his overall appearance.

His penetrating green eyes sought out any imperfections that would be pointed out in this, his final inspection. He surveyed the portrait shown in the glass noting that the many hours in the gym had paid off. The complete absence of his mother and death of his father, a man whom Zachary had never met, meant that he was an orphan. Soon, when he left Lancaster Gentleman's Academy there would be no one who would dare to order him about. He was an orphan in fact, orphan to society and an orphan to emotions. He was an orphan with virtually limitless means.

All he had to do was take care of himself and his desires, whatever they may be.

CHAPTER 5
Allison

Allison retrieved her mail and headed to her apartment. Turning the key in the lock of her townhouse she quietly opened the door, paused for a moment and listened. She waited for tell tale sounds which would tell her if Will had returned. The silence confirmed her worst fears, Will was not there. She quickly toured the five-room apartment she noted that there was no evidence that he had even been there. Anger and pain settled in the pit of her stomach.

She dropped her mail onto the coffee table, placed the camera bag onto the sofa and flopped down beside it. Tears began to well up in her weary eyes. She lay back onto the back of her couch and thought back to the earlier times. Decades ago, now it seemed. Times when she was happy with Will. The face of Andrea Cain framed an image in her memory. She could still feel the impact that seeing William Henry Dean had upon her when they first met. Seeing the memories in her mind made her long for the joy filled days of time passed.

* * *

Allison's first experience with university finals had stimulated cramming sessions that lasted like for what seemed days on end. Andrea Cain, a close friend from high school invited her to go to the club known as the Book Vault. Allison had never been into the club scene as many of the other students, she rationalized that this was a juice bar. Thus, she wouldn't feel as much of an outsider for not drinking alcohol. She wasn't a prude, but the chemical simply didn't agree with her.

Upon entering the club, the loud music pounded at her ears. She had a difficult time getting her eyes to adjust to the darkness. From out if the shadows a boisterous voice rang out. "Andi, hey Andi, over here!" Andrea grasped Allison by the wrist and pulled her through the mass of dancing and laughing students. Within a few steps, the two girls stood in front of a table occupied by two young men.

"Allison, this is Alan Dunvey," said Andi and then she pointed to the other man at the table, "And this handsome fellow is Will Dean." Andi pulled Allison down into a chair and promptly walked away to look for a server. Allison felt the flush of heat as embarrassment flowed through her face. "Relax," said Will. "Not everyone is as forward as Andi. We won't bite I promise." Allison struggled to make light of her discomfort and said, "I don't know those look like some really healthy choppers to me."

Will's laughter began to put her at ease. Andi emerged from the whirling crowd defending two orange and pineapple mock cocktails. She tugged at Alan's hand. The music was loud that Andi was forced to cup her hands to the sides of her mouth in order to be heard. "Let's dance Al. I feel like blowing off some steam." The two disappeared into the gyrating glut of bodies on the dance floor.

Allison sipped at her drink. She watched the congregation of students as they set aside the strain of finals week. She could feel the pressure of Will's eyes as he watched her intently. Her nervousness grew. An eternity seemed to pass before he broke the ice.

"I've seen you before. You spend a lot of time in Hoover."

"Yes, I guess I do. I supposed you could call me a dedicated student," retorted Allison.

Will rubbed his chin and seemed to be surveying Allison's appearance. The searching eyes made her uncomfortable. Will seemed to sense Allison pulling away from his gaze. He suddenly interrupted her train of thought, "Dedicated student huh?" Well, I suppose that's better than being called a bookworm. It's especially hard to believe when it comes to someone who looks like you."

Allison forced a nervous laugh and then felt a bit frustrated over her shyness. She gathered herself together and turned toward Will. She was determined to shed her wallflower demeanor. Allison finally relaxed and the two engaged in a long running conversation. They discussed everything from course of study to instructors both liked and disliked. The fact finding mission was interrupted by Andi's voice shouting,

"Hey now, it looks like you two are getting along just fine." Andi surveyed the room to find out where the bouncers were. When she seemed satisfied that all was clear, she asked Dean, "Will here's your bag?"

Allison watched in puzzlement as Will glanced around the room. He took Andi's glass and lowered it under the table. With his other hand, he opened his book bag and removed an odd shaped container filled with a clear liquid. He filled Andi's half-full glass to the brim and handed it back to her. Will offered the same to Allison who covered the top of her glass with her left hand and declined with a wave from her right.

"You don't know what you're missing," chortled Andi. She turned to Will and offered out-stretched hands and said, "Thank you kind sir. You're a gentleman and a scholar."

Curiosity got the better of Allison, "Okay okay what's in the bottle?"

A wry smile crossed the lips of will. He leaned over to open his bag for Allison to peek its contents. Allison's thickly lashed eyes gaped widely as she saw what the bag was concealing. The bottle was laboratory specimen jars compete with a dead frog floating in clear fluid.

Allison gasped, "Oh my God what is that?"

Will laughed boisterously, "I'm a biology major. This place has a practice of checking book bags for bottles of booze." He peeked around the room once again. "I switch the formaldehyde with vodka."

Allison recoiled and gave Will a look of utter disgust. "Oh ick," she exclaimed. Her eyes traveled to Andi. Allison stared in disbelief as Andi finished the beverage. A shiver coursed through her shoulders as Andi ordered another mock tail to be converted in the same manner. Allison covered her mouth as if to fight back the rising of bile. "How could you drink that stuff Andi, holy crap Andi?"

Andi giggled through a hiccup, "I don't think the frog minds, do you Will?"

In a contrived comforting tone, Will replied, "Believe me, that little guy suffers no pain whatsoever."

Andi began to walk away and then turned suddenly to Allison. "There are some people I need to talk to. I'll be gone for a little while." Allison was concerned and stopped her short, "Just don't forget that I'm here. We came in your car, remember?" Andi smiled through her reassurance and said, "No worries kiddo. I'll be right back." Allison was worried about Andi's lack of sobriety and begged Alan to make sure she didn't drink anymore. Alan promised he would take good care of Andi.

The long hours of study caught up to Allison by eleven thirty. She began looking for Andi. Her ride home was nowhere in sight. Allison was getting worried. She talked to several of the people discovering that Andi and Alan had left the bar quite some time before. Feeling distraught and angry, Allison headed for the pay phone. Will stopped her and told her he would be happy to give her a ride home. She conveyed a suspicious gaze. "And just how much frog juice have you had, Will?"

He held up his index finger, "I only had the one drink, honest Allison. I'm just fine. Would you like me to walk a straight line? Or how's about if I say the ABC's backwards?"

Allison fingered the coin in her hand. She really didn't want to call her parents like a child. She hated the thought of sniveling to her Mommy or Daddy for a ride in the family taxi. Allison decided to relent to Will's self-touted trustworthiness and accepted the ride home. Allison was nervous and silently vowed to herself that she would never go any place with Andi again. Unless SHE drove.

*   *   *

"Frog juice, a long, long time ago," Allison muttered to herself as she sat up. She picked up her mail and sifted through the envelopes. Among them was a letter from Sam Cook, the managing editor of the Oakland Tribune. The letter was a job offer for her. Tired and smelly from the Windover scene, she set the letter aside with a promise to think about seriously taking the job. She headed for the kitchen to grab a cola from the refrigerator and then to the shower. The smell from the Windover street murder scene permeated her clothing. She felt awful. Allison turned on the shower and undressed while the water warmed. She took a healthy gulp of her pop before stepping into the hot sprays of rejuvenation. She braced herself against the back wall of the tub surround and allowed the shower massager to pound against her back. "I'm so tired," she said aloud. The words had barely escaped her lips when she seemed to hear her mothers' voice. The familiar cadence of her speech and her mannerisms were complete in Allison's memory." Allison honey, you're too young to be tired." Allison permitted a regretful smile to cross her lips, she missed her mother and she missed her father so very much.

Allison's spell was broken by the sound of the telephone ringing. She hurriedly turned off the shower and wrapped a towel around her body as she heard the answering machine pick up the call. The voice was Will's. Allison found herself thinking, "Okay what's his lie this time." Still damp she headed for the phone, but as she picked up the receiver heard the line go dead. Allison played the message and listened as anger and resentment built inside her. "Allie, sorry I missed you. You might have noticed that I never made it home last night; a big shipment of tile came in. I was the only one available to stock the shelves. We have this big sale today," said Will.

Allison shook her head and narrowed her eyes. "Sure Will, like I really believe that crap," spat Allison toward the machine.

The message continued with Will's voice lilting over the recording, "I grabbed a hamburger last evening and got a page to report in. I'm dragging man! It took me all night to put everything away."

Allison knew she was right. It was yet another lie. Allison had called the store three times during the night and there had been no answer. It was just another in a long line of excuses, lies and half-truths that Allison had endured during their entire marriage. Allison shook her head with irritation as she retrieved a plastic bag from under her sink. She took the bag, following the rancid odor into the bathroom and began bagging the clothing she had worn at the Windover scene. She placed the bag on the balcony for later disposal. Fatigue gripped her and she headed for the comfort of her bed. She soon drifted into a restless sleep. While dreaming a pitched battle with Will filled her mind. The dark brown eyes of Will transposed into the pale blue eyes of Denise Haver. The ranting denials of her husband gave way to him suddenly grabbing at his midsection; Blood began pouring through his fingers. The pale blue eyes of the dream state Will offered Allison a tortured gaze. He dropped his eyes to gape at the rivulets of blood. He lifted his hands from his abdomen exposing a gaping wound across his lower torso. Allison started awake. She shook her head to voice the visions that remained. Visions of Denise Haver's body and remembrances of her friend DeeCee combined in her mind. She sat on the bed attempting to gain composure and slow her pounding heart. Finally, she gave way to the tears that she had been fighting to control.

After the emotional venting, Allison washed her face with cold water to drain the swelling around her eyes. She had barely finished drying her face when the phone once again rang. This time she rushed to the telephone and grabbed the receiver. She was ready to do battle with Will. Instead, she heard the voice of John Hughes, her managing editor at the Chicago Sun Times.

Allison almost yelled in the phone, "Yeah, what is it now?"

"Wow Allie, I didn't do it," said John.

Allison started laughing, and apologized to her superior and said, "Sorry, I thought you were Will."

Hughes joked with her, "I'm like so glad I'm not him." They both laughed over the banter. Allison said, "Sorry John, what's up?"

Hughes said, "I just got off the phone with Captain Sanders. He said you seemed real upset when you left the Windover scene. I was just calling to check on you."

"Oh John, that's so nice of you, but I'm okay. I'm just a little shaky right now. My stomach sort of got the worst of the scene from this morning."

"Bad news scene! Huh? Was it as bad as Sanders said when he called me?"

Allison replied, "Yeah, it was the worst I've seen."

"Sanders said that you were upset when you arrived. I don't mean to be nosy, but is it Will again? When are you going to dump that son of a bitch? You don't need this shit Allie, you just don't need it."

Allison was quiet for a few moments. She appreciated the friendship that John had always offered. But she wasn't ready to leave Will, at least not yet. She didn't know what the breaking point would be but she knew the last straw was close to the surface. "Thanks John, I hope Will and I can work this out. It just remains to be seen."

John changed the subject. "I had another reason for calling you. Your plane tickets for the conference are lying on your desk. You need to sign the travel voucher and pick them up. You're leaving in the morning, right?"

Allison let out a little laugh and said, "Yeah right, I'd forgotten all about the conference, with all this stuff going on. I'll be in the office a little later. You know John it just might do both Will and I some good for me to be gone for a few days. Three days aren't much but maybe it will give each of us some time to think things out."

"I hope so kid. I hate to see you go through this. I know it's not fun. Anyway, back to the Haver murder. You'll do your write up on the case this afternoon before you leave right?"

"Yeah it'll be ready to run before I leave," said Allison. And as for it being a nasty scene, John honey you have no idea. You know I've seen a lot of pretty bad stuff. But that poor woman was butchered. I'll never forget this one."

Allison vacillated between telling John that she knew the victim and not telling him. She didn't want to be removed from the pipeline of information simply because she knew the victim. Friends and family weren't usually the most objective in the investigation of a crime. Allison decided to keep quiet and not tell anyone of her relationship with Denise Haver.

Allison began packing for her trip. She secreted the letter from the Tribune into her camera bag. She ignored the dull ache in her lower stomach and her feverish feeling. She preferred to think about John and Betty Ann Hughes. She thought about the friendship they had offered both she and Will. Will didn't seem to appreciate them as friends, the way Allison did. "Oh well, "she commiserated, "Las Vegas will be fun and I could really use some fun."

Allison folded her favorite sweater. The pale pink turtleneck was beginning to show its years of wearing. She cradled the garment in her arms and thought about her mother once again. She reflected upon the day her mother handed her a ribbon-laden box. The box contained this sweater. Her mother had given it to her just before Allison had left for Chicago. "It's cold in Chicago. But honey, it will always, always, be warm here."

The words of Janet Kayhill had remained with her daughter. It seemed so long ago now and so much had happened to her since that day. She recalled the unwilling discussions her mother had about Will and her marriage. How is it she thought to herself that mother's have a way of undressing their child's mind? Mothers can make every thought and emotion nude and open to scrutiny. "I should have listened to you, Mom and Dad. You were right about Will," muttered Allison. She thought about the heated exchange between her father and herself.

Robert Kayhill had made it plain that he didn't like Will Dean. She began thinking about the file her father had offered her during their disagreement. He had gone through some great pains to investigate Will and his background. She remembered the pain as she read through the file. A file which had indicated he'd been suspected of theft at his jobs and had been given and passed lie detector tests. There were further allegations that Will had been married before. Further, the documentation claimed that he had given his wife syphilis. Allison loved Will then and flew to his defense. She had closed her ears and eyes to the paper trail, which had been laid out for her. Being divorced was not a crime and she was convinced there was a good reason he didn't tell her about it. There simply had to be much more to his story that what was indicated in this file.

The altercation played through her mind. Allison visualized her father standing in the den of their home. She could still see the expression of dread upon his face. She saw him fidget when he asked her, "How much do you know about this Will Dean?"

"I know enough to know that I love him," answered Allison.

Allison watched in disbelief as her mother and father exchanged stricken expressions. She had glanced through the file and looked up at her parents with questions written all over her face. "So just what is it that you're trying to say?"

Janet Kayhill had tried to soothe her alarmed offspring and said, "Allison dear, we're just trying to find out how much of the information you knew about. We love you dear and we wouldn't want to see you make a mistake that will haunt you."

Allison felt like she was standing in a cave. The way the words echoed in her mind and heart. She could hear herself saying, "I'm not a child anymore you don't need to treat me like one. I'm perfectly capable of making my own decisions."

The visage of her father leaping to his feet and pointing at her filled her mind. She remembered him saying, "Listen little one, go ahead, and ask Dean about this. But never," he repeated for emphasis, "never even think that he wouldn't do the same things to you as he did to his other wife."

She'd wanted to believe in Will more than anything. The eight names that had been given by Will as possible contact partners couldn't shake her faith in him. After all she had reasoned, perhaps they were separated at those times. A line in the sand had been drawn. Allison had chosen Will's side of the desert. The rift between father and daughter grew until Allison had chosen to accept a position more than a thousand miles from her home. Allison and Will moved to Chicago. All of these memories plagued her. Allison didn't know how to bridge the gap. All she really knew is that she desperately wanted to overcome the bad feelings.

Allison gently placed the sweater in her suitcase. She muttered aloud, "You were right mom and dad." Allison knew it was true. Shortly after they were married, their relationship began to deteriorate. All and more, much more of her parent's observations had come true. Only Allison's sense of pride had kept her from openly sharing her marital difficulties between she and Will away from her parents. Even her relocation to Chicago had been fraught with problems. Will had difficulty in finding work. The fact that he had dropped out of Stanford didn't help his cause. Financial concerns weighed heavily upon Allison. The competition between photojournalist was much greater than she had ever anticipated. She understood then, that for her talent to be marketable she would have to create a name for herself. A name she now had, due to some luck at being at the right place at the right time and Burton Sanders and the Chicago P.D.

Allison latched closed the last suitcase and set them by the front door. The thought of Sandy always brought a smile to her face. He had sort of taken on the role of surrogate father since her first meeting with him. She envisioned the warm face of the detective and back to their first meeting.

* * *

Allison, new to the Chicago Sun Times, had been dispatched with a journalist to cover a murder on the east side of Chicago. She stood at the barrier tape with all of the other reporters who were there to cover the story. Captain Sanders seemed to possess a commanding presence. Her eyes had riveted on him while he was shouting orders to junior officers at the scene. Allison watched as he threw his arms out wildly and then slapped at his sides. He leaned toward an obviously intimidated subordinate and yelled loud enough for Allison to hear, "What the hell are we going to do now?"

Suddenly he turned toward the crush of reporters and stared at each face to a point that one would think they were suspects. Reporter after reporter shrunk from his stare. All except for Allison, her instincts were telling her that opportunity was staring at her, and she had better stare right back if she ever wanted to make a name for herself. His eyes met hers and he approached her in firm commanding steps. Standing directly in front of Allison his six foot four inch full-bodied frame dwarfed her. Before she knew what was happening the huge man was point an index finger at her as he said, "You come over here."

Allison looked around the crowd and realized that he indeed was signaling to her. The reporter standing with her gave a quick push as he held up the barrier ribbon. A police officer in charge of crowd control yelled at her to get back behind the ribbon. But the big man put a hand on the officer's shoulder and said, "I asked for her, you just control the rest of these jerks."

Allison stepped forward and looked up into the furrowed face of a man whose nametag read, 'Captain Sanders'. His narrow blue-green eyes seemed to have an untold wisdom combined with a mixture of determination and inflexibility. The closer he came to Allison the more impressive his size became. He asked, "What's your name?"

"Allison, Allison Dean, from the Chicago Sun Times," she held up her press pass for him to see.

"Well Ms Dean from the Chicago Sun Times,' he pointed to her camera and said, "are you any good with that thing?"

She mustered her smile and bolstered her level of courage at the same time. "I'm the best."

He said, "I'm Captain Burt Sanders, Chief of Detectives in this thriving little metropolis. I have a problem. But before I get to that, I need to know if you can keep your mouth shut."

She gave him a bewildered look and simply nodded an affirmative.

"Fine," he said as he took her by the arm and pulled her away from the crowd. The two arrived at the steps of the building that was the focal point of interest. He began, "Our photographer has been in an accident. He isn't going to be here for quite some time" He swung his arm out indicating the crowd. "This mess has to be cleaned up before we cause a traffic tie up here at rush hour. The next things I need to know are, do you have a strong stomach? And do you have the ability to detach yourself from the sight of death. And most important of all, can you keep your mouth shut? If you can answer yes, then I have a job for you."

Allison gulped a chunk of air and steeled herself. She didn't want to sound childish. "First answer is, yes, I can keep my mouth shut. Secondly, my stomach is as strong as the next person's. And lastly, I don't know. I've never seen dead people before. But," she continued, "I'm as safe a bet as any out here and maybe even better. Unlike the other news hounds, I'm not afraid of you, the others are."

Burton Sanders laughed and rubbed his hands together as he weighed his options and then continued, "I need pictures of every square inch of this place, ceiling to floor of the murder scene. Clear and concise are the key here, can you do that?"

She nodded again and choked out the words, "you bet I can."

Sanders looked deeply into Allison's eyes. His intensity was stimulating to Allison. "You'll see evidence that we won't give to the press. Furthermore, you'll need to be able to hold your tongue, despite the insistence of your editors. Can you do that too?"

Allison could barely take her eyes off of the towering man. Beneath all of the veneer, she sensed a gentle and caring man. "That," she said emphatically stated, "I can definitely do."

Sanders began to walk with her up the steps of the building. When he stopped her short he said, "I'm taking a big risk here Ms. Dean, don't let me down. Traditionally the press and police don't see eye to eye. You people have a way of printing the sensational, even if it isn't true. I can't stress enough that this promise, to keep a lid on what you see, must be kept. It will work out best for all of our concerns if you can. Leaks cannot happen here."

Allison took every word to heart. Sanders gave her a sly look and said, "If you keep the details to yourself, I will see to it that you and the Times are the first notified of any break in the case. It will be scoop town. You get me Dean?"

She surprised herself when she strongly replied, "Yes, and I want to be the mayor of scoop town."

*   *   *

"I've kept my word Sandy. And you've kept yours." Allison said to the listening walls.

CHAPTER 6

Columns Revisited

Zachary decided he wanted to live in the spacious surroundings where he was born. The Pendrake Industries counsel tried, without success to change this mind. He was very insistent and not to be put off. He knew exactly how the corporate heads would react with even the slightest hint that he may want to become involved with the businesses inner workings. When the board of directors were presented with even the remotest thought that the young heir would want to run Pendrake Industries, made them all see the wiser course of action. They decided that giving young Zachary what he wanted was the better option.

The reopening of Columns Manor was fraught with complications unique unto themselves. The estate, which had fallen into disrepair, needed considerable work to occupy. Not to mention meeting all of Zachary's demands to be met in the restoration of the huge secluded home. The wheels however were set into motion. The renovations moved forward. New staff was hired to fill every conceivable position. Karl Jacobs saw to it that everything Zachary wanted, he got.

Karl's years with the Pendrake Industries had been financially kind to him. He prospered to a greater level after the death of Norman Pendrake. As tragically affected, as he seemed to be, Karl was an opportunistic man and a realist to the ultimate. He was not yet quite as well heeled as he intended to be. However, the deal he had been working on for well over a year would complete his financial portfolio. Karl Jacobs would then retire as one of the worlds' richest men.

Unbeknownst to most commodity brokers, Jacobs was playing his own game of hearts. The difference was that instead of a card game, he was investing a great deal of money into the world rice market. The millions of dollars invested would enrich Karl and Pendrake Industries well into the billions of dollars. From Karl's point of view, keeping the young and arrogant heir out of the business picture provided the capability to fulfill his financial aspirations.

*   *   *

The newly hired staff of Columns Manor had no clue as to the makeup of their young master. They only understood that he was the last of the Pendrakes and nothing was to be omitted from his care. All those who intended to attend anxiously awaited his arrival at the estate.

The renovated manor house was complete and boasted all of the latest in technology and modern upgrades. The pool now had a Jacuzzi as well as a new sauna. All of the living quarters were completely refurbished and rooms had been set with modern furnishings. A downstairs guest room had been re-fitted and set up as home theater. The exterior white pillars gleamed in the late afternoon sunlight.

A sleek black Lamborghini with deeply tinted windows skulked up the driveway toward the imposing estate. Zachary sat in his car with the motor running. He took his first look at the home of his earliest childhood. It was a time before Lanchester and laced with remnants of an empty time, for which he only had the vaguest of memory. He looked around the expansive lawns dotted with mature trees giving texture and cool feelings throughout the yard. The flowerbeds were filled with bright perennial and annual floral color spots. He found it acceptable. Zachary had no actual memories from this place, but whispers of an emotional past influenced a part of him that he no longer recognized. Satisfied that he had taken in all that he cared to of the grounds of the estate he turned off the ignition. He tripped the latch to the up-swinging driver's side door and unfolded his six foot five inch bulk from the cockpit. He stood and stretched out his arms and spine. He took a deep invigorating breath and filled his lungs with the air of what he considered home. The door to the manor opened and a smartly dressed man approached Zachary.

"Mister Pendrake, sir, I am Jefferson, your head staff person. Welcome to Columns Manor."

Zachary studied the exuberant man standing in front of him. His indifference toward the Jefferson became completely obvious to the manservant. Zachary looked down to him and said, "I'm ready for a tour. Were all of my specifications met?"

Clicking heels were met with a courteous nod as Jefferson said, "I believe so sir, but if you would care to inspect the work, after you sir."

Zachary stepped up onto the spacious veranda and caressed the huge marble pillars which braced the roof. His fingertips traced the rich ebony veins in the stone. Jefferson stood by without a word. He watched as if he were wondering what was going through young Master Pendrake's mind. Zachary suddenly dropped his hand to his side and walked through the double door entry. He set his first footfall onto highly polished Italian marble floors. The circular reception hall seemed to be an explosion of purity. The stark white pillars half encased in the walls surrounded the foyer. The lush red carpeting that blanketed the broad curving staircase enhanced the brilliance of the white walls. A succession of crystal chandeliers illuminated the crimson pathway to the upper floors and gave warmth to the dark furnishings. The updating of the aged mansion provided the ambiance of contemporary design.

Zachary's long legged stride combined with a tempo that radiated his militaristic training, gave lesson to Jefferson about the nature of his employer. The tour provided by Jefferson was kept at a brisk pace as they looked through room after room. Introductions to staff were made during their trip through Columns and acknowledgments were kept to an abrupt nodding gesture. Zachary seemed to focus on nothing and yet took stock of everything he saw.

Jefferson held the theater until the end of the expedition in an attempt to save the main level's finest attribute for last.

Zachary pushed past the black velvet curtains, turned to Jefferson, "These drapes are not acceptable," said Zachary. "I want them replaced with oak padded security doors immediately."

Jefferson nodded and said, "Yes sir, right away."

Royal Purple drapes girdled the semi-circle stage at the rear of the expansive room. The skirting complete with matching drapery and black tie backs accentuated the large concave screen. Near to the brocade ceiling, recessed speakers lined the auditorium to provide an enormous sound system. Overstuffed chairs, footrests, and sofas lined the room. All were provided for comfort during viewing of films. Cases of films had begun to arrive shortly before the master of the house and were stored as per his direction. Included in the film room storage was a back room in which housed films that had no title on the jackets. They instead were labeled only with a number. The only one to know what these films were was Zachary himself. When he inspected the room, he looked at the shelves holding the secret videos and ran his fingers across the stacks. The secretive nature of the films in this area fostered curiosity and conjecture from the staff members of Columns.

The two men climbed the crimson stairwell to view the upper floors that housed Zachary's as well as ten other guest quarters. Each guest room had its own private bath and theme. Jefferson moved toward the first door on the right and began to turn the knob. Zachary stopped him with a wave of his large right hand and said, "I don't need to see these rooms. I won't be spending any time in them. Just show me the master suite."

"As you say," said Jefferson.

The twosome traveled down the corridor to meet a massive double door entry into the master quarters. Jefferson grasped the curved gold handles and gently opened wide the barriers to the private sitting room for the master suite.

Zachary stepped forward into the sitting room that was decorated in the finest furnishings. The contemporary motif of the remainder of Columns gave way to the ornate curves and designs of cherry wood French provincial décor. Plush area carpets with broad light blue angular striping graced gleaming hardwood floors. Settees bordered the carpeting that was covered in rich blue velvet upholstery. The center of the room boasted an oval provincial coffee table of gold plated wrought iron and marble. Jefferson stepped across the parlor and opened yet another door which closed off the master bath. The huge jetted tub was encased by broad cabinetwork of teak wood and was heavily laden with ornate hand carved designs and patterns. The panels above the tub opened when pressed upon, to expose a wide variety of electronic equipment and still another large selection of film. A swiveling rocker arm held a wide screen television so that it can be angled toward any part of the room.

Directly across from the tub were marble counters with hand painted porcelain sinks. The 18-carat gold fixtures gently arched over the basins. A wall of mirrors cast a wide reflection of opulence contained in this private domain. Zachary dismissed Jefferson as he reached for the door handle for the entry into the sleeping berth. Zachary turned and faced the retreating servant and announced, "Dinner at seven o'clock Jefferson, menu selection five."

Jefferson turned as he began to pull the doors closed and replied, "Very good sir. Might I inquire when you would like to meet the staff to impart your expectations?" Zachary's face grew taught with irritation as he retorted, "I have no intentions of meeting with the servants. It's your job to keep them in line and out of my hair, is that clear Jefferson?"

Jefferson was adept at making himself as invisible as necessary. He lowered his eyes and said, "Precisely, Mr. Pendrake." He closed the doors and left the master on his own.

Zachary wanted to be alone while he explored his inner sanctum. He wanted to make absolutely certain that all of the equipment he had ordered, had been installed and operational. As he left the bathroom and went into the master sleeping area an enormous circular bed was the centerpiece of the room. The cherry wood walls housed hidden cabinets and closet spaces. He pressed against the embedded gold plate in the center of the doors. The panels gave way and spread apart to expose a huge walk in closet complete with drawers and his clothes that had been delivered earlier. It seemed that all his specifications had been met. The sock and undergarment drawers were aligned in the exact order specified. His clothing had been hung in the grouping according to color and style. His masses of footwear were all in the prescribed arrangements.

Zachary exited the closet areas and cycled the partition closed. The inspection of the next secluded alcove displayed his television monitors, fax machine, computer and telephone with four lines available to him. All equipment seemed to be in working order. Zachary reclined on the bed and opened the control pan located in the built in night stand. He pressed the button labeled 'drapes'. The wall of ceiling to floor curtains parted and exposed a huge bank of windows with glass doors that lead to a large private patio. He walked over and soaked in the view of the gardens and the myriad of waterfalls cascading into ponds. Walking out onto the balcony, he felt tight and needy, despite the relaxed nature of the landscape beneath him.

He returned to the closet, grabbed one of the portable telephones and reclined across the bed. He dialed 900-732-7387, the secrets line. It was early and the conversation on the party line offered Zachary no entertainment. He decided to call back during his favored night hours when he was certain that the dialogue would be more to his liking.

Zachary returned to the bathroom. He began filling the tub with hot water and prepared to bathe. He responded to a knock at his door by calling out for the visitor to enter. Jefferson walked into the room and announced. "Sorry to disturb you sir, but a package has been delivered."

Obviously irritated he asked, "Why are you bothering me with this?" He watched and was pleased as a slight quiver coursed through Jefferson

Jefferson explained, "I beg your pardon sir," began Jefferson, "the driver says that he has instructions for personal acceptance only."

"Alright, alright, go ahead and send him up here. I'll sign for the package."

Minutes later and in the privacy of his suites, Zachary opened the boxes that had just been delivered. The three cartons contained video presentations from Ebony films, a not too well known underground snuff film producer. Parody titles such as Patriot Tamers, Black Velvet Sisters, The Eroticist, and Three Men And A Fast Lady were among the titles available. He took some time considering his mood and chose the latter one for viewing. He had seen this particular video many times and craved the response wrought by the content of the film.

The tub was filled to the level he desired and Zachary inserted the compact disk into the player. He stripped off his clothing and slid haltingly into the swirling, just short of scalding water. His flesh reddened and stung as perspiration surged down his body. Zachary rolled his head in wide circles as he reveled in the pain of the torrid mist. His body became relaxed finally as he adjusted to the intense heat of the water. At last fully immersed in the water, he opened the control panel and pressed the play button on the video player.

The video he had chosen portrayed three men kidnapping a woman from a grocery store parking lot. The following scenes showed the men raping and sodomizing their captive. Very little build up preceded the ferocity of the attack. The victim's fear entranced Zachary. His own passion flourished as he watched the escalation of violence. The genuine pain the woman endured was interpreted by Zachary as the emotion of ecstasy. Snuff films always had the makings of an intensely erotic episode for Zachary. The exhilaration he felt increased his heart rate and his lower abdomen grew taught and tingly. The power the three men possessed beheld great allure. The uninhibited men as they played out upon the screen originated a purely erotic and unrestrained carnal encounter.

Fixating upon the struggles of the victim and the ardent pleasure taking of the executioners on the screen consumed him with an enormous yearning. Zachary soaped his bull blown erection to a lather. He writhed in matching thrusts with the rhythm of the assailants on the screen. His avarice attained new heights as he squeezed his testicles between his palm and fingers. The men beat, scratched, and bit the body of their captive. Her screams only served to augment his need for satisfaction. Zachary fantasized that it was he in the video and he was doing the taking of the woman. The vision of the aggressors as they simultaneously utilized every available orifice upon their prisoner's body urged Zachary's appetite on. The frenzied groans and grimaces on the screen turn to throaty screams. The bound victim bled profusely from the brutality of the beating and the sexual bombardment. As the largest aggressor sodomized the woman who could no longer scream, he reached over her body and cut her throat at the same time that he ejaculated. Zachary's lust coalesced to a crescendo when the woman's lifeless body fell limp. The end of the video and with the death of the woman on the screen, the three men and Zachary achieved a four-way climax.

He lay spent in the still churning water as the video screen went black. His green eyes were glazed in satisfaction. The discharge of his seed rewarded every fiber in his being with supreme awareness. He lay back, serene and content for a short time before he stood and showered.

Zachary had just wrapped his muscular frame into his robe when a knock sounded at his door. "Enter," he said still feeling the depletion of his energy.

Jefferson politely said through the door, "Your dinner is ready sir. Where would you like to be served?"

Minutes later Zachary's meal was delivered to the sitting room per his request. Upon the tray was an array of newspapers from around the country. Zachary picked up the Chicago Sun Times and read the publication as he dined. He paid particular attention to an article that reported upon the murder of a woman named Denise Haver. Zachary smiled with remembrance.

After finishing his dinner, Zachary retreated to his sleeping quarters. He stretched out on the bed and once again dialed the 900 Secrets line. This time the line was considerably more active, which appealed to Zachary. He listened intently to the conversations of Rocket, Satanica, Inquisitioner, and Domatra, The usual names held testimony to the particular bent each individual preferred. Normally the more ambiguous the names were, served to show indications of the scope of sexual discipline enjoyed.

Zachary had come to know the participants of this culture, at least on the telephone. They shared the same bondage and pain-pleasuring philosophies as he. Unlike the video, the conversation merely intrigued him. The chatter did not arouse his desires. The frank discussions of the methods of pleasuring continually offered him something new for his imagination and exploration. Zachary himself was known as Prince Odious, a name that he had offered when he had stopped simply listening and began interaction with the regulars of the group. Satanica discussed her latest encounter with an unwitting participant on the night before.

"She was so hot," said Satanica. "I love taking care of a curious bitch and breaking in a novice. It's like getting your first virgin." She let out a raucous laugh and said, "The taste of virgin blood is the sweetest."

"You bet," chimed in Rocket, "Where'd you meet her?"

Satanica once again laughed and said, "She came to the club on a bet. I just wonder if she won or not."

"Who gives a shit if she won or not," laughingly replied Domatra. "The real question is do you think you made it for her?"

"She'll be back for more. You just wait and see," assured Satanica. "As a matter of fact, even I would bet on that one."

Zachary officially signed onto the conversation with his trademark statement, "hello servants."

Inquisitioner spoke up first, "Prince O, you're back! Where you been ole' buddy?"

"Just taking care of some business in Chicago," replied Zachary. "But I want to hear more about Satanica's new convert."

"Yeah give with the rest of the story," said Rocket. "This sounds like a Vixen bulletin to me."

Inquisitioner blurted, "Sure as shit does! By the way, our little Vixen has either made a different scene or has dropped off somewhere. Anybody know where she's been?"

"Not me" said Rocket, and then she added, "I haven't heard from her since she made that date with the new guy. What was his name. Let me think, oh yeah Cruiser, wasn't it?"

Domatra spoke up, "Well maybe she found her ultimate mate, what'cha think gang?"

"Sure that's got to be it. We haven't heard from, Cruiser since then either," added Satanica.

All of the parties were in agreements, save Prince Odious who remained silent. Prince Odious simply smiled with a large measure of mute victory and memories teeming with his own private truth.

CHAPTER 7
Reunion

A few days had passed since the shoot of the Denise Haver crime scene. Still, the haunting dreams persisted. At times Allison was certain the sights and smells from the apartment were firmly planted in her mind. How else, she reasoned could she still smell that nauseating stench. Her emotional stability seemed to be pushed to the limit with the combination of the realization that Denise Haver was her friend DeeCee, combined with the ever-present problems she was having with Will. Until recently, Allison had expended much of her time agonizing over the problems. She had depleted her energy in acceptance of blame for all shortcomings within Will. Through all of the feelings of inadequacy she had laid on her own doorstep, she had only just begun to see the solutions.

Allison begged off completing the three-day conference and left Las Vegas after only two. She had met Sam Cook, the managing editor of the Oakland Tribune during the conference. They sat and discussed the upcoming opening in their staff.

Allison had left the meeting asking for time to think over the offer. "I'll get back to you in a couple of weeks. Is that alright?" Allison was grateful and relieved when he had agreed to give her the time she needed. She appreciated that he had not tried to pressure her into making a rapid decision.

Her head ached from stress and fatigue. She wanted to go home. Deep in her heart, she secretly hoped that Will would be home. Perhaps they could try one last time to settle the distance between them. In her view, there was not much left of their relationship. What had once been a good relationship was now destroyed by Will and his actions. Finally, Allison had made up her mind. Either the marriage would improve or it would end with this conversation. During her flight home, she envisioned discussion of the situation with Will repeatedly in her mind. She knew what his responses would be. She could feel the anger well up inside her again as she could hear the excuses flowing from his lips. While she despised the thought of her marriage failing, she knew that continuing to live like this was not an option. The last few weeks had seen a dramatic change in the formerly compliant Allison. I don't have 'WELCOME, ' tattooed on my forehead any more had been her latest comment to Betty Ann Hughes, her bosses wife and friend.

Without comment to anyone, she contemplated the offer from the Tribune. She had kept the letter secreted in the bottom of her camera bag. Allison reread the letter. The thought of going home created flurries of emotion, both positive and negative. She wasn't certain how the gap between her parents and herself could ever be bridged.

Allison felt so ill that it was difficult to drive herself home from the airport. Calls to Will had gone unanswered. When she did finally arrive the sun had set. She decided that she would have Will bring up her luggage in the morning. Allison felt as if her feet were trudging instead of walking. The light timers had not been properly set, which resulted in the stairwells being dark and almost forbidding. She stood at the door feeling her way through her purse to find her keys. The lights suddenly blazed on just as she located them in her purse. She chuckled at herself for dropping them into her purse in the first place. It was late and she didn't know if Will would be sleeping or not. In the morning, when she was rested and felt better she and Will would have their talk.

Quietly, Allison turned the key in the lock and tip toed into the entry hall. She heard the gentle beat of the music that she and Will played while they made love. The lights were off but the glow of flickering candles slightly lit the hallway. A smile traced her lips as she quietly walked toward the living room. Three steps into the hallway the reality sunk in that Will didn't expect her to come home until late the next day. Her smile vanished and suspicion crept into her heart. Allison rounded the corner to find Will and his co-worker, Sarah Penna making love on the floor in front of the fireplace. The glow of the flames highlighted their sweat soaked bodies. Two glasses with champagne were setting on the coffee table along with a host of strawberries and whipped cream. Will rolled over on his back and pulled Sarah on top of his body. Speechless, Allison watched as Sarah inserted his penis into her writhing body. She reeled backwards running her hands through her blond wet hair. She moaned loudly and begged for more. Will reached up to tease her swollen nipples with his fingers and palms. He fondled her breasts uttering enticing phrases and provocative challenges. Sarah clasped her hands onto Will's to guide his caresses to more sensitive areas of her body. Will took hold of her shoulders pulling her forward, demanding to be kissed.

As she leaned forward rubbing her breasts on his face the eyes of Sarah Penna fell upon Allison standing in the entrance of the room. Sarah gasped for breath and quickly rolled off her partner as she exclaimed, "Oh shit!" The words, "Damn it, damn it, damn it," rolled from her lips. She grabbed at her clothing which were strewn all about the room.

"What's the," was as far as Will got before he flexed his neck to see Allison. Tears were streaming down her face. At long last she could only mutter, "Why, Will why?"

Sarah, only half dressed skirted around Allison seemingly to avoid any potential threat. Will called out to Sarah to wait for him in her car. Allison turned her back on Will and went into the bedroom. She sat on the bed and continued to cry. The last thing she heard was the closing of the front door. Will was gone with Sarah. At least this time she thought to herself, she wouldn't have to listen to his lies and denials.

The illness that had crept upon Allison was lost in a mixture of grief and anger. Allison called John Hughes and asked for a place to stay. She simply couldn't stay in the apartment that held so many memories.

John and Betty Ann Hughes opened their hearts and their guest room to her. The next day Allison contacted a moving company. She had all of their belongings except for

Will's clothing and personal items packed. Everything she had accumulated over the last three years was now packed tightly into a security storage unit.

Allison sat in John's office at the end of the next day and showed him the letter from Sam Cook of the Oakland Tribune. He read the letter and then looked at Allison with sadness in his eyes, "I knew you would have to leave. But, I didn't know it would be this soon. What's your plan?"

"I'm going to take it John. I have to get away from Chicago and Will. All day long, I have been hearing from people who are now willing to tell me the truth. I now know for a fact, what I had only suspected before. Will has been cheating on me since our move here. I just wish that someone would have been open with me before this."

John glanced over the letter once again and said, "Allie, I know this is hard. Your friends care about you and didn't know how to tell you about that cheating son of a bitch. It's risky you know, telling anyone all of the truth. It has backfired on many. I'm sure they didn't want to risk the possibility of losing your friendship. You just watch, all of them will be there to support you. And by God that's what real friends do."

Allison was sure that she had cried all of her tears away the night before. But somehow, as she gave her notice to John more came flooding from her sore eyes.

Hughes said, "How much time are you going to give us?"

Allison dabbed up a stream of tears. "Is two weeks okay, John? I don't want to leave you in a bind, but I need to get out of here."

He countered, "Two weeks is fine Allie. I understand why you feel that this moment you must leave Chicago. But do think it over "Allie. Take some time to make certain that this is what you want to do."

She smiled and said, "I will think about it, but as it stands right now, I'm pretty sure this is what I need to do."

John slapped both hands on the top of his desk and said in his way, " Nuff said." He then turned back to his credenza and pulled out a stack of papers. "You need to see these kiddo." He handed her a stack of messages taken for her. Each of the messages were from Will. The first two simply asked her to give him a call. The second two were filled with apologies and demands for another chance. The last message left demanded to know where the furniture and other belongings had been taken.

"I had Shirley screen these calls," John explained. "I hope you understand. I just thought that you were too vulnerable to talk with him at the time. To be honest I was worried that you would go back to him if I gave these messages to you." He tilted his head slightly sideways and said, "You see Allie I'd rather lose you to Oakland, than let you lose your self-worth to the likes of Will Dean."

Allison shook her head in slow yet definite denial and managed a smile. She steeled herself and in a voice loaded with self-assurance said, "I know John, you and Betty Ann have been great. Thank you so much for caring the way you do." Allison shifted her body and leaned forward. She folded her hands in her lap. "You know John, this morning Betty Ann and I had this same conversation. I'll tell you what I told her. Will Dean is like a disease! I've had him and I'm immune."

John chuckled and said, "How right you are! Even in your comparison of Will Dean and a disease. The scary part is that it truly fits."

Allison's expression turned serious, "John is it all right with you and 'Betty Ann if I stay in your guest room until I make arrangements?"

Without hesitation he replied, "You bet!" He then leaned forward in his chair, "Allison, I know this won't be easy, but, you are going to call your parents aren't you?"

Allison slumped into the chair and shook her head in total disgust. "Yeah John, but I tell you it won't be easy. It's never easy saying just how wrong you've been." Allison began to cry once more. "I've been just too blind, proud and in love to accept what they were telling me." Between the tears, she managed some humor. "You know what I mean, telling your parents that you have been suffering from rectal cranial inversion really sucks."

Allison and John laughed together. He finally cleared his throat and said, "Seriously Allie, you're gonna be just fine. Better than that, I think you have a bright future in front of you. Don't be afraid to grab it."

She shook her head and said, "I know, but it will take some time. I have a lot of bridge building to do."

Her editor and friend rocked backwards in this overstuffed chair, interlaced his fingers behind his head and said, "I think those bridges are not as wide as you may think. My folks used to say, that I came from good stock, whatever that means. I'm sure you come from good stock too. Try not to sell your family short. They are lucky to have a daughter like you."

* * *

As controlled as she intended to be, the facade of any strength and well-being fell away the moment Allison heard her mother's voice on the phone saying, "Hello." The instant she said the word Mother, a torrent of tears fell from what felt like her soul.

Robert picked up the extension and the estranged family was once again whole. No recriminations were spoken and nothing but love and caring was in the offering. Secretly between Robert and Janet Kayhill, they were glad the nightmare was over. Robert despised Will for the injury he had inflicted upon Allison.

Allison was sure that anger would be vented. She was ready for it. She was even more surprised when not a word was spoken to her about the rage she was certain they felt. It was as if William Henry Dean had never existed. Allison's goal was to move forward and build a happier life that included a close relationship with her family.

Allison began the task of severing her ties to Chicago. Robert purchased a one-way airline ticket for the last day of Allison's employment with the Sun Times. She sold her car to a new employee at the paper and had a storage locker sale.

She kept very few of the items that were stored. Robert hired a van to transport what belongings that were not sold to their new home in Palo Alto.

Will continued to call the paper demanding to be put through to Allison. On her final day, she accepted a call from him. He began by telling her what a mistake he had made and that he wanted to work out their problems. Allison listened coldly to his pleadings. She enjoyed the power being in her court for the first time she simply replied, "I'm not interested Will. We have no marriage. Not the kind of marriage I dreamt of having. All you have done is use me. I won't be used anymore. It's a done deal."

Will apparently got the message. His prior smooth talk gave way to viciousness. He demanded, "Where's all my stuff Allie? You took a lot more than your half! And, a hell of a lot more than you were supposed to take!"

Allison burst out into a hardy laugh. "That's ironic Will! You took everything I had to give for the last three years. I think it was about time that I took exactly what I wanted. You know Will, I made up a wise old saying yesterday. It's something you might want to remember it goes like this. Time wounds all heels."

Allison gently hung up the phone. As the headset nestled down onto the cradle, Allison took her very first breath of free, fresh air in three years.

CHAPTER 8
Lady Cassandra

Conversations on the 900-Secrets line were especially tantalizing during the early morning hours. The lightless wee hours sent the fiber optic highway ablaze as the night people joined the exchange loop. True identities, cloaked by obscure pseudonyms shielded the participants. Characters with names such as Virro, Rebeck, Judas Cain and Lady Cassandra joined the swarm of voices.

Often new participants would not introduce themselves. Regulars on the 900-Secrets circuit had their own name for these outsiders. They were called 'heeders'. Heeders were the curious who listened and benefited from the dialogue and then disappeared. It seemed that one caller out of twenty became accepted by the group. Zachary signed onto the conversation early on and listened as the heeders came and went. Lady Cassandra was in rare form reading from, a new book she had purchased. The book described in specific terms the satanic and ritualistic sexual techniques practiced by witches and warlocks.

Zachary found her recitals to be incredibly intriguing. He gleaned much in the way of new and exciting tactics for later application and experimentation. A heeder was on the line who had introduced himself as Hannibal the Slayer. His glib remarks and cool wit aggravated Zachary.

Lady Cassandra however seemed to respond to the dry and caustic humor offered by Hannibal. The two exchanged digs towards each other and finally decided that they wanted to meet, face to face. All the other members cheered them on except for one quietly gleeful member. Zachary was quietly creating his own set of plans. He began recording the conversation.

Cassandra gave Hannibal a location to meet her and they set a date for the following Friday night in a small town outside of Tucson called Benson. The entire group assisted them in plotting a menu of particularly interesting games to play. A multitude of specific toys were listed down as suggestions to augment their liaison

Zachary's itinerary was being set along with the meeting that was being planned by Hannibal and Cassandra

*   *   *

Zachary's private jet set down at the Tucson airport. A rental corvette pulled up beside the lowering step platform. Terry Marsh, the steward, opened the gangway door and quietly stepped out of Zachary's path. Zachary, saturated with purpose, bounded from the jet. He signed is name for the delivery person and without so much as a glance took the keys to the vivid red sports car. He drove southeast to Benson.

The directions were concise and before long, he pulled up in front of a mailbox on a rural road. The name V. Macadam was written in faded black paint. He studied the surroundings and positioning of the vast adobe home.

A full five acres of desert land sprawled around the ranch style house. A short fifty feet from the back right corner of ranch house, was a large barn. The long rock covered driveway was lined with Saguaro cacti and curved around an ornate lava rock fountain. Sprays of water caught the light of the sun and glittered, diamond-like as it cascaded into a coy and lily filled pond below.

Zachary parked his corvette and followed a cobblestone pathway leading him to large black wrought iron gates. The gating enclosed an expansive courtyard. He spied the intercom and pressed the call button. A short time later a soft woman's voice filtered through the speaker. "Yes, who's there? May I help you?"

He smiled as he let the melodious tone in her voice wash over him. Her tenor was soft and sweet, just his type. Softly, he spoke into the intercom, "This is Hannibal. Is this the Lady Cassandra?"

Cassandra's voice sputtered, "Hannibal, what the hell are you doing here now? You're four hours early and I'm nowhere near ready."

"I know," soothed the imposter. "The only flight I could get was earlier than I had planned. I didn't want to be late. Besides, I just couldn't wait to see you in person"

Zachary listened to the silence and clenched his fists behind his back. "I guess I could drive back to Tucson, but it's a long way and I just thought we'd have more time to get to know one another." His need to win her over was step one of the predator and prey game. The challenge afoot was, not to lose this contest. Zachary spoke in low smooth tones. His voice was laced with broodiness and a hint of disappointment." Can I help it if I fell in love with you on the telephone? Can I stop myself from being attracted to someone with the same desires as I?"

The voice emanating from the speaker said, "Oh I don't know."

The time span of silence that followed their barter seemed to take an eternity for Zachary. His anticipation of victory twanged at his groin. He was about to ring the bell again when he heard the bolt give way on the massive gates. Zachary walked through the gates and pushed them closed as the front door opened. Cassandra emerged from the house and stood in the doorway. She was barefoot and wearing jeans and a tee shirt. Her long brunette hair was tied back with a pale blue ribbon. Zachary watched her reaction to him. Her expression of appraisal was obvious. He knew she would be pleased, he was perfect and he knew it. Her face blushed as he looked directly at her as she stared at him. Her head barely came up to his armpits. She seemed to be lost in the gaze he was offering her.

Cassandra looked down at herself and crossed her arms over her clothing. "I just finished cleaning horse stalls in the barn. I'm sorry that I look like such a mess. I wanted to be perfect and ready for you when you arrived. But, fate had other plans I guess," said Cassandra with a little hint of a giggle. Cassandra invited her guest inside the house.

Zachary walked through the doorway. Her eyes followed as he passed her. The appreciative stare continued as she pushed the door closed with her backside. She fixed her eyes upon the enormous visitor. Zachary could feel the pressure of Cassandra's stare. He was cautious not to project any form of threat. It was vital for success for him to seem at ease and relaxed. Alarming her at this point would be counter-productive to his game. To avoid showing any visible threat he looked softly into her eyes and smiled warmly. Inside however his excitement was beginning to build. He couldn't let her in on the game just yet, or it may be over entirely.

He walked over to her, cupped her chin in his hands. He stroked her face from the top of the cheekbone to the jawbone gently and lovingly. "I feel so fortunate," said Zachary. "Fortunate to finally meet someone who is kind and beautiful as well." He dropped his eyes to provide the appearance of being shy and continued, "I knew we would be good together, but I truly had not idea that you would be the epitome of my dreams."

Cassandra returned the compliment and added. "You know, the thought crossed my mind that I may want to keep you prisoner for the entire weekend."

Zachary smiled, outwardly to show approval, inwardly to venerate his victory. Lady Cassandra prepared a rum and cola for her guest. She excused herself saying, "I need to get the barn out of the girl." After she handed him the drink, she retrieved a towel from the linen closet. One last smiling glance provided to Zachary confirmed his plans would be fulfilled. His confidence riding high, he walked over to her and touched her shoulder. He looked ardently into her deep brown thickly lashed eyes. "Put on something enticing. We both know what we like."

Cassandra cocked her head in a playful mocking tone. "You got it, be back soon. Enjoy your drink. I'll hurry as much as I can." She turned slowly giving him her best, naughty glance and vanished into the back of the house. He waited until he heard the drumming of the shower and put his plan into action.

He left the house and backed his Vette into the barn. He grabbed his travel bag from behind the driver's seat and ran back into the house through the back door. Senses heightened, Zachary busied himself with finding and disabling each telephone. He located the intercom control panel that housed the gate lock and security system. Satisfied that he understood its function Zachary paused to discern that the shower was still running. He mentally mapped out his plans for the afternoon and grew impatient with the time that Cassandra was taking. His anticipation was growing but his desire was absent as of yet. The trigger that was needed to put him into action had not yet materialized. His patience was taxed as he checked his Rolex every few seconds. His mind tried to focus upon the pleasure he was about to experience. Adrenalin began to flow through his body as he at last heard the shower stop.

Zachary sprang to his feet and stripped off his clothing. He neatly placed his garments on the sofa and felt the first onset of the yearning. Desire was surging as he pulled out a hunting knife, a pair of handcuffs, a tube of red lipstick and a black eyeliner pencil from his satchel. His need was beginning to match his excitement. Internal fires began to tug at his groin as he walked briskly down the corridor to the rear of the house.

Zachary opened the bedroom door and listened as Cassandra hummed a lively tune. In one quick swipe, he severed the last telephone cord. Zachary's eyes leveled upon a bright red lace teddy lying neatly on the bed. Beside the teddy was mixture of matching accessories. A red satin collar embedded with shiny metal studs grabbed his attention. He picked up the collar and began rubbing with increasing furor, his inner thighs and scrotum. The shocks of pain initiated by the metal points ushered in Zachary's need for satisfaction. His erogenous zones tingled as groin muscles flexed and pushed against the pressing nodules.

The sound of a hairdryer in the adjacent bathroom heightened his pleasure. He envisioned the shock Lady Cassandra was in for, the moment she opened the door. He set down the collar and picked up his knife. Fingering the blade edge and point assured him of the instruments sharpness. He slid the knife, handcuffs and other accessories under a mass of pillows at the head of the bed. Zachary sat cross-legged as he fixated upon the closed door. He waited as an animal awaited its prey to fall into his trap. He fought back his impatience as he waited for his target to appear.

Finally, Lady Cassandra walked through the doorway brushing the last traces of moisture from her hair. Obviously startled, her eyes bulged when she spied her guest sitting nude on the bed. Cassandra clutched at the neckline of her plush velour robe instinctively as she blurted out, "Oh shit, Hannibal. You scared the hell out of me!"

Without a word Zachary balanced on the brink of rapture as a vulture anticipating a meal and unwilling to wait until death to begin devouring. He drank in the life sustaining breath brought forth by the stimulation of her sudden fear. He felt the onset of his internal stirrings once again, in his testicles with each twinge of panic she displayed. The smidgen of alarm was tantamount to kindling. But he needed more, much more to set his desire ablaze. He lifted himself off the bed with his strong muscular arms. In a flash, he stood in front of his targeted prey. Cassandra pushed off of Zachary's chest with one hand and said, "Can't wait, huh, Hannibal ole' stud?"

He stepped around her and guided her to the bed. He held the collar of her robe and pushed her onto the bed, removing her covering in one instant motion. Cassandra quickly flipped over onto her back and darted backwards towards the pillows. In a heartbeat, he was on top of her, pinning her to the bed with the length of his long encasing body.

"Listen, Hannibal, this is my bed! And my rules go here," insisted Cassandra. Zachary was beginning to feel the zeal of looming satisfaction. It was truly his game now. His heat was driven higher by her reaction as he leaned down toward her face and calmly said, "I'm not Hannibal."

She froze in terror. "Who the hell are you then?"

A tidal wave of passion flowed through his entire body as he observed the horror in her face. An evil grin crossed Zachary's full lips. He introduced himself, "I'm Prince Odious."

Lady Cassandra's face grew taught with fear. He drank in her panic as an infant with its milk. His sexual organs tingled and grew swollen, tight and heavy. His spine rippled with sensation, sending shivers of delight racing through his entire frame. He gently licked the dampness from the cheeks of Lady Cassandra and savored the luscious flavor of her fright.

Cassandra screamed, "Let me up you pervert!" She struggled to free herself from his grip. He slid his hand under the red satin pillows and produced the knife. He placed the blade point directly under her chin. Zachary watched in ecstasy as Cassandra stiffened her body and took great drafts of air through her nostrils. She muttered through clenched teeth, "Please, please don't hurt me."

Zachary demanded, "Raise your hands above your head."

Cassandra's refusal delighted him. He retaliated by slashing the left side of her face from the corner of her left eye to the top of her jawbone. The burning pain induced Cassandra's own fight or flight rush. She began a life or death battle. Anger and fear provided a burst of strength. Before he could secure her hands in the cuffs, she flung out with all her might. She struck Zachary with her elbows across the left side of his head. He rolled off her just far enough of her thrashing body for her to slide out from under him. She rolled off the bed and made a run for the bedroom door. Zachary quickly recouped and lunged off the bed and grabbed the arm of the fleeing woman. He laughed wildly while he rewarded the attempted escape with a punch to her face. Cassandra crumpled to the floor, unconscious.

As Cassandra lay stunned, he finished securing her hands to the headboard. He spread her legs wide apart and tied her ankles to the footboard with belts, which he removed from her closet. Zachary drew a line with cross-stitching across the lower stomach of Lady Cassandra. Then he circled the mock sutures with the red lipstick. Zachary went into the bathroom and filled a glass with cold water. He poured the contents of the glass across her face. Cassandra awakened to a blinding pain from the right side of her head. Tears soon blended with the streaming blood that was pouring from the gash on her face. She could hardly see straight when she heard him say, "No sleeping allowed! You need to be awake to enjoy, I know you like this."

Cassandra began to plead with Prince Odious for her life. All the begging in the world seemed to fall upon deaf ears. The toll of his pleasure taking began by Zachary running the point of the knife down her chest. He applied enough tension on the blade to slice thinly through her skin. At the apex of her breastbone, he turned the blade outward toward her breast. Slowly from the base of the ribcage he sliced in a continuous motion, surrounded her breasts up to her nipples. The wounds sent small rivulets of blood down her sides. Cassandra screamed in agony and each shriek tested Zachary's ability to proceed slowly. His need was growing beyond all proportion.

His lust grew with every pain-filled groan, every yell and twitch, each scream or whimper brought him closer to the brink of fulfillment. Anytime his playmate lost consciousness, he brought her back with splashes of icy water. Lovemaking held no satisfaction to Zachary unless he could see the fear, pain and anguish his partner endured. When she was once again lucid, he would induce more agony.

Zachary met thrust for thrust matching the wild gyrations of his lover. He lowered himself over her and savagely bit her bleeding nipples. He tore at the areola to encourage them to hemorrhage. Cassandra's screams as her vaginal canal was penetrated with a twisting and turning knife blade thrilled him deeply. He fought back the urge to climax time after time. His craving surged and ebbed as the tides until Cassandra fell silent and motionless her chest barely rising for breath. Zachary's need to ejaculate was pressing upon him with urgency. He kissed the forehead of Lady Cassandra. He gazed tenderly at the still face of the provider of his joy. He silently drew the knife downward to her lower abdomen. He traced the drawings with the blade. He uttered in smooth emotionless tones, "Just look what you have done to me."

He sliced deeply into the body cavity of Lady Cassandra and straddled her. He inserted his penis into the incision while clasping his slimy hands around her neck. He pulsed in the thickening body fluids. He plunged and writhed deeper and deeper. In his rapture, he squeezed his hands with the vigor of enthusiasm. Zachary could no longer contain his exaltation, as Cassandra's last gasp for life expelled, he climaxed and spread his seed into the wound of his creation. He lifted his bloodied and sweat soaked body off Lady Cassandra. He released his grasp on her neck. Zachary stood by the bed and looked down at his lover. The last bit of air escaped from her body, creating a series of blood-coated bubbles rising to the lips that graced the mouth of the lovely dead. He stood transfixed as the light danced on the shiny surface of bubble after bubble. He noted the oddity of the ridges formed as each one burst, leaving a bloody ring tracing her lips.

He rested, sitting on the bed for a few minutes and reveled in the complete satisfaction he felt. He felt so peaceful and fulfilled. He looked over at the clock and realized that within an hour the real Hannibal would be arriving. He raised himself from the bed and walked into the bathroom He picked up a washcloth and returned to the bedroom. He dipped the corner of the material into the abundance of blood. On the wall beside the bed he wrote, "I AM MY MIDDLE NAME."

Zachary cleaned himself in steaming hot shower water. He made certain no traces of blood remained on him or his tools. He returned to the living room and dressed himself. Zachary was tranquil and utterly complete. He casually strolled into the bedroom to take one last look at the object of his satisfaction. Zachary smiled at Lady Cassandra and blew her lifeless body a kiss.

Just steps from the door, the chimes rang out. He peeked through the curtains to see a short man standing at the gate. Zachary partially opened the front door and ran into the kitchen. He pressed the gate release and left through the back door.

* * *

The man known as Hannibal the Slayer stepped through the gate and walked up to the slightly ajar door. Hannibal knocked as he pushed the door open and called out to Lady Cassandra. He waited momentarily for an answer. When he heard nothing he reasoned to himself that this must be part of the game Cassandra was playing. He began traveling through the house, searching and repeating Cassandra's name. His search continued until he came to the bedroom.

Hannibal stood in utter shock when he saw the bloody body of Lady Cassandra. He covered his mouth with one hand, grabbed at his mid-section with the other. He bent and vomited. Hannibal staggered toward the front of the house when he heard the roar of a sports car. It sounded as if it were speeding away from the house. By the time, Hannibal got to the window he saw only the flash of red mixed with flying debris, swirls of dust and barriers of saguaro cacti.

*   *   *

Zachary boarded his waiting jet. The steward met him at the gangway with a glass of Zachary's vitamin drink.

Marsh questioned, "Did you enjoy your visit sir?"

Zachary took a long gulp from the glass and in a matter of fact tone said, "The best trip I've ever taken."

Marsh smiled, "Very good sir. We're clear to leave anytime you are ready."

"I'm ready, let's go," replied Zachary.

Prince Odious reclined in his overstuffed leather window seat. He sipped his drink and propped his feet up. Zachary Payne Pendrake felt content and serene as he watched the ground surrounding Tucson as it disappeared from sight.

CHAPTER 9
Oakland

Janet Kayhill had a hard time maintaining her decorum as Allison walked up the gangway from the airplane. Allison suffering from sleep deprivation and stress burst into tears as her father wrapped his arms around her. The three years that had separated them dissolved in their comforting embrace.

While they were in the airport, Robert kept his comments regarding Will within the confines of his own heart. Both he and Janet knew that their daughter suffered in ways they couldn't fully comprehend. They had decided to simply be there for their daughter and offer supportive shoulder and listening ears.

Allison fell into a deep slumber during the trip back to Palo Alto. Janet looked at Robert and said, "I hope Allison stays longer than the couple of weeks she talked about."

Robert nodded in agreement and added, "It'll take longer to get things into place than a couple of weeks."

"Robert dear, I know you want what's best for Allie," began Janet. "But I don't want you to push your feelings on to her. I mean, let Allison be Allison."

Robert stopped the car at a red light and looked at his wife with confusion showing on his face. "I don't think I do that, Janet."

She shook her head in dismay. "Robert, the main rub between you and her is your tendency to interfere. She reached out and took Robert's hand. "Sweetheart, I know you want the very best for her and I know how much you love her. But you don't seem to understand that sometimes, people have to fall all by themselves. Then they find the way to pick themselves up and go on. You simply can't shelter her from life and learning. She won't let you nor should she. Just think of how having Burton Sanders 'keep an eye out, for Allison worked out.'" Robert clinched his teeth and took a quick look into the back seat of the Fleetwood. He drew in a relieved breath when he saw that she was still fast asleep. "Yeah, my Marine brother really messed up. He got her involved with this murder stuff." He glanced once more at Allison and said quietly, "You don't think she knows do you?"

Janet shuddered and shook her head, "no."

The light changed and Robert proceeded toward home and said, "I tell you, that is the last time I ask my friend a favor. Semper Fi."

"It's that kind of obstruction I'm talking about, Robert. That's my point! If you hadn't had your fingers in the pot she would never had been doing this stuff."

Robert gave Janet a frustrated look. "Okay, so what you're saying is that I'm supposed to simply sit by and watch her make mistakes. Is that what you're saying to me? Mistakes, that I can help her avoid? Janet, if I can save my child heartache, I'll do it."

Janet rolled her eyes and squeezed his hand. "Please dear, for me, please try."

He rocked his head backward onto the headrest and said, "Okay, I'll make you a promise. I'll try not to interfere. I'll try but you know I just don't see why she can't learn from the example of others."

*   *   *

The first seven months of Allison's new beginning was a time of self-exploration. Her goal of finding her own place in a couple of weeks had been abandoned. She insisted that she pay her own legal fees for her divorce, despite her father's offer. It was her responsibility even though it lengthened the time she stayed at her parents' home.

A major argument erupted when Robert was caught by surprise with Allison's decision to keep the name of 'Dean' instead of taking her maiden name back.

Robert yelled as his fist crashed onto the library desk, "Why?"

At first, Allison began to shy away from his tirade. Suddenly she stiffened her back and looked directly into her father's eyes. "I'll explain if you will listen to what I have to say. Otherwise Dad, I think this discussion is better left for later."

The response from her was outside of the character Robert identified as his daughter. He saw her in a very different light for the first time. He sat down, calmed down and decided that perhaps he should listen.

She said, "I'm keeping the name of Dean, because I have worked very hard for recognition in my field. I have succeeded in my job under that name and I am not ready or willing to start all over again to build a reputation with my maiden name."

Robert opened his mouth to speak, but Allison cut him short. "Dad, this is my decision. This is my choice. It's what I'm going to do and no amount of argument from you will change that decision."

Robert was forced to accept his daughter's decision. He made it clear that he didn't approve, but there was little else he could do. He ended the battle saying, "You may call yourself 'Dean', but to me you will always be Allison Diane Kayhill."

*   *   *

In the months that passed, Allison had gone through many alterations of self-image and she had reasserted her drive to succeed. Her new job with the Oakland Tribune afforded her the opportunity to flex her journalistic muscle. She began writing articles in addition to photography and worked to be honored with her own by line.

Will was now a part of Allison's distant past and their divorce was now final. His relentless calls had slowed, as she didn't respond to his tirades. He had continually tried to convince her that he'd changed. The final insult to her sensibilities was a comment offered by Will indicating that she owed him a second chance. The three years they were married were times of constant demoralization for her. The thought of owing anything to the likes of Will Dean nauseated her beyond belief. The only benefit Allison could derive from her time as Mrs. William H. Dean, was the strength which fired her soul and drove her to triumph over adversity

Allison had always heard that once you leave home and live on your own, you could never truly go back. She found, this to be true. Her philosophies had grown beyond the established boundaries of the wants and demands of her parents. While she felt grown and fully capable, it seemed that her father compared her age as the terrible twos' revisited. Allison found that annoying and funny at the same time. She was grateful for the regrouping time afforded her by her family. The time was put to good use as she struggled to heal her heart and regain direction and composure. Allison felt strong and more self-assured than she ever had.

The day that she moved into her own apartment was a day of emancipation for her. For the first time she was totally on her own and experiencing the pressing reality created by the consequences of her own decisions. Her new life back on the home ground had been work, work and more work. Her talents, much to her dismay, were assigned to the society pages. At least writing was included with the position. Allison photographed and wrote about engagements, weddings and births of the wealthy. She hated her assignments and longed for the hard news she had covered in Chicago. In the opinion of the seasoned reporters, Allison was a cub journalist and would not be ready for the city desk for years to come. Allison decided that she would bide her time and depend on the good sense of the paper to eventually offer her a lead story.

Allison was beginning to lose patience as Sam Cook, her editor summoned her to his office. He offered her a story outside of the of the society page and into the business section. She was to cover the arrival of a foreign dignitary. Harry Satto was a well-known and powerful commodities broker. He controlled vast quantities of rice, beans and other such staples. He was instrumental in maintaining the price controls on a world-wide basis. At last, Allison thought to herself, a story with teeth.

The initial meeting with Mr. Satto proved to be extremely cordial. The power of the world trader while not understated was secondary to his purely humanistic values. Allison found him to be a consummate gentleman. His personal charisma combined with his genuine openness fueled Allison's aspirations and enveloped her with a deep appreciation for the man. Her admiration of him and his successes filled Allison with a drive to be equal and on a level square footing with this man.

The interview generated a full two-page spread, complete with pictures. Satto's warm and genial manner allowed her to compose a story that benefited her with recognition of her peers. Mr. Harry Satto and Allison Dean became trusted friends and allies. New assignments began to come her way.

* * *

Allison found a note on her desk when she arrived at the paper. The note was a request for her to meet with Sam that morning. She pushed her way through the double swinging glass doors to his office. He was talking on the phone but motioned for her to sit and wait. Sam hung up the phone and looked at Allison with a mysterious expression on his face. Until finally she said, "What, Sam, what is it?"

He began, "I've been intending to give you a story which challenges your talent. I have one now."

Allison felt a surge of excitement. She leaned forward to match Sam's posture.

He said, "Have you heard of the Sunday Torch?"

"Why yes of course! Who hasn't?"

Sam leaned back and dropped his pencil on his desk blotter. He smiled and said, "I think it's time that I got you completely away from the society page and let you do what you do best. I'm going to assign you to cover this torch story."

Allison could have leapt for joy. "Oh Sam, thank you so much! I won't let you down."

He gave her a mock gruff expression and said, "Don't thank me, the brass upstairs ordered me to put you on this story."

Sam's pretended demeanor didn't fool her. Although she didn't challenge his statement she knew Sam was the champion in her corner.

Allison played it cool, and contained her excitement as she listened to the available information regarding the 'Sunday Torch'. The detective on the case was Sergeant Phillip Hall. Detective Hall normally worked in homicide. He had just been assigned to the case. Hall had the reputation of being less than communicative with the press. The strength in the story was that this particular crime had been confirmed to be the fourth fire set by the same arsonist. The latest blaze took the life of a fifty- six year old woman. The perpetrator's crime now was first degree murder as well as arson.

Allison was sort of 'cop-wise', she thought, especially after her years working with the Chicago P.D. She knew she'd never get a word out of Hall at the scene of the crime. Allison decided to take a different tact in pursuing her assigned story. The 'Sunday Torch' was front-page news. That opportunity spurred her determination to get the facts. She accessed all of the information regarding Hall from the database of the Tribunes records. She read about everything from his beginnings on the force to his divorce five years prior. She gained what she thought was an understanding of the motivations of Detective Sergeant Phillip Hall.

Allison pushed her chair back from the keyboard and looked over at one of her fellow reporters. "Scott," she began, "where are the police bars?"

Scott Dennis contorted his face and responded, "Bars? I'm assuming you're not talking about the jail."

Allison giggled and said, "No, not that kind of bars, not the jail." She laughed again and said, "You know where all of the cops go after their shifts."

"Well, let me see," he began; "There's several haunts they frequent. But probably the most popular hangout is Archer's Haven. It's over on one eighty fifth by Humboldt."

Allison stood and slipped on her jacket, picked up her purse and said, "Thanks Scott. I'm on my way."

Scott yelled after her, "Hey Allie, that place is like no mans' land for civilians and reporters! Watch your toes!"

As she walked out the door, she raised her hands high over her shoulders and gave double thumbs up, to wave off his concerns. The fact that she was not a familiar face amongst the unusual scores of reporters was a distinct advantage. At least, that was the way she had it reasoned.

She arrived at Archers Haven within an hour of leaving the Tribune offices. She pulled open the heavy black walnut door and entered into a dimly lit club. Before her eyes could adjust to the half-light, she heard the rhythmic hum of conversation and the clack of pool balls as they smashed into one another. The club reminded her of the Book Vault where she had met Will for the first time. Allison shook off the negative feelings that memory evoked and sat at the bar where she could see the entire room. She was confident that she would recognize Hall from his pictures in the paper archives. Her search of the customers for his face was interrupted by the bartender. "Good afternoon, Miss I'm your bartender Russ. What'll it be?"

"Club soda with a lemon twist," she replied.

Allison continued her inspection of the room as her drink was delivered. She took a long gulp through the straw as the door opened once again. Through the door walked her target, Phillip Hall. He was better looking than his pictures had portrayed. He seemed to be well over six foot tall. His husky build made him appear even larger. His dark eyes seemed to radiate the ability to be either very gentle or exceedingly hard. She thought back to a term that she and DeeCee had developed. When the duo saw someone that was particularly interesting, they would call that person a 'brow wiggler.' Although sadness crept into her heart at the thought of DeeCee, she admitted to herself that Detective Phillip Hall was definitely a 'brow wiggler.'

The detective joined three men sitting in a booth near the far end of the pub. She watched his interactions intently. He animated his conversations with lively gestures with both hands and his square-jawed face. Allison enjoyed watching this highly spirited man. Suddenly one of the men in the group turned and looked at her directly. She averted her eyes and started into her drink. Allison had tried not to be obvious. "Damn," she muttered under her breath. From the corner of her eye, she saw the man stand, then fall back onto the chair. All three laughed loudly. Allison turned her back to the man.

Suddenly she felt a heavy tap on her shoulder. She turned around in the barstool to see one of Hall's companions standing next to her.

"I've never seen you in here before," he slurred his words. He reeked with the smell of beer and was obviously intoxicated. "I'm Ron, Ron Smith." He leaned toward her face.

She felt the invasion of her space and with a quick shudder pressed backward into the chair. She wanted no contact as the man was pushing forward. Allison played her role coolly, even though she wanted to cut and run. "I'm new in town," she said. "I've never been here before, so that would be the reason you don't recognize me."

Allison was feeling trapped. Her spine was pressed against the chair back as Smith leaned ever closer. She placed her hands on Ron's chest and gently nudged him away. She was just beginning to slide out of her chair when another hand slapped Ron on the shoulder. "Enough Ron, let's leave the lady alone." The hand of her rescuer belonged to none other than Phillip Hall.

"Perfect," she thought to herself.

Hall placed both hands on Smith's shoulders, turned him around and guided the drunken man back to his table. Hall walked a short distance from her then pivoted and looked at Allison questioningly. In a few steps he was standing next to her. "I'm sorry Miss. I hope he didn't scare you. Believe me, he is harmless."

She smiled with the purpose of appearing, inviting. "No, I'm fine. I think your friend has had a bit too much fun this evening."

He looked down at her, his eyes appeared soft and curious. "I'm Phillip Hall and who are you? I've never seen you here before."

Allison chuckled and shook her head. "Is this a private club or something? Your buddy just asked me the same question."

Phillip Hall looked around the bar. "Well," he began, "I guess in some respects you could call it that. Almost everyone in here is a police officer with one agency or another."

"Oh I see," said Allison. She liked the soft tones in his voice and the depth of caring shown in his eyes.

"I guess my buddy thought you were either a new cop on some beat or a groupie that likes to date cops."

Allison held out a hand and said, "Hi there my name is Allison, Allison Dean. And no, I wouldn't call myself a cop groupie." She continued, "I'd ask you to sit down, but it looks like your friends are leaving without you."

The tall ruggedly handsome man turned and looked at his cohorts as they gathered their coats. The former intruder, Ron, walked over and whispered something in Hall's ear. He smiled and patted Ron on the shoulder. The strange thing was that as Ron Smith walked out with the other two in the group he didn't so much as wobble, let alone stagger. Allison let the observation go and returned her attention to Detective Hall.

Hall held up his glass to the bartender and pointed to Allison's glass. "Two more, Russ. We're going to go to a table. If it's alright with the little lady, that is."

Allison nodded an affirmative.

Russ said, "You got it, I'll send the drinks over with Lydia."

Time flew by as the two buried themselves in deep conversation. Phillip talked about police work. He asked Allison what type of work she did. Allison stammered, she'd almost forgotten her goal for the evening. She didn't want to outright lie to him so she replied, "I'm a writer and photographer."

Over dinner, they exchanged their views on everything from police matters to political problems. They found they had much in common. The comfort of the evening allowed Allison to push her hidden agenda to the back of her mind. Dessert and coffee continued until 9:30 p.m. Phillip escorted Allison to her car. He asked, "May I have your phone number?"

Allison reached into her purse and pulled out a pen, tore a sheet from her day timer and scribbled her number while saying, "I'm out a lot! But I do have a message machine. Be sure you leave me a message if I'm not there. How about if you give me yours and I'll give you a call."

Hall reached into his breast pocket and pulled out his shield wallet that contained his badge and business cards. He removed a card, wrote his home number on the back and gave it to her. As he gave her the card, he leaned seductively close to her, "I hope I hear from you, very soon."

That evening Allison dreamt of Detective Hall. Stirring visions waltzed through her dreamscape. Scenes, which left her breathless when at last, she awoke. She wrapped herself in soft, warm, blankets and watched through the window as the sun broke the night's hold upon the sky. The last time she had thought of any man this way seemed to be long, long ago. She felt awkward because she hadn't been completely honest with him about her work. She felt embarrassed at her own actions.

* * *

For a couple of weeks Allison avoided his messages. She was torn between her interest in Phillip and her fear of being hurt again. Like it or not she was still very tender. The only contact she would have with Phillip Hall was during her slumber. The warmth she felt each time she awakened stirred her deeply. Allison had asked Sam to re-assign the Sunday Torch story. Sam had made it clear that he was not pleased with her decision. "It'll be quite some time before I will assign you another story of that importance," he told her. Apprehension and fear of another painful relationship cloaked her heart with a cape visible only to the trained eye.

Allison had finally sought counsel of the one person with whom she could share her feelings, her mother. Janet and Allison had shared many confidences in the past but the subject of Will Dean seemed to be a banned topic. Finally, an opportunity presented itself and Janet charged in, determined to open and treat her daughters' wounds. Janet knew that as long as Allison kept the pain buried inside of her, it would continue to fester. At first, during their talk about Will and the awful things he had done, Janet was greeted with a glaring eye from 'Allison. Janet was not going to be put off any longer. Her daughter had been home for almost a year and yet had never ventured forth with any relationship other than professional. In Allison's mind, the advice her mother was giving to her was correct. Nevertheless, she simply didn't know how to implement the healing process. The echoing of her mother's words resonated in her mind.

"Get back out there and try!" Janet had told her. "Not all men are like Will."

* * *

The advice played and replayed through Allison's consciousnesses as she sipped her early morning cola. Her ringing telephone brought her back from her thoughts. The answering machine picked up the line on the third ring.

"Good morning," she heard Phil's voice say.

She could no longer resist and found herself running to the living room to pick the phone before he hung up. Allison grabbed the receiver as he was reciting his number for her to call.

"Hello, Phil. Here I am."

Phil said in a joking tone, "Ms. Dean, its 8:35 in the morning. Do you have bankers' hours or what? I know that you said you were out a lot, but this was going to be my last call."

"Phil," she interrupted. "I was going to call you today." Allison looked at her clock and saw that it was really barely 7:00 in the morning. "Give me a break, will you please, it's not after 8:30 in the morning."

Hall chuckled.

"What's with this banker's hour's comment? I just got out of the shower," fibbed Allison.

Hall said, "I was calling to see if you are free for dinner this evening. I really enjoyed the evening we spent together. You do remember me don't you? I know it was weeks ago but I want to get to know more about you."

A three-way struggle began within Allison. Her mind, heart and libido went into hand-to-hand combat. Her heart won and the time was set for six that evening. "There's something I have to tell you tonight, Phil. But I want to tell you in person."

"What could it be," chided Phil. "Oh wait I know, you're really married and just haven't had the time to tell me." Phil laughed.

Allison matched his laugh and said, "No nothing like that. We'll talk this evening."

She gave him her address and directions to her apartment. Throughout the day, Allison commiserated over the veiled truth she had given Phillip. She held out little hope of building a relationship that was based on half-truths and distortions. Allison decided to tell him the truth about who she really was and what she did for a living.

She scheduled herself to leave the Tribune by 5:00 p.m. sharp. She wanted to look extra special for Phil that evening. It was going to be difficult because all day long her stomach felt like it was in her throat. The tension of having to confess worried her. At 4:45 p.m., she felt a tap on her shoulder. Allison swiveled in her chair to meet the warm gaze of Detective Phillip Hall.

"Phil," Allison sputtered, "how'd you know where to find me?"

He handed her a single white rose. "You forget what I do for a living."

Embarrassment flushed Allison's face. "Honest Phil, I was going to tell you tonight. I've been avoiding you because I hadn't told you the whole truth."

Phil laughed. "We've both done our share of hiding the truth."

Confused she looked at him and said, "What do you mean?"

He learned forward and whispered, "You remember Ron Smith?"

Allison thought for a moment and said, "Oh yeah, the drunk guy with you the night we met."

He pulled the companion chair over next to Allison and sat down. "Ron is a close buddy of mine. We play good cop, bad cop very well. Especially, on the job and while we're interviewing perps. I saw you at Archers' the moment I arrived. Ron wasn't drunk. He was just helping me to meet you. So, you see, we both did our share of covert operating that night."

Allison laughed, "You got me I guess. So who owes who? I know, how about if I pick up the pizza?"

"I'll get the pizza," he countered." I know where the best take and bake pizza place in this city is. How about if you get the wine?"

Allison tilted her head and cocked an eye at him. "Take and bake. Whose place yours or mine?"

He leaned forward in the chair and looked deeply into the bright eyes of Allison. "Your choice! But I'll have to warn you about the bachelor pad ambiance that my apartment epitomizes." He exhaled a rapid breath, "It can be really scary, trust me on this one."

Allison quickly suppressed an urge to unleash a wildly nervous giggle. "I don't think that's a real good idea. I don't know you very well."

Phil held up two fingers and crossed Allison's lips to shush her. "I'll be on my best behavior, scout's honor."

She looked at him suspiciously, "Were you really a boy scout?

Hall quickly shook his head. "No, but it sounded good. Don't you think? I really would like to know a lot more about you. You could single handedly save me from the priesthood. Since my divorce, I just haven't found anyone who interested me, then you come along and I am completely gone."

Allison weighed her options. Her mother's voice echoed in her head. She could hear Janet yelling, "Not every man is like Will Dean. Get out there and find someone!" She swiveled her chair back into working position and said, "Hang on here a minute and let me finish this projects and then we're outta' here." Her fingers raced over the keyboard until she struck the save command. Allison backed out of her computer, flipped off the power switch and said, "Okay, let's go."

The two talked and shared each other's history as they munched on pizza and drank their wine. Phil talked about his former marriage and the affairs his wife had with numerous men. He confided that the feelings of failure had plagued him since first learning of her infidelity. He in turn listened intently as Allison poured over her marriage and the details of her life. She opened her portfolio and declared that one day she would have a one-woman show. The book of pictures was a long portrayal of her personal and professional history. Included were the letters from the Chicago Sun times, Burton Sanders of the Chicago Police and District Attorney Sandoval. The glowing reports germinated as seed of an idea in the mind of detective Phillip Hall.

As case hardened as he was, Hall was sickened at viewing the pictures of the Denise Haver murder.

"Denise was a friend of mine. We went to high school together," she explained. "We did everything together," she managed a slight chuckle, "We formed this club named 'The Triple M.'

Hall scrunched up his face, "Triple M?"

"Yeah, the M's stood for money, men and Marlboro. It was DeeCee's idea.

"What's a DeeCee?"

"That was her nickname. Her real name was Denise Carmen Park. Her mother had always called her DeeCee and it stuck."

"Okay," said Hall, "back to the Triple M story,"

"Stupid I know,"said Allison. "We were just kids. Neither of us smoked. We thought it was so cool at that time in our lives and we swore that we would never smoke anything but Marlboro."

Phil laughed out loud.

"DeeCee's father was in the military and was stationed at Moffitt field." Allison's eyes misted. "Her father was transferred in the last two months of our senior year. We wrote for a while, but life being what it is, we lost contact. I didn't hear from her again nor see her again until I photographed her murder. " The tears resurfaced and Phil held her in his arms and stroked her hair, and let her cry. Finally, she stopped crying and straightened herself up. "The worst thing is that I didn't even recognize her. She looked so very different. To be straight I felt ashamed of myself. You know, I swore that I would get this guy and at times I feel like I'm letting DeeCee down."

"Why, on earth would you feel that way, Allison, you aren't a detective or a police officer."

"Because he's still out there and I'm sure he's still killing. But most of all I made a promise to DeeCee, that I would find him."

Within the confines of Phil's strong arms, Allison felt safe. For the first time she felt as if she could crawl right into the pocket of his shirt and be protected from the world. It was the feeling she'd wanted to find all of her adult life. The scent of his musk cologne drifted into Allison's mind. Her skin felt like sheets of warm satin. She heard every word he said to her, but absorbed nothing. Allison somehow knew that their friendship could easily turn from the closeness of friendship to the partnership of love. Allison let her pain go and blended into his arms.

He lifted her face to look into Allison's eyes. His ardor found hers resting upon the tenderness of the first kiss. Allison's wounded and hardened heart softened. Her willing eyes and gentle touch invited him without uttering a word. The pain each had endured at the hands of another fueled their closeness. A brand new love began in the gentle and loving touch of their hearts. From the very first kiss to an early morning embrace, Phillip and Allison quenched their need for someone to love.

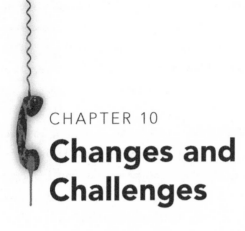

CHAPTER 10

Changes and Challenges

During the next six months, Allison's reputation grew. Phil's respect for the talent and tenacity of Allison Dean opened the door for a new alliance between herself and the Oakland Police Department. The Tribune, just as the Sun Times, eagerly accepted the prospect of having one of their staff work closely with the authorities.

She became a vital contributor to both the newspaper and the law enforcement agencies. Her affiliation between the Tribune and the homicide squad flourished into a lucrative and impressive profession.

Her letters of reference from the district attorney helped pave the way for this new collaboration. She had been credited with stunning pictorials of crime scenes and her journalistic talents were now a favorite among readers of the Tribune. Oakland's district attorney was now boasting the same high rates of conviction as claimed by Salvador in Chicago. Being given her own byline was a reward given to Allison. It was an accomplishment at the tender age of twenty-seven. She worked very closely to provide her readers with the gist of the events she covered. But she also withheld enough to guard the integrity of the investigation processes. The Tribune consistently scooped the Chronicle.

It was a game, but one which was beginning to grate upon her nerves. The only fly in the ointment so to speak was a reporter for the Tribunes' rival paper, the San Francisco Chronicle. Most people in the news business considered Steven Morris as a self-centered, ambitious and totally without scruples, individual. While having his own readership and fan base, his less than straight shooting style generated much in the way of sensationalism. In Allison's estimation, Morris, being a small man of about five foot five, was plagued with an ego that would have trouble fitting into someone seven foot tall. The competition between the two newspapers was well known and at times exploited by the smaller presses.

Whenever their paths crossed, Allison acted condescending toward him simply to infuriate and agitate Morris. Upon her arrival at crime scenes where he was assigned, his sarcastic jabs and cat calling would be loud and clear. He continually commented that Allison should return to the kitchen. "Take off your shoes and pop out some puppies," was one of his favorite chants. Allison laughed and mocked Morris for the most part. When she wasn't in the mood to banter with him, she simply ignored him.

"Someday, Morris would yell, "Someday I'm going to best you."

Allison would produce her expression of complete pity. A face she developed exclusively for him. With mock forbearance in her tone, she would turn to him and say, "Stevie, Stevie, you should live so long." Allison developed a number of stock phrases to be delivered while he was standing in a crowd of his peers. One of her favorites was to call him a munchkin and warn him about the possibility of him being flattened by a house."

Allison responded to a call from Lieutenant Jones of the Oakland police department. She arrived at the address as requested within twenty-five minutes of the page. The normal traffic blockades were in place. The usual gathering of officials and the ever-present curious citizens milled about the area. Allison searched the crowd for the familiar face of Jones. Surely, she thought to herself, she would see Phil at the scene. Allison was more than a little disappointed when she discovered that the Detective Joe Biggs and the homicide B squad had been assigned to this case.

Joe Biggs was an abrasive officer who treated her like a schoolchild. He had been suspended more than once as charges of excessive force were levied against him. His ill-tempered mannerisms created embarrassment for his department on more than one occasion. His personnel file was replete with internal affairs investigations and findings labeled him as a borderline officer. On many occurrences, Joe Biggs came just short of being terminated.

Allison clipped her press and police passes on the lapel of her blazer. She waited outside of the building for her contact to let her know when and where she was needed. Lt. Jones wasn't much bigger than Sandy, but their dispositions seemed to be identical. Allison caught herself several times about to call him Sandy. The appearance of the large Irish officer signaled her that everything was ready for her to begin her work. He, as Sandy had done in the past, tried to prepare her for the scene that she was about to photograph. The difference was that Jonesy, as she called him, was vocal about what and where to focus attention of the camera. Allison would assure him regularly that she knew what they wanted. She learned just to agree with Jonesy and follow her own patterns. She would assure him that she would capture exactly what he wanted her to cover and then thank him for the advice.

Jonesy grinned and patted her on the back. "Hop to it short stuff. We don't have all day you know."

Allison carried her equipment to the apartment and took a quick look inside to distinguish the light quality in the crime scene. She then snapped the appropriate lighting in place on her light-bar. Her gear would provide all the illumination required to enhance the surroundings and bring clarity into every corner of the apartment. Shielding the scene from possible contamination was vital prior to her walking anywhere in the townhouse. To protect existing evidence, she placed protective shoe coverings on her feet, prior to her going into the apartment. As Allison entered, she began shooting frame after frame to begin her system of full coverage. She had done this so many times before that it was almost automatic. Her habitual chatter continued with questions to which she paid little attention to the answers. It was mindless and kept her focused. Like ambient noise to aid in concentration.

"Who's the victim, Jonesy?"

Jonesy looked at his black note tablet and read the information to her. "JoAnn Campo, age thirty four, single and a very, very kinky lady." The term 'kinky lady' caught Allison's attention. She paused momentarily and dropped her camera to her waist. She offered him a curious look. Allison remembered the last time that the word kinky had been used to describe a victim's lifestyle. She dismissed the shudder that coursed through her body and continued her business.

The rooms were ultimately tidy and organized. No sign of violence was visible on the lower level of the townhouse. The team from Scientific Investigations Department followed in her footsteps. They proceeded with their evidence gathering as she moved along.

Allison began to move up to the second level of the townhouse. She stopped and photographed a small table next to the stairwell. On top of the table was the telephone with a cord that had been severed near the base of the unit. The left corner of the telephone held open the victims' personal address book. The listings showing were under the letter, 'S' Allison murmured to Jonesy, "It would be nice if this book could talk."

Jonesy simply grumbled an affirmative and stood aside as Allison ascended the stairs. When she reached the landing, the scene changed from quiet orderliness to one of mayhem. Blood splatters dotted the gray carpeting that lead her eyes to a damaged and bloody door casing. She sharpened her frames on all of the visible evidence and included the tag id numbers in her pictures.

"Did any one hear her or the noise?" questioned Allison.

Jonesy once again shrugged his shoulders and replied, "Not that have come forward yet. I hope someone can help us with this one. But you know how it is, Allison."

Clicking another frame into the record, she said, "How'd you find her?"

Lt. Jones checked his report book again and responded "Ms. Campo had a visitor stop by tonight. A former roommate, a guy by the name of, let me see," he checked his note pad and replied, "Patrick Wilder."

Allison cocked an eye toward Jonesy, "Any connection to the murder? You know a possible suspect?"

"No, I don't think so. He's really shook. He's the one that called us. He had to go to a pay phone down the block. No one would let him use their phone."

Allison said, "So he's out as a suspect all together?"

Jonesy looked off at some imaginary point in the wall and said, "Yeah, you know, after working as a cop as long as I have, you develop 'blue sense.' That sense sort of tells you who is likely and not. This guy was so sick to his stomach over what he'd seen; I really doubt he could have been the sick son of a bitch that did this."

So, this Blue Sense tells you that he's not the killer, and that's all you need?" Allison continued, "he'd be pretty smart to act that way don't you think?"

A wry expression crossed his aging face as he conceded the point. "This Patrick guy says that when he arrived he found the door slightly ajar. He came on in. He's well, in my opinion a bit weird, but clearly not the maniac that did this."

She faced the closed bedroom door and said, "Okay, I'm ready, open the door."

Jonesy turned the knob near the spindle to preserve evidence. The latch gave way and with a slight tap on the top panel, the barrier revealed the bedroom, where the fight for life had ensued.

The door moved from right to left and she began taking her shots from the floor moving up to the walls of the room. As her camera focused on the far wall in the bedroom, Allison gasped for breath. "Oh my God, No." she cried. She covered her mouth, her eyes riveted upon bloody writing on the wall. The words spelled out "I AM MY MIDDLE NAME."

Color drained from her face. She stepped backwards bumping into Jonesy. Her arms fell limp and the camera dropped onto the carpeting depressing the flash button. The burst of light startled Allison. She turned away from the doorway. Graying swirls of dim light clouded her vision and made her feel faint.

Lt. Jones steadied her and reassured her. He tried to calm her by saying, "I know it's pretty awful."

Allison waved off his assurances and said, "No, no, no Jonesy, I've seen this actors' work before!" The memories of DeeCee and the horrible scene back in Chicago flooded back to Allison.

Jonesy turned Allison's face to his and demanded, "What? Where? When?"

Allison steadied herself by holding onto the doorframe as she reached down to pick up her camera, "In Chicago, Jonesy, in Chicago."

Jonesy calmed his voice. He held both hands straight out and level and said, "Are you sure Allison? Try to take it easy and tell me about it."

Allison went down stairs and sat on a chair in the living room, away from other police and definitely out of earshot of the news hounds that were outside of the townhome. Jonesy sat next to her. He asked, "What is going on Allison?"

She gathered herself and said, "The writing, it's the same as it was at the Denise Haver murder scene. I did the photo work up on the case a little while before I left Chicago. Jonesy, Haver was a friend of mine. She was so messed up that I didn't even know who she was until I saw the obit information. The murderer wrote the same words on the wall, just the way it is right now upstairs."

Allison looked directly at Jonesy. She signaled toward the upper floor and said, "You been up there?"

The Lieutenant looked at her and nodded a grim affirmation.

Allison stared off into space and began to describe the remains of Denise Haver. With every word, a tear tumbled down her cheeks. Each similarity wrought a long drawn out "yes" from Jones. "I have copies of the crime scene shots from the Haver killing at home in my portfolio. You can contact Burton Sanders for reports on their investigation." Allison cleared her throat. "Jonesy, Phil should be on this case. He saw the pictures some time ago. He knows about this guy." He rested his hand on her shoulder and gently asked, "Can you continue? Or would you like for me to call someone else in to do this one?"

146

She shook her head and said, "No Jonesy, I will get it together in a few minutes. I really need to finish this job. It's just that I know this will be a duplicate of the most gruesome murder I have ever seen." Allison took a deep breath, stiffened her shoulders and checked her camera to make sure it wasn't broken. When satisfied that everything was fine she entered the room and photographed the bloody demise of JoAnn Campo.

Police officers at the scene had a quick caucus in order to decide what information was going to be let out to the press and what evidence they would withhold. In agreement, Lieutenant Jones stepped out to meet the mass of reporters, all demanding answers to their questions.

"If you'll all just quiet down I have a statement for you," shouted Jones.

The press people surrounded him in a semicircle as he relayed the following information.

"The victim here is a twenty-eight year old woman by the name of JoAnn Campo. The cause of death has not yet been determined but it will be listed as a homicide. Ms. Campo died sometime within the last twenty-four hours. There were no signs of forcible entry." The Lt. turned and started walking away as the reporters followed him yelling a myriad of questions at him. When he reached his car, he turned and said, "That's all the information we have at this time. When we find something new that we can release we will be happy to do so."

Allison arrived back at the Tribune. She turned in her film for development and called Phil. She was told that he was out in the field on an investigation. The person on the phone promised that he'd give the message to Hall as soon as he returned to the precinct.

Her next call was to Sandy. He'd want to know about this, she reasoned to herself. The murderer of Denise Haver was not limited to Chicago or to Illinois alone.

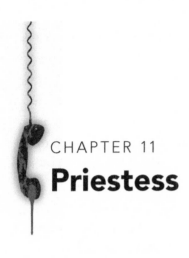

CHAPTER 11

Priestess

Zachary listened in to the secrets line as he had for weeks without obtaining satisfaction. He was growing increasingly discontented. The video productions at his disposal only served to provide temporary quenching of his desires. He lingered each night on the conversation highway. He listened for opportunities to present themselves. At last, Zachary heard from Priestess.

*   *   *

A fanatically religious family had raised Sharon Glass. The pleasures of life according to the doctrines taught by the 'Children of Light' were not to be enjoyed. In their belief, God's children were placed upon this earth to work and atone their sins to the father. The group shunned modern conveniences as they labored on farms and sweated in their mills. The grandparents of the children arranged marriages amongst those of their society. Every woman child was married by the time she was fourteen years old. She received the Lord's blessing in form of a child by the age of fifteen.

A good child, according to the teachings, was only produced by the pious. An unruly child was considered spawn of the devil. The disobedient children were chastised severely for their shortcomings. Likewise, the parents of the undisciplined child were either shunned or subjected to the cult's hammering indoctrination.

Sharon had been a much less than reverent child and rebelled against the strict codes of conduct as depicted by the members of the cult. It was at the age of thirteen she left the compound and her family's convictions behind her. Life away from the influence of her family began on the streets of Chicago.

She lived by stealing food and seeking shelter in abandoned buildings. The networks of homeless were not tolerant of her lack of survival skills

Sharon did indeed give birth to a child by the age of fifteen. However, the child was a product of rape and was taken from her only moments after birth. She had no means of support and the Children's Protective Services arranged for an adoption. Sharon slipped back onto the streets and through the cracks in the system. The shelters were full and had no room for her.

Difficult as her life was, she counted herself fortunate that she wasn't trapped by the disciplines of the church. The real rub was that while away from the influence of the cult, she was still a product of the ultra religious sect. She felt since she was a disobedient child she must be the spawn of the devil. Sharon set out to make contact with others of her kind.

Sharon was a beautiful youngster and attractive to the men who patrolled the streets seeking temporary dominion over the bodies of the lovely young. Her sky blue eyes contrasted her thick auburn hair. Sharon's petite figure attracted those who would pay for her companionship. Sharon learned quickly how to choose the men she would accommodate. She had at one time, a keen sense of self-preservation. But, as the years slipped by and she moved from one pimp's domination to another, one man's stable to another, Sharon lost her zest for living.

By the age of twenty-one she had lived a lifetime and it showed upon her face and demeanor. Her only companions were a small mirror, a razor blade and a white powder that removed her from the world of reality. She constantly begged the heavens for escape. The thought of suicide plagued her. Death seemed to be the better alternative. Yet, as often as she prayed for life's end, Sharon could not bring herself to take her own life. She still firmly believed that souls of a suicide were damned to eternal torment and endless emptiness.

Sharon's established customer list included regular visits from several men who were financially secure. The procurers of her body paid well to satisfy their unnatural tastes in sexual amusement. One of her customers gave her his calling card as incentive to perform especially daring or insidious acts. Sharon despised beyond words, the dirty little cravings she satisfied for this host of eccentric degenerates. The only thing she hated more than these people was herself and her life. Over the years, she had several encounters, which left her beaten and left for dead. Sharon Glass prayed that one of her attackers would finish the job and finally end her turmoil.

In search of companionship from those who would understand her, Sharon began calling the 900-Secrets line. At first, she assumed the role of a heeder and took in the aberrant conversation. On the third call, she spoke for the first time. She announced herself as Priestess. For the first time in her life, she was accepted. Sharon felt that she had finally found others of her kind a society in which she belonged.

The members of the call-in group included her in their fantasies and ideas for pleasuring. Priestess tried some of the suggestions on a few of her customers with some measure of success. She couldn't understand why her biggest supporter, Lady Cassandra, had dropped off the line. Sharon missed her, but there were others to take her place. The acceptance of the other members gave her a group of confidantes for the first time in her life. She felt she knew each member of the crowd and longed for some personal contact. While online, Priestess set a date with a new member Maxmillian.

Sharon felt excitement as the day for the date approached. She was sure that meeting Maxmillian would change her life forever and provide her with an entirely new life partner. Confined within the boundaries of her own heart, she sought a completely different path of life. Visions of a home and family of her own were secreted within the hope of dreams come true. Sadly, as she considered the prospect and how appealing it was, she knew it was truly only a dream. Everyone knows that dreams never come true for the wicked at heart.

*   *   *

Knocking at the door awakened the night creature from her slumber. Sharon Glass staggered to the door and opened the peephole to see who was demanding entry. She saw a tall younger man standing at her door. She was exhausted and felt frustrated that a John would come on her night off. She pulled back the slide bolt from the door. But before she opened it, she drew the security chain across and secured the bolt into the holding bracket. Opening the door as far as the chain would permit, she said, "Yeah, what do you want?" She liked his looks but was just too tired to bring on a new customer right at this time.

The visitor smiled and said, "Priestess, I'm Maxmillian."

She twisted her head to look at the clock. She rubbed her sleep heavy eyes and questioned, "Why are you here now? We're not supposed to meet till much later."

The enormous good-looking man offered a gentle smile. "It sounded like you needed a friend the other night when we were talking on the secrets line. I came early because I want to be that friend."

Sharon sighed, released the chain and opened the door. After closing the door, she turned to look at her visitor. He seemed to be very interested in her surroundings. Maxmillian pointed onto the small kitchenette and said, "Do you think I could have a drink of water?"

"Just water? Nothing else in it, plain water."

The pretended Maxmillian nodded.

While running the tap to flow extra cold, Priestess thought about her visitor. "Wow, what a hunk," she commented to herself, "he's clean and wearing very expensive clothes. Perhaps this really could work into something close to my dreams." Sharon returned to the living room and handed him the glass of water. "You're sure you wouldn't like anything in it?"

She watched as he began to drink the water down. She stepped over to the door to slider the bolt closed. When she reached for the bolt, she was surprised that it was already secured. She didn't remember locking it. Then she settled the issue within herself that she must have automatically locked it out of habit. He thanked her as he handed her the empty glass. Sharon took the glass and excused herself. "I need to get dressed," she explained. "I'll be right back."

Sharon quickly walked into her bedroom. She began pulling her nightgown off over her head. Suddenly there were hands helping her. Startled, Sharon wheeled around to face Maxmillian. She quickly grabbed her robe and pulled it up to cover her nakedness. "What the fuck are you doing? Get the hell out of here, Maxmillian! You don't come in here until I invite you! Get it Max!"

Her eyes betrayed no hint of fear. Her only expression was one of command. A dark mask seemed to fall over his face. Instead of heeding her warning, he grabbed a handful of her hair and flung her upon the bed. Priestess rolled over and lifted herself off the bed. She casually walked toward her guest. "You like it rough, huh?" Then in a matter of fact tone, she said, "fine, whatever."

Maxmillian looked surprised at her undaunted attitude and began to clench his fists and narrow his eyes as he peered coldly at her. Sharon dropped her hands to her sides and lowered her head. She shook her head in disgust. "Oh I get it," said Priestess, "you can't get it up unless I get scared." Exasperation began to take hold of her as she glared back at her visitor. "Well, just fucking forget it prick! You don't scare me, Maxmillian. I don't care what you do. All you are is just another cunt jumper, hump this and jump that, you're all just fuckin' alike."

Her visitor leaned forward until his face was within inches of hers. "I'm not Maxmillian, I'm Prince Odious. I'm here to make your dreams come true."

Priestess simply gave out with an empty laugh, and said, "What would you know of my dreams?" She pushed away from him and walked back into the bedroom. She reclined and continued. "You're no different than all of the sick fucks around this damned town." She sat up and shouted at him as she pointed to herself. "The big difference is, pal, I don't frighten. Whatever you are planning on doing won't be much different than I have had before. She leaned into him and said, "Give it your best shot. I'm beyond giving a shit."

Prince Odious looked down at her, and spoke in low menacing tones, "And if you die in the process?"

She looked up at him and then sat on the bed. She reached for her vile of cocaine. Speaking without emphasis, she said, "In that case, you prick, you'd be the angel that I've prayed for." She drew a line of the white power up into her nose through a tiny straw. She then fell back upon the bed and laughed with intoxication.

Priestess giggled as he moved about the room as a cat ready to strike at an unsuspecting bird. She mocked him as he tried varying methods to instill fear into her. Each failure seemed to aggravate him more. She watched as he opened his travel bag and brought out a large hunting knife and said, "I want you to meet my friend."

She took another snort of cocaine and then stood and placed the blade against her own throat. Without emotions she said, "I've seen this game before too. If you are the angel that I've waited for, get on with your business."

Odious was obviously perplexed and his confusion seemed to be leaving him cold.

She plopped onto the bed lying on her back and said, "I was right. You can't get it up till I act all afraid of you." She rolled onto her side and propped her head up with her hand. In a sneering tone said, "What do you want me to do, plead with you? To cry? To beg you not to hurt me?" she then yelled, "It ain't gonna happen shit face."

He climbed on top of Priestess and slapped his open hand across her face as he straddled her. She cleared the swirling in her head and smiled saying, "You can do better than that! A guy your size should be able to pack a better punch."

Anger knotted his face. He began pummeling her with his fists with ever-increasing furor. She could feel the bones in her body give way with each strike. Priestess looked up at Zachary just before she lost consciousness and said, "Maybe you are the prince of death."

*   *   *

Zachary returned to the private airfield and boarded his jet. His early arrival was not anticipated by the crew. His lack of fulfillment fed his frustration and anger. Rage was in total control of his body and mind. When the steward didn't meet him at the door, he inquired as to where he was. The pilot explained that Marsh was visiting his family that lived nearby, just outside of Chicago. The pilot paged the steward and called for a rush return.

Twenty-five minutes later Marsh walked through the door apologizing for the delay. Zachary was not to be consoled by the excuses offered. The flying fists of Zachary met Marsh's emphatic regrets and adamant denials of incompetence.

The pilot, hearing the commotion ran into the cabin only to see Marsh bleeding and almost incoherent. He pulled Zachary off Marsh. In turn, Marsh made a break for the door and escaped with his life. He stumbled away from the jet and stood on the tarmac as he watched the jet taxi and leave. The beaten steward filed a police report from the hospital.

* * *

The light of day had long since gone before Sharon Glass regained consciousness. She moaned with pain and regret as she realized that she was still alive. She tried to move but it seemed that even taking breath was agony. She heard faint knocking at her door and finally gave out with a groan loud enough for the visitor to hear. The words, "Oh my God, Sharon" reached her ears as darkness once again closed in on her.

It took three full days for the next excruciating shards of light to touch her swollen eyes. She found herself in a hospital surrounded by doctors, nurses and police. She didn't remember the sounds of the sirens as she was brought to the hospital.

Sharon Glass didn't know that a timely call from her neighbor had saved her life.

In a coma-induced dream, she stood before a bright warm light. The surrounding tunnel was filled with people who were more glowing energy than substance. They were beckoning to her to come forward. Some of the visions she recognized and others she didn't. She moved through the tunnel as a wisp of air travels freely and endlessly. The warmth from a light in the distance pulled her into a doorway to another state of being. She traveled effortlessly through until one of the beings drew her to a halt. She heard spoken words in her mind, "It's not your time, you will have to go back." Sharon knew she could not enter. Slowly she felt a gentle reverse pull and faded from, the light and the powerful glow. She felt more than heard, a voice saying, "You have lessons before you, Sharon." At last, she understood that she did have a purpose. There was a task in life that she had not yet fulfilled.

Police investigators waiting to question her met her emergence from the world of light. Sharon wept to the depth of her soul as she recounted what she could recall. Her ordeal with the prince of death was fed to her bruised mind in fragments. Her incoherent rambling were a mixture of sadism and religion.

She at first couldn't recollect the name of her attacker. Sharon could remember a face and worked with a police sketch artist. The two worked hard attempting to compile a decent likeness to the face of her assailant. The portrait of the aggressor took on unrealistic features. The artist gave up and told the waiting officers that she didn't think the victim was mentally capable of recalling truly, what the man looked like.

The police artist said that the battered woman would ramble, "My Bible, my Bible, he's in there."

Janet Damon, Sharon's ICU nurse, tucked the blankets snugly around Sharon and said, "You poor kid. Whoever did this to you is truly evil."

Sharon's entire body began to quake and shiver, "Yes, that's him. You do understand he was the prince of evil."

Nurse Damon soothed her patient by gently rubbing her forehead and said, "Yes, I understand, try to rest now."

Sharon managed a half-paralyzed smile from sausage-like lips and said, "The Odious one, the Prince." She slipped once again into her shadowy void. Sharon Glass, in the face of her own mortality decided that life was the better option.

*   *   *

Marsh and his attorney rode the elevator up to the offices of Hastings, Kilmer and Brock.

Marsh declared, "I'm going to nail that son of a bitch!"

David Nelson, Marsh's attorney said, "Calm down. " He continued, "Listen to me very closely, Terry. I don't think you really know whom we're dealing with need for you to calm down and be very quiet during this meeting. We can find out more by listening at this point than we can screaming."

Marsh exploded, "Calm down! Look at what that asshole did to me!"

The elevator reached its destination and the doors popped open. Nelson held on to the arm of his client "Look," Nelson warned. "I'm your legal counsel and you pay me to protect your rights and give you advice in your best interest, right?"

"Right."

Nelson tucked his briefcase under his arm. "Either you let me do the talking, or you will go into that den of lions by yourself. Do I make myself clear? Do you understand?" Nelson leaned forward to make strong eye contact and said, "Right?"

Marsh steeled himself and said, "Okay, I'll keep quiet."

The receptionist guided Marsh and Nelson into a large conference room. At the far end of the twenty-five foot oak conference table sat both Kilmer and Brock. In front of them, lying on the table were two manila file folders. Kilmer and Brock both stood as the duo entered the room and introductions were made all around.

Nelson began by stating their grievances with the young Pendrake. He culminated with their ability to seek damages according to the law. He produced as a part of their evidence a police report taken on the day of the assault, hospital records and the sworn testimony of a witness who had been a short distance from the jet.

Kilmer and Brock listened quietly and nodded at the receipt of the copies of the records listed. "We have all of this," began Kilmer. "However, you may not be aware of what our rebuttal will be." Brock walked over and handed copies of depositions offered by the pilot of the jet, Dick Clayton and by Zachary Payne Pendrake.

Kilmer explained, Clayton's statement indicated that Mr. Pendrake was protecting himself from your client's assault. It seems that Mr. Pendrake discovered Mr. Marsh's drugs that were secreted on the aircraft." Brock summed up their position in the matter by saying, "Zachary Pendrake's sworn statement agreed completely with those of Clayton."

Marsh jumped to his feet, "Drugs, I didn't have any drugs on that plane then or any time. I don't use drugs and never have."

Nelson pulled Marsh away from the conference room and quietly said, "Just listen to them. And for God's sake, keep your mouth shut."

Marsh objected, "David, it's a lie and they know it."

Nelson shook his head and quietly said, "Can you prove it?" His question was met with a blank look from Marsh. Once again, he put his fingers up to his lips hushing his client, "Again, just listen."

They returned to the meeting room. Brock began to explain the solution as offered by Pendrake Industries. "Neither our client Mr. Pendrake or you want to see your client in jail. Nor do we feel that we want to waste the money it would take to defend Pendrake industries against Mr. Marsh's wild accusations. Therefore, we have been authorized by Karl Jacobs of Pendrake Industries to offer your client a cash settlement in the amount of one hundred thousand dollars.

Our clients will take care of all medical claims incurred by the altercation. And Mr. Marsh will need to sign a waiver of prosecution in favor of Pendrake Industries. "Kilmer spoke out, "Understand Mr. Nelson if you take this to court you will lose. Pendrake Industries feels the argument between our clients was unfortunate. They would like to put an end to this business. Mr. Pendrake wishes no links to your client's behaviors. Furthermore wishes him the best in the future."

After a short but heated discussion, Marsh signed the release and accepted their check. The only record of the incident was a single page police report.

CHAPTER 12
The Link

Allison waited for Sandy to return her call. She paced the floor in her office and waited for the lab to deliver the pictures from the JoAnn Campo slaying. Nothing seemed to happen fast enough for her. The enormous tension rewarded her with a gigantic headache. Her mind reeled with all of the fearful possibilities. She knew if this could happen in two different states this killer may have struck in others as well. DeeCee's murder wasn't an isolated crime. Finally, Allison dropped onto her chair and buried her face in her hands. Turmoil of emotions filled with the memories of Denise Haver's death were less prominent than her memories of DeeCee, the friend she'd been so close to. "Something," she said to the ever listening walls, "has got to be done."

The clerk handing her the developed Campo pictures interrupted her personal debate. As usual, she'd ordered three sets of prints. One for the police, another set for the paper and the third for her own portfolio.

She called Jonesy to let him know she had pictures in hand. She would be leaving shortly to deliver them. She stuffed the photos into her brief case and began to leave. The ringing of her desk phone called her back to her desk. Allison picked up the receiver and said, "Dean."

"The hell you say! Hi there Kiddo!" Sandy's familiar voice bellowed out. Allison circled her desk and leaned back cradling the headset to her ear. "Yeah, Hi Sandy thanks for calling me back."

"Well," began Sandy, "how the hell are you. And how do you like sunny California? Are they treating you well?"

"Listen Sandy," she interrupted, "I'd love to chat with you bur right now I don't have time. I think we have a problem."

"Okay kid, what's going on?"

Allison tried to shake off the feeling of dread. "Sandy, do you remember the Denise Haver murder?"

"Of course I do! Christ, who would forget it? Why?"

She stroked her temples hoping to alleviate her aching head. "We have another death out here Sandy, same MO as Denise Haver. I just photographed the murder scene of a woman named JoAnn Campo. Sandy, I know it's the same guy. She was butchered in the same way."

Jonesy could only mutter, "Sweet Jesus."

"So Sandy, where are you guy's, with the investigation. Do you have any suspects or leads?"

Sandy's voice lowered. "No, Allie. We haven't been able to ferret anything out that we didn't know before you left. I tell you, the press isn't letting up on us at all either. They're like a pack of starving dogs smelling meat."

"When I did the Campo shoot I told Lt. Jones about the Denise Haver murder. He's going to call you and want to put your heads together I'm sure."

"I'll get ready for the call," replied Sandy. "I'll get all the information to them as soon as I hear from, who did you say it was, Lt. Jones?"

Allison arrived at the police headquarters. Lt. Jones was talking on the telephone and hung up as she approached his office. Allison waited outside of the glass partition for his signal to enter. He wheeled his chair around and stared out the fifth floor window.

She stepped into the doorway quietly. Slowly he turned around to face Allison. She handed over the manila envelope and kept silent as he looked through the portraits of savagery. Jones looked up at Allison with a pained expression. Dread reflected in his voice as he said "Chicago! What do we have in common? What's the link?"

Allison knew his question was rhetorical but couldn't help trying to answer it. "I honestly wish I knew!"

Jones pulled himself up to his desk and in a quick jerk said, "Well, I guess we had better go about the business of finding out! In double time!"

Allison locked eyes with Jones, "Have you talked with Burton Sanders yet?"

"Yeah, I was talking with him while you were waiting outside. He's faxing data and shipping over night copies of their files. We'll be working the cases jointly and bringing in the FBI." Jones looked up into the worried face of Allison and he took the packet of pictures. "Thanks, Allie we'll be in touch very soon. Are you okay with all of this? You look very tired and harried."

Allison fought to control the turbulent emotions fighting for control. "Yeah, I'm good."

Jones's expression indicated that he didn't buy it for a minute. He knew that it wasn't his place to play the role of father confessor. "Try to stay loose."

*   *   *

Allison returned home and added the pictures of JoAnn Campo along side of the Denise Haver crime scene photos. Her emotional state was precarious and she knew it. She needed to sleep and rest her mind from the brutality that she had seen. Building her own murder book in this now series of murders was incredibly taxing. Her heart ached again as she placed the pictures in sequence. Jonesy's words kept repeating through her mind, "What's the link?"

Each graphic was placed adjacent to the correlating photograph for each scene. She created a comparison from room to room. Allison noticed the telephone book on the desk in JoAnn Campo's foyer. She enlarged the writing with her magnifying glass and saw the notation, "900-Secrets. " Read the script. Allison sat back in the chair and said aloud. "What on earth is 900-Secrets?" She pulled out the photos of the Haver living room ad focused on the papers strewn over the living room floor.

Amongst the papers was Denise Haver's telephone bill. The numbers were much too small to make out. Quickly, Allison collected the photographs and drove back to the Tribune.

Her arrival was just in time. Allison caught the lab tech walking out the door. "Bill! Bill, can you do something for me? I really need your help."

The tech frowned in a manner that was exaggerated. "Com'mon Allie, I just finished and it's been a bitch of a day. How about if I do it first thing in the morning?"

Donning her best begging expression Allison pleaded. "Bill, this is really important or I wouldn't' ask:" Allison watched as he wavered, "I tell you what, Bill. You help me on this and I will buy you tickets for the 49er's game coming up this weekend.

He exhaled a petulant breath, shrugged his shoulders and said, "Box seat?"

Allison grimaced and said, "yeah, okay."

"Deal, whaddya' need?"

Allison brought out her photographs. She circled in red ink the areas of the pictures she needed enlarged. Bill took the paperwork and said, "Twenty minutes or so. Is that soon enough for you?"

Allison grabbed him by the forearms and gave him a grateful shake. "Thank you so much Bill. I really appreciate it."

He gave her a wry smile and said, "No problem, when I'm at the game I'll be appreciating you!" He laughed and headed for the lab.

True to his word, Bill handed her the enlargements within the time frame he had mentioned. Allison gave Bill a quick kiss on his cheek and returned home.

Once again, she began her comparison. The numbers billed by the telephone company were repeated calls to 900-732-7387. She looked at the photo of JoAnn Campo's address book that had been lying open in the apartment. A bit of confusion washed over her as she read, '900-Secrets' until she looked at the alphabetical listings on her own telephone. She transcribed the 900-737-7387 and found that they translated to 900-Secrets.

A shudder ran through her as she realized that she had discovered the link. She immediately picked up the telephone to call Jonesy. Her heart sank when her call was re-directed to his voice mail. She waited for the prompt and dialed zero to leave a message for him. What seemed like hours passed and still no call came in from Jonesy. Allison felt the surge of nervous excitement. She was certain this was the elusive 'link' Lt. Jones had talked about. Allison fidgeted and fretted. She paced the floor and concentrated upon Jonesy. It was as if she were trying to make a psychic connection. She spun mid-rack and uttered in frustration, 'Ring telephone, come one Jonesy call!"

The more she weighed the likelihood of that being the true connection the more doubt began to creep into her mind. Allison decided to call the line and listen in. The nine hundred number rang as Allison looked at the billing rate showing on the Haver invoice. "Crud, almost five dollars per minute." she said and hung up the telephone before the connection went through.

Allison sat cross-legged on her sofa. She rapped her fingernails in cadence upon the handle of the receiver. She worked at balancing out the black and white facts she had in her full color pictures. While her sensibilities told her, the 'link' could not be so simple; her intuition told her that it just might be exactly that easy. A slightly mercenary glint filled her eyes as she considered the scope of the story. Allison knew the 'senior' writers with the Tribune would have to take a back seat on this story. It was hers and hers alone.

She glanced at her watch. 9:00 p.m. and she still hadn't heard from Jonesy. She reasoned that being an investigative reporter, it would be her job to follow up on the information she had acquired. Allison pressed redial on the portable telephone. This time she allowed the call to go through. A woman's provocative voice said, "Welcome to the Secrets line. You must be at least eighteen years old in order to participate on this line. Using the keypad of your touch-tone telephone, you have five seconds to dial in your birth date. "Allison dialed in a random birth date. The seductive voice on the line said, "Thank you." Her call was thrust into the mainline gathering. Her ears slipped into the party line during boisterous laughter of the countless participants. People with strange names like King Wolf, Avenger, Queenie, and Domatra were discussing the newest club scenes. The current topic was the outrageous dress of the so named club kids. Allison could decipher at least ten different voices coursing over the highway. The raucous discussions were lurid, complex and decidedly deviant. Frank descriptions of the viability of using the club kids for their own strange practices sickened Allison. She listened to the stories of the man who referred to himself as Demon Seed. He conveyed with distinct and precise language his latest encounter with a club kid who called herself 'Trixi.' The description of his evening with Trixi caused Allison to gasp audibly.

Suddenly one of the members blurted out, "Heeder on the line!" Allison listened for the voice of Heeder, but heard no one new begin to talk. Midst the conversation, a beep sounded. A new voice rang into the conversation. The voice was strong and smooth and said, "Hello servants." In unison, most of the members greeted the joiner. "Prince Odious! Where you been, Bitch!"

Allison looked at her watch and realized that she had listened in for ten minutes. She figured she had just spent a good chunk of money and hung up the telephone. "Fifty dollars," she sputtered, "and for what? Just to listen to a bunch of weirdoes with even weirder names get themselves off."

She returned to her task of cataloging the photos of JoAnn Campo along side of the Denise Haver film. She was still in the process of comparing the two scenes when her attention was drawn to the tattoo on DeeCee's ankle.

"Vixen," she said to herself, "Weird names, with even stranger interests." The thought made her sit back and reflect upon the life style of DeeCee and the outrageous culture she was into at the time of her death. Once again she said, "Vixen." She went back to her phone and again pressed re-dial. She waited for an opening in the conversation and said "Hi Gang! Vixen's here!"

Two of the people on the line welcomed her as a regular member of the group. "Vixen girl, where have you been? Makin' someone else's scene or what?" Domatra, said, "Hey Prince O, did you hear who's back?" Prince Odious didn't respond. The smooth voice that heralded his arrival was absent from the conversation. Suddenly another voice broke in. "Wait a minute, this doesn't sound like Vixen to me. Vixen, dropped off the line more than year ago. This vixen doesn't have the same Brooklyn accent."

Allison hung the phone up, breaking the connection. She lay back on her sofa, her mind spinning with the reality of the connection she had uncovered. She jumped when he telephone rang. Apprehension enveloped her as she wondered if the secrets line was calling her. Common sense then took over and she answered the phone on the third ring. Still she listened before she spoke.

Jones's voice rang out, "Allie, this is Jones. Allie are you there?"

She swallowed and shook her head, feeling silly about her worries. "Yeah, Jonesy, I'm here."

"So what's the story? I got a message to call saying that it's vital."

Allison took a deep breath, steadied herself and dove right in. "I know this is going to sound crazy, but, I think I may have found the connection you were talking about earlier."

Jones was quiet and then said, "Go on, I'm listening."

She began, "I think our connection is a 900 sex talk line."

"What?

She could feel the disbelief in Jones's voice and said, "Jonesy, just hear me out. I think you may find this interesting." Allison began her explanation by describing

how she found the information that led her to 900-Secrets.

Jonesy said, "Hang on a minute, my pen ran dry, I need to make some notes."

Allison provided Lt. Jones with the number for the 900 secrets line. She told him of the pseudo names used by the participants who were on the line during her call. The final connection settled into place when she explained the response she got from the crowd when she introduced herself with the name of Vixen.

"Jonesy, Denise Haver had the word Vixen tattooed on her ankle." Allison caught herself close to calling Denise Haver, DeeCee. She couldn't do that now. Now that some leads were showing up in the case. She still felt strongly about making sure that the killer of her close friend paid the price.

"Jonesy, Denise Haver had the name Vixen tattooed on her ankle."

The tone of Jones's voice indicated to Allison that she had his complete attention. "Very interesting idea, kid. You've given me enough to start the investigative ball rolling. We'll do some checking and see where this leads."

Allison asked, "Jonesy, have you gotten the pictures yet from Sandy in Chicago?

"No, not yet, it may take them some time to get it all together."

"Jonesy, I have a set of the crime scene photographs here in my portfolio. I could bring them over for you to see if you'd like."

"That might be a good idea."

Allison started gathering her portfolio as she'd offered to share them. When he agreed she simply grabbed them all up and said, "I'm on my way."

* * *

Claire Lang, Jones's administrative assistant came in and handed him a stack of faxed transmissions that had just come in from Chicago. Lt. Jones paged Phillip Hall and Joe Biggs with a message to return to head quarters at once. He had barely finished his page when Hall came walking through the doors of the squad room.

Hall joked, "This fast enough for you?"

Jones looked up from the papers he'd been reading and said, "Yeah Phil, I didn't know you were in the building. I have a call into a Captain Sanders in Chicago. There have been some developments in a case that had been assigned to Biggs. Chief Adkins should be arriving any time. I want you to wait out by your desk and come back in after the Chief and I talk with Biggs"

Hall furrowed his brow and said, "Sanders, from Chicago? What's going on?"

Jonesy half glared at him. "You'll be filled in a little bit later. But for now just let it alone."

Seemingly perplexed by the forbidding attitude from Lt. Jones, Hall returned to his desk. A short time later the Chief of Detectives walked through the door and headed straight in for a closed door meeting with the Lt. Jones. Chief Adkins settled himself into the companion chair and said, "Okay Chuck what's so important that I needed to shag my ass down here so fast."

Jones looked intently at Adkins, "We have a situation brewing here. I need to have you on the same game plan as I."

"Fine man, spit it out," replied the Chief.

"I need to shift a case around. To re-assign it." Jones dropped his pen on the desk pad. He took a sharp breath and said, "I want to take a high profile case from Joe Biggs and turn it over to Hall."

A concerned furrow formed across the forehead of Adkins. He asked, "Why do you suspect or have any evidence of incompetence or personal detachment being compromised with Biggs on the case?"

"No, nothing like that. It's just that I'm sure Hall is in a better position to accomplish two things."

Adkins shifted in his chair and said, "Okay enlighten me. What two things are you talking about?"

Before Jones could answer, there was a knock at the door. Jones looked up to see Claire holding pictures. He waved her inward, she handed the pictures to Jonesy and said, "Excuse me for interrupting, but Allison Dean was just here and gave these to me to get to you. She said that you were waiting for them."

Jones took the pictures and asked Claire to let Allison know that they would be returned as soon as possible. He turned to his desk as Adkins sat waiting. Jones handed him the pictures of the JoAnn Campo murder scene. Adkins grimaced at the all too vivid pictures.

Jones extended his index finger. He pointed to the Campo shots and said, "This was this morning here in Oakland." He opened the file from Allison and laid out the corresponding pictures. "And," he continued, "This was in Chicago about a year ago."

Adkins recoiled slightly and said, "Christ, How did you make this other case so fast?"

"Allison Dean, that's how. You know the Trib photographer. She moonlights for us. She photo's most of our homicides. She's good, real good. Anyway, she used to work with Chicago's PD too. And she shot both of these cases. When she went in to the scene, she instantly recognized the MO as being from the same actor."

Adkins said, "Can she keep her mouth shut?"

"Yeah, I'm sure. Dean worked very closely with the district attorney in Chicago. He raves about her ability to work with the police and the press at the same time. She's done a great job for us as well." Jones offered Adkins a wry smile, 'not like most of the press clowns that are out there."

"We also have a couple aces in the hole," explained Jones. "She's paid by us on a part time basis. She really seems to have a drive about her regarding this killer. But most importantly, I want to be able to control the information that comes out about this maniac."

Jones grinned, "Beyond that, she is dating Sergeant Hall. I'm sure he can help keep a lid on anything going out to the presses."

Adkins said, "And right now, Biggs is assigned to this case, right?"

Jones nodded a grim affirmative, and then added, "Biggs can be a real abrasive son of a bitch and a hot headed asshole to boot."

Adkins rubbed his chin thoughtfully. He finally looked up at the waiting Jones and said, "Okay, Jones. We'll go ahead and make the changes. Put Hall on the case effective immediately."

*   *   *

Allison arrived home, exhausted from the revelations of the day. She played her messages and found that Sandy had returned her call. His sense of humor was still in place she noted as he said on the recording, "Tag you're it. Call me when you can, but I'm bummed that I missed you." She smiled warmly as she remembered the genuine caring relationship they'd had when she lived in Chicago. She put her coat away, situated herself on the sofa and dialed his number. The hurried chat they'd had with him earlier, made her miss him even more. He answered the phone and she began, "Hi Sandy! I got your message and who's it now?" He laughed as she continued. "Listen, I want to apologize for having to run away like I did."

Sandy laughed and said, "I'm glad you called. I was sort of worried about you."

"Awe Sandy, you know me, I'm always on the run. By the way, I hear you've been talking with Jonesy."

"Yeah I have, and he seems like a real sharp guy. And what's with this Jonesy bit? Another nickname?"

Allison laughed, "You know how I am. Those people I really like get their comfy nicknames. She laughed louder as she said, "know what I mean Sandy? Actually I can't tell you how much he reminds me of you."

Sandy jibed, "That good looking huh?"

Allison played along, "And almost as brilliant as my master crime fighter in Chicago." The two friends laughed at each other's comic banter until finally Sandy drew the comedy to a halt. "Okay," he said, "what's going on with that Campo murder there in the big city?"

"Oh Sandy," she began, "you should be getting a memo from Oakland PD. I found what I think is a link to the two crimes."

"You're shitting me. Fill me in."

"I'm sure you've seen my portfolio and all the pictures I've saved from my work with Chicago. Well, I've been keeping the same sort of records here."

Sandy interjected, "Ah yes, the only lady I know that will have a one woman show of the macabre."

Allison chuckled, "I was arranging the new photos of the Campo murder next to the Haver crime. I noticed something peculiar. Anyway long story short, both victims were calling the same nine hundred number."

"Really? The x-rated sex lines?"

"Yep the very same. Anyway, Sandy, do you remember the tattoo on Denise Haver's ankle?"

"Sure, I think so. If my memory serves me right, the word Vixen was tattooed on her ankle, right?"

"Absolutely right," she said. "I followed a hunch Sandy. I called the nine hundred line just a little while ago. I introduced myself as Vixen to see what reaction I'd get.

"And did anything bite? Or was there no response."

"Boy howdy, did I ever get a bite on my bait. A couple of the people on the line asked me where I had been. It was going fine until some other guy mentioned that Vixen had a Brooklyn accent. DeeCee was raised in Brooklyn before moving out to California. She could put on an accent and take it off like I do a sweater.

"Okay and the Brooklyn part has been verified."

"Now get this part. The same guy that said Vixen had an accent also said Vixen had dropped off the line about a year ago. How's that for a coincidence?"

"Too coincidental to be random! You know kiddo you just might be on to something. Keep me informed will you. I'll work it from the same angle on my end."

"You bet, Sandy."

"Well kid, I hate to say goodbye but I really have to get going. I am helping in the planning committee for Chief Ory's retirement party. But I know we'll be talking again real soon."

"Ory's finally giving it up, huh? Boy howdy look out little fishes, here he comes!"

Sandy gave out with a belly laugh as he hung up the telephone.

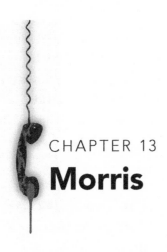

CHAPTER 13

Morris

Steven Morris, a senior reporter for the Chronicle, snapped the lead in his pencil while he read the account of the Campo murder. The article written by Allison Dean infuriated Morris. He knew there was much more to the story than she had written.

Morris was a competitor of major standing who was not above offering bribes in order to get a story. His methods while controversial had largely been successful. Pete Canada, a fellow journalist, was seated at the desk across form Steve. He watched as Morris's color changed from normal hues to vibrant tones of red.

"Problems, Morris?"

Morris sneered, "Oh this Dean bitch. This really pisses me off."

Canada warned, "Best watch your blood pressure. And just what is it that pisses you off now?"

179

Morris leaned back in his chair and folded his arms across his chest. "Ever since the Trib took this little priss off of the society pages, the Chronicles' been scooped on almost every front page story. I'd like to know who she's sleeping with."

Canada offered Morris a sympathetic sneer and asked, "What's wrong Stevie, feeling like you could be kissing your Pulitzer goodbye?"

Morris was not amused by the cajoling of his office mate and glared back at Pete. "I'll clue you in. I'm going to find a way to blast that little bitch off of the front page. And to top it off, I'll do more than just a little damage to her credibility. You just watch me!"

Pete retorted, "And just how do you plan to do that?"

Morris nabbed his tape recorder and placed it in his pocket. He snatched up his briefcase and began to walk away. At the last second he turned to Canada and grinned a toothy smirk and said, "I'm working on it. I'll find an opening. I don't know where it will come from, but I'll find the opening I need. Trust me I'm working on it."

*   *   *

Across town the meeting between Adkins, Jones and Biggs began. Phillip Hall waited, confused and curious about the talk that was going on. Adkins elected to break the news about the Campo case reassignment. As anticipated the change in commands didn't go over well with Biggs. A slamming noise caused Hall to jerk his head up and look in the direction of Jones's office. He could hear shouting but couldn't make out what the angry Biggs said. Biggs stood up and leaned over the desk. His face was virtually purple with rage. Phil craned his neck to try to see the Lieutenant and the Chief. He knew Adkins fairly well. Jones, he knew even better. Hall read the expression of ultimate control on both commanders' faces. Claire LeTang walked by as the shouting continued. She looked curiously over at Phil and pointed towards the closed door. Hall offered a stumped expression and shrugged his shoulders.

Suddenly the door to Jones's office flew open slamming into the adjacent wall. Biggs came screaming out of the room. He stomped up to Hall's desk and pointed his tobacco stained index finger in his face. "You wanted it," yelled Biggs, "It's all yours. You ass kissing prick." Biggs spun about and started heading for the exit.

Gagged with surprise, Phil didn't have a chance to respond. He stopped just short of the door and said, "Screw you, Screw all of you."

Adkins and Jones crowded the doorway to the Lieutenant's office and watched Biggs's tirade. The two commanding officers stood as silent and immovable as gravestones.

Jones shouted out suddenly, "Biggs! Biggs! Make that four weeks suspension, without pay. Another outburst like that and we'll be discussing your future with the department. Am I understood?"

"Completely sir," Biggs snapped.

Phil watched the swinging doors until they came to a stop. His confusion evident, he turned and looked at Jones. "Hall, now!" The come hither waive of Jones's hand, the tone of his voice and the scowls on their faces concerned Phil. He followed

Jones into his office and joined the two superior officers. Lt. Jones motioned for Hall to sit down. Hall touched the seat of the chair in jest as if to test the temperature. He noted his superiors were not amused by his attempt at levity. Phil sat down prepared to listen; when he was seated he spied Brigg's shield and identification wallet sitting on the desk. Phil narrowed his eyes and asked, "Lieutenant Jones sir, I don't mean to be pushy, but what the hell is going on here?"

Adkins reached over and picked up Biggs' wallet and shield and placed it in the top desk drawer. He began, "Biggs has decided to sign off of a pretty important case that he's been working."

Phil was well aware that Joe Biggs would not have chosen to drop an important case. He was also very cognizant of the politics involved. Not lost on him either was the fact that the Chief referred to him as 'Biggs' instead of Detective Biggs. He simply replied, "Interesting decision, sir."

Jones looked at Hall over the top of his reading glasses and said, "Close the door Hall and then cut the sir."

Adkins handed the Campo case file to Hall. "We are assigning you to this case."

Suddenly, the reasons for Biggs's eruption became clear. He wasn't however, going to ask too many questions at this point, except," Why me?"

"Three reasons," began Adkins. "First of all you're a top notch investigator. Number two, your lady friend has become involved with this case. We need for you to keep a handle on Allison, so that she doesn't become a liability to our investigation."

Jones added, "She's also involved in another case, a year old in Illinois."

Hall narrowed his eyes in concentration. He opened the campo packet. He instantly saw the similarities in the pictures. "You're talking about the Denise Haver murder in Chicago," replied Hall.

"Yes. How did you know about the Haver case?"

Hall's one word answer was, "Allison."

Jones nodded in understanding. "The department needs to handle the press delicately or else those sharks are going to have a feeding frenzy about this Campo killing."

"Burton Sanders of Chicago tells us we can depend on Allison," added Adkins. "But the only reason you should need is the fact that it's our call and that's the way we want it! Or would you like to get into the same discussion we just finished with Biggs?"

Phillip Hall opened the three-inch thick file and began to read through the ongoing investigation in Chicago. He was surprised at the amount of information Chicago Pd had documented. The maze of paperwork included a complete set of hand and palm prints, along with DNA information regarding the murderer. The summation pinpointed the perp as a white male, most possibly between the ages of twenty-five and forty-five. The strands of hair found in the shower tested out as a male with sandy blond wavy hair. His blood type was identified as B positive. Semen analysis revealed that the killer was a secretor and exhibited no sign of venereal disease. The soap marks on the shower ceiling suggested that the subject in question was well over six feet tall. Handwriting analysis of the bloody words on the wall above Denise Haver's body implied formal education and more than just a hint of compulsive neatness. Further indication of the killer's compulsiveness was offered by the precise folding of the face cloth he had used to clean himself after the killing.

All of the evidence, handprints and complete DNA profiles were useless without someone to match them up with. And so far, no matches had been found.

Hall questioned, "Has this data been given to the FBI for a predator profile from Quantico?"

Jones responded, "They have it now; we're just waiting for their reply and to return the profile to us. Now this actually could be a federal case since the same killer has crossed state lines. They are offering us assistance in any area we feel necessary."

Adkins added, "If Dean hadn't brought the other death to our attention we would have presumed that this was an isolated incident. The feds don't like to spend time for homicides until they are listed as a serial killer. And then they give the states a wide berth for investigation and jump in only when the individual police agency cries for help."

Hall turned the page to reveal the autopsy report. Again the details surrounding the physical evidence astounded him. Each of the individuals grew silent as they read the report. The analysis of the wound in the body cavity and the surrounding area suggested the perp had ejaculated inside of the gash itself. There was no indication of vaginal penetration except for the cuts and slices of a sharp blade. Further statements given by the report stated that the large laceration which disemboweled the victims was not done post mortem. The markings on the exterior of the incision turned out to be tracings of eyebrow pencil and a common formulation of red lipstick. The same instrument that had penetrated the vaginal canal evidently created the wounds on the breasts. Defensive wounds and bruising indicated that Denise Haver had struggled to save her life. The cause of death listed for Denise Haver was strangulation.

Jones broke the silence, "We don't have the autopsy results from Ms. Campo yet. I'm sure however, that they will parallel each other."

Adkins nodded in agreement and added, "Get a hold of the medical examiner's office and put a rush on those reports."

Adkins' voice betrayed emotions he rarely allowed anyone to see. "You know something? Many times I have wondered why every child born in this country is not finger printed and had their DNA mapped and listed on a national data base. Fuckers like this guy would have been caught by now and JoAnn Campo would still be alive."

"We can catch them. Then the system will let them back out on the streets faster than we can haul them in! Bleeding heart, fucking liberals, "said Jones.

Adkins ended the meeting telling Hall, "You have thirty six hours to provide us with your investigation plan."

*   *   *

Steven Morris skidded his car to a halt at the corner by Archer's Haven. He waited impatiently for the light to change. He was still agitated by the comments from Pete Canada. He balanced his forearms on the top of the steering wheel. Tapping his left foot he looked around at his surroundings. Movement and noise off to his left garnered his attention. The door to Archer's was standing open and two bouncers escorted Joe Biggs from the bar. "Cool off Biggs, your taxi will be here in a minute," demanded one of the bouncers. Morris's attention was cemented upon the scuffle taking place. "I'm okay you suck-ass bastards. Just give me my fuckin' keys or else," raved the drunken cop.

"Or what? You'll arrest us?" Both men laughed.

Morris saw a taxi turning into the parking lot. The light restraining Morris turned green. Morris accelerated quickly, squealing his tires in an effort to cut off the cab. As soon as his car was stopped he humped out of his Cadillac and intercepted the cab driver. He quickly handed a ten dollar bill to the driver. Morris yelled to the bouncers, "I'll take care of him, we're old friends." Biggs was much taller and heavier than Morris and so drunk that he could barely stand. Morris opened the passenger side of the Deville and guided Biggs into the seat. He jogged around to the driver's side. As he slid into the seat, he quickly reached into his pocket and pressed the record button on the tape recorder. They held Morris's departure up while they fastened the seatbelt around Biggs.

Dave the bouncer closed the door on the sedan and slapped the side of the car saying, "Okay, he's all yours."

Biggs looked at Morris with glassy eyes and an unsteady head. "Who the hell are you?"

"Take it easy detective. You know me. I'm Morris, Steve Morris from the Chronicle."

Biggs leaned over the seat trying to focus his blurry vision on the driver.

"What are you so upset about, Joe?"

Biggs slurred his words, "What the fuck do you care, you fuck."

Morris aligned with Biggs to get him to talk. "I care because I know you're the best detective in the department."

"You're God Damn right I am." Biggs tried to focus on his surroundings. "Where the hell are we going anyway?"

Morris said slyly, "Anywhere you want big guy. Hey, how about if we go somewhere and get a drink? Whaddaya think?"

Biggs rested his head on the window, "Sounds like a plan."

Morris took Biggs to a restaurant and gave him enough food to wake him up but not enough to sober him. He learned that Biggs had been removed from the Campo murder case. He was elated when the drunken officer told him about the relationship between Hall and Allison. He had found his opening. Morris's intrusion continued with questions relating to the slaying. "What did you see in the bathroom at the Campo house?"

Biggs gave out with a laugh, "Awe shit, she wasn't found in the bathroom. She was in her bedroom. You know, they think I'm stupid. We told the press she was in her bathroom so we could weed out the asshole, confessors. They think I don't know what all that crap found in her bedroom was for."

Morris pulled himself close. "What crap are you talking about?"

"Fuck, you know. Whips, handcuffs and lots of really freaky toys there in that place. They think I'm stupid and don't know that this stuff is for sex."

"Your right Joe, I can't believe they under estimate you."

"Under estimate me, you bet they do. I bet they think I don't remember the writing on the fucking wall."

Morris feigned a laugh. "They're the one with no brains. They couldn't remember what was written. But you do! Don't you Joe."

"You bet I do. Christ, it was as big as day. The son of a bitch wrote it in Campo's blood." Biggs held up his hand as if to trace the words. "I am my middle name. Yep that was it, I am my middle name."

Morris smiled, "No, they wouldn't want anyone to know about that."

"Right," said Biggs. "They didn't want anyone to know about that or how he really sliced her up."

"Yeah, but you can tell your friends. Here Joe, have another drink. You can tell me how she was killed."

Biggs was beginning to fade and Morris was so close to getting all the information he needed to scoop the Tribune and boost his own career. Biggs began to sink into unconsciousness. Morris was sensing that he was close to the full story so he shook Biggs enough to rouse him.

"Joe, I heard she was bludgeoned, is that true? Or are the fuckers painting shit about that too?"

"The little bitch was strangled and had her gut slit wide open"

Morris drew his hand up the center of his torso and said, "You mean like this? Like gutting a deer?"

Biggs said, "No, no, no, like this," he leaned back in his chair and drew a vague semi-circle on his lower abdomen. "And get this shit," he continued.

"The bastard that killed her thought he was some sort of fuckin' artist."

Confused by the comment, Morris said, "What do you mean an artist?"

"Yeah the guy drew on her stomach with some lipstick and a pencil of some kind before he slashed her open."

"Good God," said Morris. "This guy is one sick bastard."

Morris looked over to see Biggs slump forward, hitting his head onto the table. He lifted Biggs's head by his hair and looked at the closed eyes of the man that just helped him scoop the Tribune.

"Thanks asshole," Morris turned off his tape recorder and called for a cab for Biggs.

To Morris, Biggs was simply a means to an end and just loose cannon enough to take advantage any opportunity for a career boost.

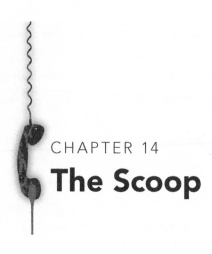

CHAPTER 14
The Scoop

Allison slumbered peacefully, wrapped in a cloak of fresh love making. Her sleeping ears began to hear voices calling her name. She rolled off of the bed in an attempt to find who was calling her. Faintly at first she heard her name, then louder and louder until the gentle calling had become an anguished scream. Tension filled her body as she wandered through her apartment. She was drawn to the living room where the voices seemed to emanate. The bookshelf was glowing an eerie green aura. As she approached the voices beckoned her to find them. Taunting words and phrases filled her with resolve. "I'm with you," one of the voices repeated. The other voice simply seemed to sob a pain filled wail. Allison stood in front of the shelf. Her portfolio fell to the floor and opened to the facial portraits of Denise Haver and JoAnn Campo. The eyes of both victims rose from the photos and hung suspended in mid air. Both stared through Allison's soul. The voices combined to say, "We're with you." A flash of pale green light illuminated the room and suddenly she was back in her bed. Phil was cradling her and uttering reassuring phrases. It was just a dream.

The nightmares that had plagued Allison for the first six months after DeeCee's murder had returned. Night after night she would bolt upwards, breathless and sweat soaked. It took her a long time to go back to sleep. Sometimes she simply stayed awake. She would tell herself that everything would be fine if they could just capture the man responsible for killing her nightly tormentors. Phillip seemed concerned and talked directly to her about the dreams. She tried to dismiss his concerns and insistence that the murders had become an obsession.

*   *   *

The first Sunday Allison had taken off in the weeks since the Campo murder began as a sunny spring morning. Phillip had spent the night with her, locked in a gentle and loving embrace. She awakened early and lay next to him. She watched his chest rise and fall in deep slumber. His love making from the night before, still created fresh and warm feelings throughout her body.

"I love you Phil," she whispered. She slipped quietly from under the sheets. She crept from the room and gently pulled the door closed as he rolled over and covered his head with her pillow. She picked through the unopened mail from Saturday and found a letter from Harry Satto. Allison busied herself putting coffee on for Phil and opening her soda. The warming breezes invited her to surprise Phil with a breakfast served on the patio. She set herself about the task of slicing fresh fruits and setting the patio table. She stood back and appraised the appearance of her table setting. "Something is missing," she said out loud "flowers and the Sunday paper, that's it."

All in readiness, Allison slid the patio door closed. Suddenly Phil's arms were sliding around her waist. He gently pulled her tighter to his body and whispered, "I love you too." Allison was happier than she ever thought she could be. Turning in his arms she willingly met his desire. The lover's lips met in a tender gut demanding kiss. She teasingly bit at Phil's lower lip just as the telephone rang.

"Shit," he cursed softly. She picked up the receiver, still locked in his arms. "Hello," she said with a playful giggle. Phil returned her playfulness and caressed her body. She gave him a look of mock warning and slapped his hands away.

The caller said, "Allison, this is Lt Jones. Is Hall there with you?"

"Sure Jonesy, he's right here," she said as she handed Phil the headset. She stuck out her tongue as she pulled away.

"Yes sir. What's going on, Lieutenant?"

Allison went out to the patio with the coffee pot and closed the doors behind her. She poured the coffee and cream over the berries and fruit. Phil opened the sliding glass door. "Allison, where's the Sunday paper?"

"Out here Phil, why?"

He didn't seem to hear her question. She watched intently as Phil said, "Okay Lieutenant, I'll read it right now. He finished his conversation by saying, "Okay first thing in the morning,"

He pulled out a patio chair, picked up the paper and scanned the front page. "That son of a bitch," ranted Phil.

Suddenly his eyes darted to the top of the cover page. "No, no, not the Tribune, I need the Chronicle."

"My neighbor takes the Chronicle. I could borrow it. But what's wrong, Phil?"

Her question went unanswered as Phil darted toward the door. I'll be right back. You'll see what's wrong in a minute."

A few moments later he walked back through the door with the Chronicle in his hands. He read the headlines out loud for Allison to hear.

CHRONICLE PRINTS TRUTH ABOUT CAMPO SLAYING
By Steven Morris

Six weeks ago this paper as well as others, reported on the murder case of JoAnn Campo. Ms Campo, an Oakland resident was found, slain in her apartment. The investigation is Spear-headed by Detective Phillip Hall of the Oakland Police Department. We have been Informed of some new facts about the case. Ms. Campo's body was located in the bedroom of her town home. Not in the bathroom as was reported by the Tribune. Ms. Campo's body had been disemboweled and mutilated. Her torso had been sliced by what appeared to be a sharp knife across her lower abdomen. Above Ms. Campo's body were words written in the victim's own blood. "I am my middle name." The wound in

the abdomen of Ms. Campo was smeared with what appeared to be red lipstick and some form of drawn lines appeared along the borders. The killing of Ms. Campo may have been related to a sado/masochistic cult due to the presence of varied sex devices located in the victim's bedroom. The Chronicle feels it is always in the best interest of the community to be as fully Informed as possible. If we have the facts we print the truth to protect the citizenry. We wish Oakland PD the best of luck in Solving this heinous crime. Anyone with any information should contact the investigating officer, Detective Sergeant Phillip Hall.

"You wish us luck, my ass," raved Hall. He handed over the editorial for Allison. She read the article written by Morris in total disbelief. "How could he do this? I don't understand why they would allow this to go to print."

"Money, Allison, money." He continued, "What the hell do they care if they destroy the case. The competition between the two papers will bring in bucks and lots of them."

"My question is," said Allison, "how did he find out about all of this?"

Phil clenched his fists and narrowed his eyes. "I have an idea, but I'll hold off saying who I think leaked the information."

She looked at him in surprise, "You're thinking it was Joe Biggs, aren't you?"

Phil stared off into the cloudless morning sky, "It seems to me that all of the information given in the article, were things that someone working the scene would know. The details about the autopsy weren't included. Those reports came in after Biggs was taken off the case. The leak was someone on the case in the beginning, but not now. Who else does that fit, except for Biggs? So yeah, I think it was. I'm pretty sure it was."

The telephone rang once again. This time it was Sam Cook. "Allie, have you seen Morris's editorial?"

"Yeah Sam, I'm on it. I'll have a response for your clearance first thing in the morning."

"Okay, but I want to be careful about what we print. I don't think we should give this kind of press too much space. I would like some additional information printed about what is going on with the case. And, Allison since they printed their philosophies, I feel we should print ours. Understood?"

"I understand Sam. You might like to know that Morris didn't divulge everything there is to know about the case. Just some of the information gathered earlier in the investigation.

"Anything new the police are willing to release for publication?"

"Let me talk with Phil, Jonesy and Adkins. If there is anything to print I'll get it to you right away."

Phil contacted Lt. Jones at his home for Allison. She was given permission to print a story about the Campo murder being linked to the Haver death in Chicago. Allison wrote the story for publication on the following day.

CHAPTER 15

Connections

CAMPO MURDER LINKED WITH CHICAGO SLAYING

By Allison Dean

Detective Sergeant Phillip Hall disclosed today that there is a possibility that the death last month of JoAnn Campo, a resident of Oakland and the death of a Chicago woman, Denise Haver, may be linked.

According to Detective Hall, the crime scenes have much in common. The Chicago resident, Ms. Haver, 23, suffered the same sort of wounds as those found by the Oakland Police homicide squad when Ms. Campos' body was discovered. The two police agencies, Oakland and Chicago respectively have banded together and are working this case on an information shared basis.

The FBI has become involved through their "Domestic Police Cooperation Program", and are providing technical support via the Behavioral Sciences Division. When asked if there was any other evidence to support their theory, Hall refused to comment except to say that they are following upon all leads at the present time. Anyone with information should contact Detective Hall from homicide division. Feature stories printed in other presses have released information which was purposely withheld by the police to protect the integrity of their investigation. Horribly the reported slashing of the lower abdomen as well as the lipstick smears and pencil lines drawn upon the body prior to evisceration is true. The writing on the wall which read, "I am my middle name" is also true.

Our readers need to understand that some facts are usually withheld in order to make certain that when there is an arrest in a case, they have the right person, not simply one of the hundreds of 'professional confessors' who step forward for every crime. You, the public can only be protected if they have the genuine article. The citizens in our publishing area are not served by inappropriate publicity. It is the tradition of the Tribune, which demands that your safety and security are more important than the scoop.

The staff of the Tribune believe in and practice responsible reporting by all measures.

*   *   *

Kathy St. John-Cocheran read the latest article in print about the Campo murder. She wondered why the police had never called her back. She was sure her information was important. She reflected upon her conversation with Detective Hall. "Perhaps," she thought to herself, "the police considered the story she had to tell as too old to follow up." Kathy sat wringing her hands, wondering what she should do now. "I know this is Zachary," she told her husband Steve.

"How do you know? How can you be so certain? You haven't seen or heard anything about him since he was taken away. That was over twenty years ago."

Kathy sat herself down on the sofa next to Steve. "If I hadn't read the Chronicle account of that murder, I would never have considered it."

Steve rubbed his wife's tense shoulders. "Look honey, if the police would have thought the information would help, I think they would be breaking down the door to talk with you. They're not, so please just let it be."

Kathy held Steve's hands still upon her shoulders and said, "Steve, you don't understand. You have no idea of how abused that poor child was. I tell you his mother was absolutely insane."

"What's one abused child, more than twenty years ago have to do with this case now?"

"It was the way he was abused. Not so much that he was. The things that his mother did to him were horrible. I have never forgotten it." Kathy's emotion took over as streams of tears began to spill from her pale blue eyes. She remembered Zachary being taken from her by the large uniformed woman as if it were yesterday. The pain she felt then was renewed as she trembled in her spouse's embrace.

"The Pendrakes' are a very rich family, Kathy. They have more than ample means to get the best help in the world for the little boy. You really have no idea where he was taken, you've said that yourself. So it would seem to me that with such vast resources he could have been taken care of wonderfully."

"You don't know Steve, that baby's family didn't give a damn about him," she blew her nose and continued, "I only saw Norman Pendrake once. And believe me once was plenty for me. The man was an ice cube. Steve honestly, I don't know what to do. When I read about the lacerations on that Campo woman's body. Then add the red lipstick, I was pretty sure then. But the icing on the cake was the pencil drawings. I knew, understand I just knew it was Zachary."

Steve let out a frustrated sigh and said, "Why?"

"Because the marking sounded like the same markings Adelle had drawn on Zachary, and in the very same area!"

"Kathy, you've already told this to the police haven't you?"

"Yes but they didn't listen," insisted Kathy.

Steve furrowed his brow and leaned close to her and said, "Okay, so they didn't listen then, what makes you think they will now?"

"I don't know. But," she declared, "I do know that if I don't come forward and make them hear me and another woman dies, I'll feel guilty for the rest of my life." Kathy dropped her hands onto her paper in her lap and looked once again at the headline of the story. She saw the By-line and pointed to the article. "I'll call her, this Allison Dean. You know the reporter who wrote the story. I'll be very careful about how much I tell her, but just maybe she'll listen."

* * *

Archer's Haven was hopping with the celebration of Claire Lang's forty-fifth birthday. Officers from every department crowded into the bar and grill. They offered their tips on old age to the Chief's administrative assistant.

Allison and Phil had written a funny poem about the problems surrounding the onset of aging. Allison read the poem as Phil handed to Claire, a myriad of products such as dry skin cream, vitamins, fiber bars and suppositories. The roar of the laughter assured that all were having a great time poking fun at the birthday girl.

Allison and Phil were getting ready to leave when the bouncer known as Dave approached and talked to them about the poem. "I really enjoyed your poem. My sister is turning forty in a couple of weeks. I was wondering if you'd mind if I used that poem and gave her the same kind of presents?"

Allison dug into her purse and handed Dave the paper with the poem and said, "Sure, here it is, have fun with it." Dave followed them to the door and held it open for them. Outside a line of taxicabs waited with their engines idling. "Ah yes," said Hall, "a few designated drivers I see." He smiled and said, "good thing too! The last thing we need is for a bunch of cops being hauled in for drunk driving."

Dave smirked as he shook his head. "At least they're happy drunks, Not like Biggs a few days ago. By the way where's he been? I haven't seen him since the day he rode off with Morris from the Chronicle."

Dave turned and walked back into Archer's Haven. Phil and Allison simply smiled and shrugged their shoulders. As soon as they got into their car, he turned to her and said, "Gotcha, you son of a bitch Biggs."

Monday morning Hall met with Captain Adkins and Lt. Jones to fill them in on what he had found out. The Biggs case was referred to Internal Affairs Division.

*   *   *

The Chicago Hilton was the location for the retirement party for Chief Ralph Ory. Ory had been a dedicated civil servant for some 35 years. The last fifteen were served in the capacity of the Chief of Police. It was said that he was retiring at the age of sixty because he had political aspirations. Those who knew him knew he simply wanted to go fishing for the rest of his life. Ory liked the press talking about his possible running for office. He liked anything that kept them off of his officer's backs and out of the cases they worked. Now it was time to celebrate, time to revel in his opportunity to finally go with reel in hand to any body of water and watch the sunrise and set.

The dinner had taken on the form of a roast, which was in keeping with Ory's keen sense of humor. Everyone laughed at the jokes. The one who laughed the loudest was Ory himself. During his tenure, most of the cases had been successfully closed. The massive amount of solved mysteries gave Ory pride in his department's achievements. One of the cases that remained on the books as unsolved was the death of Denise Haver.

Chicago's finest had set the case on the back burner. After a rapid beginning and mountains of physical evidence, the investigation had ground to a halt. The trail had gone cold and new leads in the crime were eating into an already strained budget. The search for the madman faded as the investigation ran into one dead end to another. The memory of Denise Haver and her horrific death was now just a file in cold storage.

At the conclusion of the evening all of the party goers lined up to shake hands with the retiring Chief before they exited the doors. Sandy felt like he was in a herd of chattering geese. He overheard more small talk than he wanted to. The conversations of secretaries and file clerks buzzed as the line gradually came close to Ory's hand. The shoptalk, normal between police officers at any function was particularly pervasive. Sandy overheard bits and pieces of cases being worked by other departments such as vice, burglary, traffic, fraud and violent crimes division. The latter was an off-shoot of homicide his department.

Standing behind Sandy was Detective Kidd. An officer assigned to violent crimes. He was discussing with several other officers, an assault case he was investigating. The victim was a woman by the name of Sharon Glass. He described the beating that the woman endured in detail. He ended his roster of injuries with the comment that he was surprised that she was actually still alive. Sandy only half listened until he heard Kidd say, "And get this! She met her dream date on one of the nine hundred sex talk lines."

Sandy excused himself from the parties that were talking at him. He turned to hone in on the conversation of detective Kidd. He placed a large hand on the shoulder of Kidd and said, "Pardon me, can you repeat what you just said?"

"Sure, you mean about the Glass assault?"

Sanders led him away by the arm and encouraged him to leave the group behind. "Exactly," he said. As he guided Kidd back into the now empty dining room. Sandy looked intently at the junior officer. "If Glass is the victim that met her date, as you called it, on a nine hundred line, then the answer is a definite yes."

"Well, as I said, the victim in the case, a woman by the name of Sharon Glass. She made a date with one of the men on a nine hundred line. When he arrived he beat the holy hell out of her."

Sanders listened carefully, "Any motive for the beating that you know of?"

Kidd replied, "That's not clear yet. She's still in pretty bad shape and can't take a lot of interrogation yet."

"But she is alive, right?"

"Yeah, just barely. It's really a miracle that she made it. If it weren't for the doctors working overtime and her guardian angel being over worked, I don't think she would have lived. They just don't know how her mental stability will hold up. She's over in county right now. She's been there for over a week."

Sandy asked, "Has she been able to name or identify her attacker?"

"Well, for all it will help, yeah. She's drifted in and out of consciousness for the last few days. Her memory seems at times like it's coming back, but then she pops up with weird things."

Sandy held up his hands, palm up and shook his head questioning, "Weird, like what? How weird?"

"She refers to her Bible a lot of the time. And then just recently she says that the angel of death visited her. His name, is according to her, and get this, is Prince Odious."

CHAPTER 16

Kathy St. John

Allison arrived at her desk and found a memo from Sam. The message indicated that he wanted to see her in his office when she arrived. Allison quickly organized her notes for the story she was working and called Sam's extension. Roberta informed her that he was on another line, but was waiting to see her.

Moments later she tapped on the glass door to Sam's office. He waved at her to enter. She slipped into the office and sat in the companion chair and waited for him to finish his phone call. As he hung up, she brightly said, "Hi Sam, what's up?"

He grinned and handed her a copy of the article that she had written in response to the accusations of Morris. The story had been picked up by the Associated Press and had been carried nationwide. The story was complete with her by-line. The introduction of the piece touted a strong sense of cooperative journalism. The article concluded by stating, "All too often an adversarial relationship is developed between the members of law enforcement and those of the press. It is important to understand not only the power and rights of the people but to further understand that the two industries exist for the betterment of society. Therefore we would like to commend the rapport that works so well for the Oakland Tribune's Allison Dean."

"You know Allie, I think this is suitable for framing. I'm sure you can find space for it on your wall."

Allison giggled with excitement as she stared at the article. "Oh man, my first A.P. Thanks a lot Sam."

Sam laughed and said, "Hell kid, don't thank me. You wrote it. I've sent out an office memo about your story and the A.P. pick up. Congratulations journalist Dean."

Allison returned to her desk with several pauses to show off her commendation. She rifled through her messages and read them off. Phil, Jonesy, Ms. Kathy St. John-Cocheran and yet another from Phil. Before she could pick up the telephone it began to ring. It was Phil on the line and she excitedly told him about her story.

Phil interrupted her, "Allison, I know about your A.P. pick up and all of that. Congratulations sweetheart, but I thought you might like to know that we have received communications from twelve different cities so far this morning.

Confused, Allison said, "About my story?"

"Well I guess it's related. The different police agencies read your article about the Campo and Haver murders. It seems that our boy has been very busy."

Allison's mood plummeted, "You're telling me that this same killer has definitely killed in other locations. See, I was right, this is serial just as I told Jonesy!"

"Yeah, the earliest report is about a murder which is just short of two years ago."

Alison took a deep breath and closed her eyes, "Tell me that there is a suspect in at least one of these cases."

She could hear the frustration in his voice as he said, "Nope, nothing but dead ends. Each of the departments was surprised to find out about the other killings. We'll be combining information to see if anyone has a piece of the puzzle that we don't and vice versa."

"So what's next, where do we go from here?"

Hall replied, "Well, some of the guys think our perp is a long haul truck driver. That would explain why so many different states and cities. But I'm not so sure."

Allison interjected, "I wonder if the same nine hundred number is involved with the other killings. If it is, that might be the one lead that can be followed."

Phil was quiet for a few moments and said, "I guess it's possible. If there is a link, no other agency we know of has put it together. But then again, they may not know to look for it. I will let the reporting agencies know about this. If their case is hot, then they'll get right to it. But, if they have a heavy case load with more recent cases it may take them some time. So far it looks like this guy has only struck one victim in each city. There's been no repeats in any place reporting their information, at least so far."

"You'll get him Phil, I know you will."

"Sure, it's just a matter of time. And by the way young lady, have I told you this morning that I love you?"

"I think I heard something to that effect this morning. Are we still on for tonight? Tonight and every night, lady. Every night!"

She felt as if he were standing right in front of her looking into her eyes. She shook her head to clear the vision as he said, "I gotta' run honey. You know fight crime and all of that.

*   *   *

Allison sat at her desk, and started thinking about DeeCee and JoAnn Campo. She had another nightmare the night before. She saw the eyes of Denise Haver turn and look at her with a pleading expression. From her blue eyes a single tear silently rolled into nothingness. Now in the background of the dream was the harangue of a ringing telephone. It was the persistent ring of danger, a ring that she couldn't dare answer. Then the ringing flowed into a man's laughter. The insidious sounds of his laugh echoed in her ears. She could still hear the sounds clearly in her waking hours.

She felt the tug of sleep deprivation. At times she felt as if she would never be able to keep pace with the demands of her work. She shook her head and said to herself, "Cut this out, Allison." She began to fill in the holes in her article about the now captured Sunday torch. The buzzer on her desk phone pulled her attention away from the article. It was the receptionist from the city desk. She was calling to tell her that a visitor was there to see her. The visitors' name was Kathy St. John-Cocheran.

Allison said, "I don't have time right now to talk to anyone Roberta" The receptionist almost whispered over the line, "Allie,

I really think you should see her. She says she has information for you about the Campo and Haver murders."

Allison was momentarily taken aback. "Well, I guess you're right. Okay, send her back and thanks Roberta." The name of her visitor yanked at her memory. She picked up her messages and looked through them once again. There it was, marked urgent. "Kathy St. John-Cocheran."

Moments later, the door to the pressroom opened and Roberta pointed toward Allison. A blond woman walked up to Allison and said "Ms. Dean."

Allison replied, "Yes and you're Ms. St. John? Tell me, how may I help you?"

"St. John-Cocheran, Kathy," corrected the nervous woman.

Allison watched as she sat down in her chair and began to fidget and look around the offices. Perplexed by her nervousness, Allison looked closely at her. Allison tried to get her to relax and kidded with her. "Well, Ms. St. John-Cocheran Kathy, would you like some coffee?"

The woman laughed, "No, Kathy, please. And thank you, but no to the coffee. I think if I had more caffeine in my system I'd climb right out of my skin. Kathy leaned forward and pulled on her purse straps. "I really don't know if I'm doing the right thing. But I need to get someone to listen to me."

"I'm listening Kathy. Roberta said you have some information about the Campo and Haver murders."

"Yes," she began, "several weeks ago I talked briefly to an officer by the name of Hall, detective Hall. You know the one in charge of the Campo investigation."

"Yes, I know him."

Kathy began, "Anyway, let me start at the beginning. Some time ago I read an article in the Chronicle. It was a story about the Campo murder. You know the one by Steven Morris. Well, right after I read the article I called Detective Hall and gave him my information. I haven't heard from him since. And now with the case being linked with yet another death, you know, the Haver woman in Chicago."

"Exactly! That's why I came here to see you. You see I think I know who killed these women. I thought maybe if the police don't think the information is important, the press just might."

"Tell me what you have. Believe me, you have my full attention, I'm listening closely."

Allison took notes and listened. She was entranced by the story of Zachary Pendrake. She couldn't understand why this woman hadn't been listened to before. The saga continued from the time of her first involvement with the Pendrake household through the tumultuous ending with Zachary being pulled from her arms. Of special interest was the recital about the bath Zachary was given for his pictures to be taken. The red lipstick and drawn line descriptions were eerily similar to the wounds found on the bodies of both DeeCee and JoAnn Campo.

Allison decided to test the credibility of Kathy and her story. She held up a hand stopping the flow of information and pulled out a piece of paper. Allison drew an amateurish sketch of a child and handed it to Kathy. "Can you draw the markings you saw on this child?"

Kathy gave her a quizzical look, shrugged her shoulders and said, "Sure. I'll never forget the markings. But," she added.

"You'll have to forgive my lack of drawing skill. My husband says that even my stick characters look like they have a case of the shakes. The lines looked like this," she turned the paper to show Allison her rendition. Then she reached over and took a red pencil from the holder on her desk. Kathy began drawing circles around the stitches and said, "Circling the black pencil marks was a smearing of red lipstick."

Allison shook inside as a visual playback of both crime scenes washed over her. Allison fought back the urge to react, and maintained her objectivity, at least to the onlookers view. She set the drawings aside and picked up her note pad. She urged Kathy to continue her story. She scribbled wildly as commonality after commonality rolled from a new very emotional Kathy. The final fiber that linked the murders was when Kathy looked deep into the troubled eyes of Allison Dean and said, "You know the writing on the wall that the Chronicle mentioned?"

"Yes, go on."

Kathy swallowed hard as she said, "Zachary's middle name is, Payne."

Not getting it, Allison scrunched up her face. "You mean pain like in p a I n?"

"No, P a y n e. Zachary Payne Pendrake."

Kathy dabbed at the corners of her eyes with a tissue. "I remember so well playing the love button game with Zachary."

Allison smiled strangely, "Love button game?"

"Yeah," explained Kathy. "Zatch, that's what I called him. You see he had a strawberry birthmark here." Kathy pointed to the inside of her right forearm. "You see, I'd press his birth mark and whenever I did that I would give him a hug and a kiss. I called it his love button."

Allison pulled out the message slip and showed it to Kathy. "Is this the right number for you? Is there any time in particular that it's best for us to contact you?"

Kathy read the number. "Yes, that's it. But here," Kathy handed Allison a business card. "My cell phone number and voice mail are here too."

Allison hid from Kathy her suffering from tattered nerves from strong personal attachment she had with the case. The two women rose and walked toward the office doors. Kathy turned to face Allison as tears formed in her eyes. "I know that it may sound silly to be so involved with this child. But I could never have children. The good news is that I married a widower with two children. But, you know, it's different when they're your own." Allison watched closely as Kathy continued. "It saddens me to think of the way Zachary was treated and how he's turned out." Kathy started to push her way through the glass doors and stopped, looked right at Allison. "I hope that when he is caught, that he gets some measure of humanity. Kathy touched Allison's arm and said, "He wasn't born a monster, Ms. Dean, the monster that he is, was created."

Allison could see the genuineness of her feelings. "I'm glad that at least some children were lucky enough to have you love and play with them. You seem like a born mother to me. It sounds like he was fortunate to have you caring for him for as long as you did."

Allison said, "Thank you Kathy. I promise you I will be in touch. I know that it took some courage to come in here. It takes involvement from people like you to solve these cases. I'm sure you know that though. Thanks again."

"No, thank you for listening. I couldn't seem to get anyone to hear what I had to say. I would have hated going to that twerp, Steven Morris. But honestly if you hadn't seemed to be receptive to the story I had to tell, he was my next stop."

"I'm glad you came here first!"

"You know," Kathy revealed, "those poor women were tortured and violated in such personal ways. I don't know if I could've discussed it with a man and not be embarrassed."

Allison reached out with her left hand and grasped Kathy's arm. She looked intently into the face of the weeping woman. "I know Kathy, I've seen the results of this guys' punishment first hand. I know how it has devastated me. Again, thank you Kathy."

Kathy St. John-Cocheran gave Allison a soft smile and walked through the doors of the pressroom. Allison watched her until she turned the corner exiting the building. She returned to her desk and cleared the Sunday torch story that was on her screen. She wrote a report directly from her notes. She wanted to get it all down while the conversation was still fresh in her mind. Allison's eyes wandered to the sketch constantly as she drafted her report. She set an appointment with Sam and called Phil. Allison was told that Phil was out of the office. She asked to be put through to Jonesy. As soon as he picked up the line, she blurted, "Jonesy, I just spent an hour or so listening to a woman by the name of Kathy St. John-Cocheran. She thinks she knows who killed JoAnn Campo."

Jonesy half sneered as he spoke, "Another one? Allison we've been flooded with calls, it seems that everyone knows who killed her."

"Listen Jonesy, she makes a lot of sense. There are a couple of details which are going to make following up on this difficult. But I do think they should be looked into. Just a minute, hang on Jonesy."

Allison flagged down a passing copy girl as she passed by. She scribbled a telephone number on the top corner of the picture. Covering the mouthpiece of the receiver, she said, "Fax this picture to that number for me. And please, right now." The copy clerk walked away with the paper and Allison shouted after her, "Get that paper back to me right after you're finished, please."

Lt. Jones was saying," what difficulties would that be?"

"I'm sending you a fax. You should be getting it any, minute. If Claire is around, have her bring it to you right away. When you see this picture I am sending I think you will understand better. Now, for the problems. First of all this information is twenty plus years old. The second problem is who she is suggesting the killer is."

She heard Jones say, "Thanks Claire." He paused for a moment and said, "Where'd this come from?"

"Jonesy, these are markings my source saw some time ago on a child she used to take care of. The child was an infant at the time. She thinks the now grown man is the one we're looking for. Jonesy, I think she might be right."

"Who does this source think our actor is?"

She took a deep breath and let it go. "The Pendrake heir? The son of the late Norman Pendrake, his name is Zachary."

Lt. Jones angrily barked, "Jesus jumped up Christ. The Pendrakes, really Allie, the richest family in the nation, those Pendrakes?"

"I know, I know," countered Allison. "I covered a story about Harry Satto the Asian commodities broker. You may not remember it was during my stint in the society pages. I met him just shortly after starting with the Trib.

"Give me a break Allison, the society pages aren't exactly my type of reading. But, if you say so," continued Jones. "What has that got to do with the Pendrakes and this case?"

"Harry Satto had flown in to meet with the Pendrakes over some rice deal. He's a hell of a guy. We got along great. I still write to him and still receive letters from him."

Jones sounded exasperated, "Allie get to the point. I don't give a damn whether this Satto guy is a gem or not. What's this got to do with the case?"

"Well it's just that he was my first introduction into the world of the Pendrakes. My source used to work for them."

"Listen Allison, this source of ours says that they used to work for the Pendrakes right?"

"Yes that's right."

I think what you have is a disgruntled employee hoping to create problems for the Pendrakes. Most of the information she gave you matches the story written by Morris. Besides that there isn't much new information she is passing on."

"I'm not so sure Jonesy. According to this source Norman Pendrake had a son some twenty-six years ago. Kathy St.

John-Cocheran, the informant told me a story about the abuse the child suffered. His monster of a mother left markings on him like those on Denise Haver and JoAnn Campo. Jonesy can you guess what this kid's middle name is? No wait don't bother guessing. His full name is Zachary Payne, spelled P A Y N E, Pendrake. He is his middle name.

Allison listened quietly as Jonesy grew silent, seemingly to ponder the connection. Jones took a deep breath. "Has Phil told you about the teletypes we have been receiving?"

"Yes, I spoke to him before he went out into the field this morning. He said there were twelve murders now being connected to this same perp."

"Well, there have been two more since that time. Everyone and I do mean everyone has an idea who this killer is. None of them have suggested as suspect even remotely close to the stature of the Pendrakes'. You really need to think this one over."

Allison barely even heard Jonesy's comments. She focused on the fact that two more deaths had been reported with the same method of operation as the Haver and Campo slayings. Her gut wrenched with the thought.

*　　*　　*

Captain Sanders and Sergeant Kidd entered Cook County Hospital and headed for the bedside of Sharon Glass. As they ascended to the fifth floor, Sanders read through the case file. The medical reports that described the victim's injuries were lengthy. He winced as he envisioned the violence described in the report. "I really don't know how much help she's going to be, Captain," stated Kidd.

Sanders gave Kidd a sorrowful look and said, "She's alive and that's an accomplishment Kidd. Especially when you read all of the reports that have been coming in. I'm just wondering why she was left alive. What's different about Ms. Glass?"

"Well it could be that she is already half in the bin now. Mentally I mean," said Kidd. "After talking to her neighbors it seems that our victim is a real different sort of person."

Sanders cocked his head sideways and looked closely at Kidd. "What do you mean a different sort of person?"

Kidd explained, "According to the psychological reports, Ms. Glass is caught in a real paradox. She was raised by parents who were true believers. They lived in a commune called the Children of Light. But at the same time she affiliated herself with the underground sex networks."

Sanders questioned, "Children of Light?"

"Yeah, it's a really stiff fundamentalist group. I guess some people, me included, would call them fanatical."

The door to the elevator gaped open and the officers soon stood at the bedside of Sharon Glass. The departing nurse told them that her patient was still very sore and tired. She asked them not to stay too long. Both Sanders and Kidd gave assurances they would not tire out Ms. Glass.

Sanders looked at the battered face of Sharon Glass. He bit back hard and suppressed any look or appearance of surprise at how badly she was injured. Sharon's jaw had been wired shut to permit the broken bones in her face to heal. Her eyes were swollen to the size of tennis balls and colored with a mixture of bruising in from black to blood red. For the first time Sanders understood the medical staffs amazement that she had indeed lived through her attack. He looked at Kidd and wanted to say, "Christ, how could anyone do this to another human being. But he kept that part to himself. He gently touched her hand. He began, "Ms. Glass, you may not remember me. I'm Officer Kidd. I was here a day or so ago. I have someone here who needs to speak with you."

Sharon slowly opened her eyes as far as the swelling would allow.

"I know it's hard to talk but this is Captain Sanders. He has some questions about your assault. Do you think you can talk with him?"

Weakly Sharon mumbled through lips that only too closely resembled over cooked sausages. "I'll try."

Sanders began, "I know you're in a lot of pain Ms. Glass. I will try to make this brief. I'll ask you questions that you can simply answer yes or no. If at any time you feel too tired to continue, we'll stop. Is that alright with you?"

Sharon slightly blinked and gave a nod.

"The person who beat you was someone you met on a nine hundred line?"

Sharon closed her eyes as a tear tumbled down her cheek. She nodded.

"You had a date with this individual?"

"No," murmured Sharon.

Sanders looked over at the perplexed Sgt. Kidd. "No, you didn't have a date arranged with the man who attacked you?"

"No, another," answered Sharon.

"I know you have been working with a sketch artist to try to come up with a likeness of your assailant, can you?"

"My Bible," Sharon mumbled. "My Bible, a picture in my Bible."

Glass nodded once again and released a long sigh.

"Where's your Bible, Sharon? Where?"

"Home, box in closet it's a purple box," responded Sharon as she faded into sleep once again.

Sanders called dispatch and had a cruiser stop by Sharon's apartment to find the Bible. An hour later, with her bible in Sanders's hands, he and Kidd sat next to her bed. They waited for Sharon to once again become conscious. "The officer who brought this said they had a real difficult time finding it," said Kidd.

Sanders looked at him with uncertainty painting his expression. "Why? She told us where it was."

"Man, I tell you, her place was torn to pieces. Whoever beat her up took some of his anger out on her belongings as well. He must have taken some considerable time wrecking the place."

Sandy's only comment was, "Interesting."

"Believe it or not, she's getting better," said Kidd. "I mean from what she was like last week. I don't understand what she is talking about though." A picture in her Bible?"

Sanders flipped through the pages of the large King James version. The book was filled with glorious pictorials of the scriptures. He looked through the pages for a photograph and said, "Many times in families, Bibles hold the history of their lineage and family snap shots." Sanders found no photograph inside but did notice the numerous underlining of passages that dealt with Satan and his reign upon the earth.

Sharon saying, "My Bible," made them realize that she'd awakened. He held up the Bible to show her indeed it was there.

"Ezekiel," Sharon mumbled.

Sanders turned the pages to the book of Ezekiel. He held the scriptures close enough for Sharon to turn the pages with her fingertips. Across from the scriptures of 28:11 through 28:19 was a full color pictures which depicted the casting out of Lucifer from the heavens.

"There," she said, "There he is." She pointed to the recreation of the descent of the Angel of Light.

Sanders looked at the picture and slumped as all his hopes of an identification dissolved.

Sharon reached out and touched his arm and said, clearly. "I was visited by the Angel of Death and he called himself Prince Odious." As soon as she'd uttered the words, she slipped back into the depths of slumber. The two disheartened police officers left her bedside feeling certain that the woman was useless to them in solving this case.

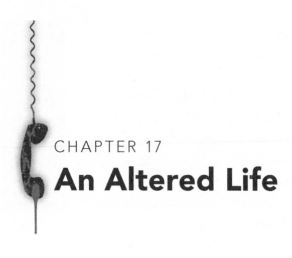

CHAPTER 17
An Altered Life

Marshall Kreger reclined in his worn easy chair. He read the Sunday edition of the Arizona Republic. The early morning hours watching the sunrise were his favorite time in the desert. He was at peace then, in these quiet moments. It was his time to digest the latest news before heading off to work. He glanced at each headline watching for a combination of words that would grab his interest. He stopped when he saw the Associated Press story written by a California reporter named Allison Dean.

He read and re-read the story ensuring he had not missed any detail. He rocked his head onto the dark leather headrest, closed his eyes and remembered Lady Cassandra. He felt the resurging of feelings of accountability and responsibility.

No one knew of the personal recriminations Marshall Kreger lived with since the day he found Lady Cassandra's body. He'd told himself many times since, that had he not called the nine-hundred lines in the first place, she'd never have been butchered. His temples began to throb as the events of that day began a slow motion replay in his memory. The image of the telephone falling from the table as he hastily dialed 911. He listened for the connection to go through as he hyperventilated. He fought back the gagging reflex that sought to overpower him. The moment before he realized the line had been cut seemed excruciatingly long.

He could still see the images of her butchered body so vividly. He thought about his run from the house toward the nearest neighbors to call police. His panic and nausea resulted in a stumbling arched half run. He was forced to stop every few feet to steady himself. When the police did finally arrive they looked at him with suspicion in their eyes and accusations written on their faces. They had found the piece of notebook paper that he'd dropped in the bedroom doorway. The writing on the paper held the directions to the house in which Lady Cassandra was murdered. On the top of the paper Kreger had written, "Hannibal the Slayer and Lady Cassandra."

When the police questioned him about the strange names, Kreger had said it was just a game he and a pen pal had begun. He didn't want the police to know about the nine-secret line. Had he not been as rattled and sickened as he obviously was, Marshall was sure the police would have arrested him immediately. The vivid recollection of Cassandra's lifeless body had deeply affected him. Since that day Marshall had gone through major lifestyle changes. He had totally stopped calling the secrets line. He could no longer stomach the typical deviant conversations. Kreger's reaction to the discussions evoked powerful negative emotions he didn't want to own. He handed the pain to his alter identity as Hannibal the Slayer. He learned through the news reports on the investigation that Lady Cassandra's real name was Sherri Connelly.

He refused to accept any identity except for that of her pseudo name. Lady Cassandra was not real. She was a figment of someone's imagination. It was easier for Marshall to divorce himself from the horror he'd witnessed with that special tool. If Lady Cassandra was really Sherri Connelly, he could not distance himself. That would mean that she truly had existed. Worse, he lived with the fear of being charged in the murder. The police questioned him so many times that he knew the Chief of Police by his first name. Still the case was unsolved and remained that way on the books.

The article outlined by Allison Dean was a shocker for him and was forcing the hidden side to emerge into the light. Surely he thought to himself, the police would read this article and see the connections just the way he did. Marshall decided he would call when he had the time just to make sure they had seen the similarities. When he had the time he would do just that.

*　*　*

Phillip Hall walked into his office to see stacks of faxed information on his desk. He quickly rifled through the mound of papers and asked the department secretary to organize the file in chronological order. That was the only way they would make any sense to him. The only file he held out were the newly arrived forensic results from the Feds and the Predator Profile put together by the Behavioral Sciences Division of the F.B.I.

The profile as offered by the Feds was full of solid psychological and trend based information. Hall had a difficult time masking his disappointment regarding the profile as it was. Virtually everything on the forensic report agreed with the determinations of the local labs. The Bureaus psychobabble indicated and suggested that the perpetrator most likely suffered from an over abundance of Serotonin and Noradrenalin. The chemical imbalances were thought to produce violent obsessive/compulsive behaviors. The terms Psycho/sociopath were bandied about in the report. The two descriptive terms were to imply the bad guy held neither mercy nor remorse for his actions.

His psychosis would demand he continue upon his self-centered quest for his own satisfaction. Even the educational comprehension was the same. The hand writing analysis provided indicated a highly intelligent, emotionless killer. The script and it's meticulously paralleled letter formation suggested an enormous power of concentration. A specific section discussed the likelihood of some form of military training due to the intricate folding of the face cloth found at each scene. These facts gave credibility to the findings of obsessive/compulsive behaviors even as they compared to the hand writing analysis.

A frank discourse was offered in regards to the confidence of this killer. The fact that he killed these women in their own homes showed that this man was arrogant. Most serial killers take their victims to secluded areas where they feel in total control. For the culprit to feel this control in his victims home indicated either his inability to feel fear, or exhibits his delight with the prospect of being caught. More often than not, these predators relish the thrill of being nearly caught. A summation of the attitudes surrounding him struck a cold vein in Phillip Hall. This person is brazen and not affected by the danger of being captured. He has no remorse and will continue until he is either apprehended or dead. Because this predator is brash it followed that he was not withdrawn nor was he depressed. However he was described as highly unlikely to be a party animal or social butterfly. The decision based upon the biological labs analysis agreed with the Federals, opinion. Both agencies described the killer as a male Caucasian between the ages of twenty-five and forty-five. The physical descriptions were of a male over the height of six foot three inches. He had sandy colored blond wavy hair.

Despite the fact that the murder scene yielded full handprints and palm prints as well as a complete DNA panel, there were no arrest records for anyone who matched the data. Interesting parts of the assessment was the list of occupations that might be held by the killer. Typical hobbies and interested opened doors to speculations Hall had not considered prior to the report. Professions that would require or involve travel were discussed. Everything from the assumed long haul truck driver through airline pilots and even sales representatives were on the list. Hobbies listed by the report included pornography, travel and even taxidermy.

Hall's assessment of the profile was that it was a confirmation that they were on the right investigative track. There was some good news that he could discern form the pages. And part of that good news was that they had so very much evidence against this man, that when they arrested him there would be absolutely no doubt as to his guilt. Detective Hall drew in an exasperated breath. He looked off into space and said to himself, "A name, I need a name and a face."

The secretary handing him the completed file that listed the cases according to the dates reported interrupted Hall's thoughts. The earliest murder thus far indicated that the killer had begun his career over two years prior to the murder of Joann Campo. Each of the scenes in the beginning had major similarities but the last five were virtually identical. No forced entry, the gutting of the victim and the writing on the wall. Even the folded wash cloth was the same. The semen in the area of the wound combined with the fact that he always showered in the victim's dwelling after the carnage were all the same. This indicated to Hall that the first nine cases were experiments in growth for refinement of his method of operation. Once set, he had not deviated his pattern. He was now an accomplished killer.

Hall picked up the files and headed for the office of Lt. Jones and Chief Adkins met him half way as he walked down the corridor. "Lieutenant," called out Hall. "I have the files on the duplicate murders. They're all in chronological order and ready to build the murder map."

Adkins's expression was glum as he said, "Let's you, Jones and me get some coffee and have a bit of a talk. A problem has cropped up and we need to deal with it like yesterday."

Hall shifted the eight-inch file in his arms and turned in the direction of the lunchroom. The three men passed the usual courtesies during their jaunt. Each sat at a table staring into dark steaming liquid a long time before any of them spoke. Finally Adkins broke the tension by saying, "Hall, your Lieutenant had a chat with your girlfriend while you were out."

Phil leaned back in his chair and sipped his coffee. "Is that right?"

"Yes, "said Adkins. "She had a visit from an informant this morning. This person swears she knows who the killer of JoAnn Campo and Denise Haver is. I thought you might like to know. I don't give much credence to who she accuses, but Allison has happened onto something that just might give us a real lead."

Hall's eyes darted back and forth between Adkins and Jones as he waited for the explanation to begin.

Jones reached into his breast pocket and brought out his note pad. He flipped it open and began to read through the doodles on the paper. "Allison's informant, a woman by the name of Mrs. Kathy St. John-Cocheran, believes that our actor is a man by the name of Zachary Pendrake."

"Pendrake," sputtered Hall. "The same Pendrake that I'm thinking of? You know the rich."

"The very same," interrupted Adkins.

Jones broke in, "Personally, I find it difficult to believe. And what's even harder to stomach is that she apparently thinks this is due to some incidents which occurred over twenty years ago."

Hall snorted, "Well I'd call that a cold lead, we're in total agreement," explained Adkins. "But, she also said her contact commented that this Ms. St. John had talked to you right after the article Morris wrote in the Chronicle."

"I can certainly check the lead sheets to find out. You know we received well over two hundred calls after that stupid ass move of Morris's. Everyone thinks they know who the killer is. Shit, it's everyone's Aunt Bertha. I even had some asshole accuse Santa Claus. That stunt wasted a lot of time for us."

Adkins peered at Hall with a cautionary look on his face. "Regardless of whether she did call or not, I think it would be advisable for you to follow up and at least give the appearance that we are interested in what she has to say. Understand this, Hall, I don't want her going to Morris feeling like she isn't being listened to."

Jones interjected, "If Morris had the balls to print what he did, he may just be asshole enough to print this St. John bullshit information. These kinds of things could get this department in to so much trouble that we would never see through it. I'm telling you that we'll go down faster than turds into a flushing toilet."

Hall laughed at the analogy despite the frustration he felt.

Jones jutted his chin forward and pointed a bony finger in Halls face. "I'm telling you, Hall. You need to get to this woman or those turds going down the shitter drain will be the Chief, the commissioner and me. And the friggin' Mayor will pull the handle.

Adkins leveled the temper being shown by Jones. "I'm just glad she did go to Allison and not to Morris. At least with Allison we know what we're dealing with and can maintain some measure of control."

The department clerical worker walked into the lunchroom. She handed Phil a stack of faxes and said, "Here's some responses to our request."

Phil took the papers while looking momentarily confused.

"You remember the telephone bill comparisons you had asked for from the other cities."

Hall slapped his forehead and said, "Oh crap. Yeah, yeah, okay thanks. He quickly flipped through the pages, then looked up at his commanding officers, raised his hand to the ceiling and said, "Thank you, Allison."

Hall hastily spread the communications out on the table. Each man picked up several pages. "This is the tip Allison suggested." He continued, "It looks like it paid off big time." Jones looked at the telephone bills of eight of the fourteen reporting departments. All eight of the bills included calls to a nine hundred number. It was the very same number that appeared on both Campo and Haver's invoices.

Jones tapped the papers on the table. "You know she just might be right about this part of it." Adkins stood and tossed his empty cup into the trash bin. "Let's see what we can do to subpoena the records from this chat line." Possibly we can come up with a link between the calls and find our killer that way. But in the meantime Hall keep on plugging.

Claire stuck her head into the lunchroom and said, "Sir, I'm going to lunch now unless you need me." Adkins nodded his approval and she started to leave, but at the last minute she turned and said, "Oh, by the way, Captain Sanders from Chicago called and left a message for you to return his call."

Jones plucked at his neck as he said, "You know Hall, the reason you got so many calls after that Morris stunt, is because the public wants this bastard caught. They want the case closed with an arrest and a conviction."

Adkins ended the meeting with the statement "Get in touch with that St. John woman right away, will you Hall? Give her some time and make her feel that we're checking on all the information. We need to quiet this one like yesterday!"

Jones provided Hall with a stern glance, "Understand Hall, we don't want this St. John woman going and talking with Morris. If she doesn't get what she wants that could be her next step."

"Yes sir, right away."

*　*　*

Jones returned Sanders's call as soon as he returned to his office. After the normal pleasantries Sanders said, "I should have waited to call you until a bit later. It looks like I jumped the gun. But a piece of this puzzle dropped into our laps. Or at least I thought it did."

Jones questioned, "How do you mean?"

"Violent crimes here, has an assault case that sounded suspiciously like the same M.O. I thought it may be linked to Haver and your case."

"Assault! Your victim is still alive?"

"Yeah, she was badly beaten but she is alive. I went to visit her in the hospital with the officer who's working her case, Officer Joe Kidd. The connection is that she also met her date on a nine hundred line."

Jones pushed, "The same number?"

"We're not sure yet. We're working on that now. Anyway I had some real hopes with this until I met her."

"Why, what happened?"

"Well get this shit, she kept asking for her Bible. She indicated that there was a picture of the bad guy in there. I sent an officer by her place to get it. When we brought her the Bible she pointed out a picture of the devil as he was being tossed from heaven. She swears the devil attacked her. I mean this woman doesn't even have a porch let alone have the light on. Get me, nobody is home, and I don't know if there ever will be.

"Do you think her beating is connected with the Haver and Campo cases?"

Sanders began to hedge and then said, "Yeah, I really do. But she can't even describe her attacker to a sketch artist. When questioned she simply gives us some sort of weird name that couldn't be based in reality. I think we'll have to look somewhere else for our answers. You know, it's possible that she can come out of this state as her healing gets along. I'll kinda' keep an eye on her and see if she does come around. Maybe we're not totally lost yet."

Sanders asked, "How's the investigation going out there? I hope better than ours."

Jones gave out with a half chuckle and replied, "Oh hell man, you know how it is. With publicity and all of the pricks that step forward to claim responsibility. That article of Morris's brought out a lot of the normal leads but strangely very few confessors."

Sanders responded, "Even the sickest of the bunch don't want to have this one pinned on them."

"For some reason, I'm not sure why," said Sanders, "this case gets more and more involved. Try this one on for size.

One of the leads that called in swore that the culprit was the Pendrake heir. A guy by the name of Zachary Pendrake."

Sanders grew quiet and said, "Jones, the same Pendrakes' that I'm thinking of? Pendrake Industries, Pendrakes?"

"The very same."

Sanders chortled, "Why mess with the little guys when you can go right to the top."

"Yeah I had to laugh too. I haven't seen the report myself and only have the information third hand. But it caused a real good laugh around here too. Do me a favor and check with your assault victim about the nine hundred number for me will you?"

"You got it, I'll let you know if I find a connection there."

The allies ended their conversation with a vow to keep in close touch as the case continued. Sandy twirled in his chair and began to stare out of the window. He slowly rotated his chair from right to left taking in a wide sweeping gaze of his city. Someone, he was sure had the key to finding this maniac. Maybe it would be someone in his home city of Chicago. He reflected upon his conversation with his Oakland counterpart. Sandy knew all too well what an out of control publicity hound could do to an investigation. Pendrake he thought, Pendrake.

Sanders pulled himself up to his computer keyboard. He typed in the name Zachary Pendrake and hit the search icon. The screen indicated that as file search was in progress and he muttered to himself. "Well, we know every family has a black sheep. Maybe the Pendrake's off color lamb is Zachary. Suddenly the computer brought up a file. The report taken by Officer David Patterson was an assault complaint. The complainant was a man by the name of Terrance Marsh.

The report stated that Mr. Marsh had been in the employment of Pendrake Industries as a steward on their private jet. Term of employment, three years. Marsh complained that Mr. Zachary Pendrake has assaulted him upon his early return to the aircraft. Officer Patterson's report indicated that Marsh's face showed visible contusions and lacerations which were consistent with his claims. Sandy read the follow up investigation by the district attorney and found that the matter had been settled out of court. Mr. Terrance Marsh had officially dropped all charges.

Sandy exhaled briskly and said, "Well, nothing of consequence there." He tried to continue to search but the computer files showed no other entry. He set the matter aside to concentrate on better evidence. Sanders put in a message to Joe Kidd. He requested him to verify the telephone number of the line Sharon Glass had been frequenting.

* * *

Harry Satto dictated a letter to be sent to his friend Allison Dean. He had to let her know when he would be in town. His time frame in his last letter was vague. He had closed with the words, stating he would see her whenever he got to town. Now he would definitly be there within the next five weeks. Harry wanted to make certain they would meet for dinner. His chauffeur, in keeping with Harry's usual flair for the dramatic made sure that Satto's invitation was delivered in person via messenger.

Satto's administrative assistant reminded him that he had scheduled dinner with Karl Jacobs from Pendrake Industries on the same evening. Satto told his assistant to cancel the Pendrake dinner. Any business they had about the rice futures he controlled would be conducted during normal business hours. He insisted the meetings be put off until the following Monday.

*   *   *

Allison was excited about having Harry meet Phil for the first time. Harry had become a staunch supporter of Allison, a close friend and confidant. Allison knew it was always good policy to be friends with powerful people. But somehow Harry Satto was more than powerful, he was just good people. Heads would turn whenever anyone saw them together. The two would laugh about the talk that would circulate anytime they met. Allison respected his high moral standards and honestly. "The introduction of Phil to Harry would prove to be a great deal of fun.

The evening was scheduled to take place on Saturday the twenty second of May. Allison mused to herself that Harry would choose the date that was significant for her. May twenty second marked a year to the day Allison had begun her new job at the Tribune. After all of the pressure upon her about the Campo murder and the death of DeeCee, a pleasant evening with Harry would be a great change of pace.

CHAPTER 18

Dominoes Fall

Karl Jacobs crumpled the dinner appointment cancellation message from Harry Satto into a tight ball and hurled it across the room. Jacobs angrily shouted, "Christian, get in here Prentiss."

The huge mahogany door opened and a lanky young man trod up to the massive desk of Karl Jacobs. "Yes, Karl, what's wrong?"

"Wrong," spewed Jacobs. "Did you know about this message from Satto?"

"Yes Karl, I knew it would cause a problem. I researched our buying window and I am sure we have enough room to breathe."

Jacobs hissed, "Have you tried calling Satto?"

Christian circled the desk and stroked the quaking arm of Karl. "Absolutely, Karl, I tried reasoning with him. His mind was made up. It seems he has an engagement with some close friends and won't break it. I didn't push the issue because we don't want him to wonder why the urgency."

Jacobs pushed the caressing hand of Prentiss away and dropped his head in thought. "I suppose you're right. If Satto figures out what we are doing we could lose the deal. Where are we in that window?"

Christian interlaced his fingers and said. "It will be close, but if we get Satto's signature on the paperwork by Monday the twenty fourth of May, we should be fine."

Karl visibly steeled himself, "Should be? That's not good enough, Prentiss." Jacobs turned in his chair and stared up into the eyes of a life size portrait of Norman Pendrake. After a few, moments he seemed to collect himself and renew his composure. He was once again the cold calculating businessman Christian knew so well.

Jacobs rose from his chair and without a word walked across the posh office. He picked up the paper wad and tossed it into the burning oak. He watched as the paper disintegrated and concentrated upon the flames in the huge marble fireplace. "You're sure of our time frame? If you're not absolutely positive you need to take the steps to secure that certainty."

Karl's piercing gaze bore deeply into Christian's as he said, "You had better be right. I have worked for over two years putting this bit of business together. I have invested millions of dollars in this deal."

"Understood sir," replied Prentiss in strong and clear words.

"We stand to make billions in profit when this purchase is consummated. The last link in the buy is Satto's rice futures. We will own the world's rice market and control the pricing.

If we don't get his shares, Pendrake Industries will lose every dollar invested."

"Relax Karl," soothed Prentiss, the last heart in your deck of cards is in the palm of your hand."

Karl dismissed Christian with a wave of his hand saying, "That's all for now. I'll see you later tonight at the condo."

Prentiss shivered ever so slightly and left the office of Karl Jacobs.

Karl poked at the flames and prayed that his plans for his more than comfortable retirement were not following the path of the white smoke and sparks as they wafted up through the flue.

*   *   *

Allison lit candles that bordered a pastel colored spring floral table arrangement. Phil was due to arrive at any time. She wanted everything to be perfect. Allison had prepared a special dinner for Phil which included all of his favorite dishes. "Silly," she thought to herself, just how a small thing like a six month anniversary could create such warmth within her. In this short time frame she had been happier with Phillip Hall in her life, than she had been the entire marriage to William H. Dean. For so very long the mere thought of her former husband turned her stomach and made her head ache.

Now, at this time in her life, she simply didn't care. All feelings about Dean were long since gone. In her own philosophy, even to hate someone was an emotion. However to simply not care whether another human being lived or died, was the lowest of human responses and how she now reacted to the thought of Will. The ringing doorbell interrupted her wandering mind. Allison opened the door and gasped when she saw a huge flower arrangement of yellow Mums obscuring their deliverer. Each flower was as large as her hand. Their stems were held together by an ornate crystal vase. Suddenly the vase lifted and Phil was standing there grinning as largely as she'd ever seen him do. "Oh, it's you," she said. "I thought the vase and flowers had grown legs."

Hall grinned and countered, "Well truth be known, I found these homeless flowers and I thought they may like to live with you."

Allison stepped aside and in a grand gesture waved him in, "Welcome to the house of homeless flowers. I hope you enjoy your stay. "Allison's eyes were enhanced by the golden color of the blossoms. She set them down carefully on the entry table and gently fondled the petals and greenery.

Phil tapped her on the shoulder and said, "Do I get a thank you for rescuing these lovelies or at least a 'my hero?"

"I think that can be arranged. Allison parted her lips to receive his. The gentleness of their kiss held mute testimony to the desire each one felt. The timer on the oven blared and she slowly pulled away. She winked at him as she ran her fingertips down the buttons of his shirt. She offered him the most radiant smile she could and said, "Food first, fun for dessert."

A summery evening breeze played gaily with the loose strands of hair that encircled her face. The flickering candlelight brightly promised of lovemaking to be fulfilled. They talked of small things and around subjects with hidden messages. The evening was gloriously warm and scintillating. Allison excused herself to bring the dessert. As she passed him she let her hand draw slowly over his palm. She returned with raspberry cheesecake to find an envelope lying next to her plate. Allison giggled and opened the envelope. A simple card read:

To the woman I love and will adore for life.
A golden ribbon holds my promise to you.
If you can discover its green lush hiding place.
And tell me yes or no, Allison will you.

Allison playfully jutted her chin forward and said, "Will I what?" Phil simply smiled and said, "You'll have to find what's hidden in some greenery, now won't you?"

Instantly the Mums skipped across her mind. She left the table pulling Phil by the hand. Allison searched the huge flower arrangement and finally found a yellow satin ribbon tied to the center blossom. She gently pulled the ribbon up from the base of the flowers to discover a beautiful solitaire engagement ring.

The card attached read: "Be My Wife." Moist droplets of joy trickled down her cheeks as she wrapped her arms around his neck. "Yes, Phil, in a heartbeat, yes."

*   *   *

Allison sported her ring with the usual pride and displayed her left hand at the least provocation. Talk of weddings and bridal showers filled the offices of the Tribune. The merriment was cut short by a telephone call from Lt. Jones asking if she could come to headquarters.

Upon her arrival she was hustled into a conference room by Jonesy where Phil and Chief Adkins waited. "Well I hear congratulations are in order," commented Jones. Allison lifted her hand for the officers to view the half-karat Princess cut, diamond engagement ring. "Well," kidded Adkins, "seems like George has finally got off his duff and popped the question."

Allison blinked and shook her head in confusion. "George? George who?" Suddenly the joke sunk in and all four had a big laugh as she followed the lead of the police commanders and took a seat at a circular table. Adkins began, "Allison I know that you have been deeply involved with the Campo murder. I also know that you've been responsible for some of the leads that we have received."

"Yes," agreed Allison.

Jones looked directly at her. "Frankly most of all of the leads that we have ferreted, have turned out to be dead ends."

Phil chimed in, "Except for the information about the nine hundred line. So far eight of the other departments."

Adkins interrupted, "Now ten reporting agencies."

Hall stopped momentarily and said, "Okay, ten have all found definite connections to this same nine hundred line. We're working to get a hold of this company's records. Naturally they're fighting us and screaming about their customers rights for privacy. We'll get the records, but it will take some time."

Jones agreed with the lines of conversation and added, "The bills we've seen indicate the people involved call on a regular basis. It's going to be difficult to narrow down the suspect because we don't have the specific date and time the callers made their plans to meet. I never knew so many people called these phone lines." Allison felt a shudder run through her body.

Jones took over the conversation. "From everything we have gathered the actor makes a date with these women and then does them in during their date."

Allison furrowed her brow and said, "You're sure that it's the date that kills them?"

Adkins leaned forward, "It's only logical. None of the murders have been found as a result of the date calling the police. A neighbor or a friend who couldn't get a hold of the victim has reported every murder. It seems to me that if these dates didn't have anything to hide, they would call. If someone else had killed these women, why wouldn't they?"

Allison had to agree with the logic. She sat back in her chair and rotated her engagement ring and seemed to zone out of the conversation. Suddenly she bolted forward and said, "This is how we catch him! Don't you see?"

Hall jumped into the talk, "Whoa there pale face, what's with this we bit? We, is not part of this investigation."

"Wait a minute, Phil," Allison's eyes were wild with excitement. "Listen to me, how about if I make a date with this guy? You guys stake out the place where we are going to meet and we can catch him. Bing bang boom!"

Phil grabbed Allison's hand and stopped her. "A police woman, yes! But you, absolutely not."

Adkins and Jones exchanged looks once again as the couple argued her involvement. "I wouldn't be in any danger," said

Allison. "I would know he's coming and most importantly, I know what he is."

Hall shook his head emphasizing his adamant feelings that she not be involved with the apprehension of this perp. "Allison, any number of things can go wrong. I just won't risk you. I won't hear of it."

"Phil the place can be wired. Nothing would happen because everything going on would be heard by the stakeout team."

Phil would not listen to her, which infuriated Allison. She turned to the two silent commanding officers. "I can do this." Allison stiffened her body. "And what's more, I can do this with or without your help. Either way boys, I'm going to do it." Allison shot them a challenging look. "I may get the Pulitzer for the story." Allison dropped her head for a moment and then looked right at Phil and said, "I owe it to DeeCee."

Hall abruptly stood and paced the room. "You could get killed, Allison."

Phil continued his objections until Allison sat him down and looked deeply into his eyes.

Filled with resolve, she said, "Nobody here but you really knows how important this is to me. No one else understands how I've been haunted by the ghosts of these murdered women. And only you know how I suffer through the nights of seeing these victims begging me to help. I have a personal stake in this Phil, please, please try to understand."

Allison turned to face Jones and Adkins. "Listen to me. I can describe what Denise Haver's eyes and JoAnn Campo's eyes looked like the day they were found. I see them every time

241

I close mine." She stood and leaned over the table in an effort to convey her need to help solve this case. "What you don't know, is that every time I sleep I dream of Denise Haver. I see the narrowest band of pale blue circling the most massive pupils I have ever seen." She slumped back into her chair, and looked at each of the three men. "Don't you get it? Denise Haver looked at me then and she looks at me now. Someone else will die unless I take the opportunity to stop him."

"I know Allie, but I don't think you're taking into consideration, what I call, the 'unpredictables!' Random things, that can and do happen all the time! Stakeout situations are always volatile at best, the worst can happen at any moment."

Allison covered his mouth with her fingers and hushed him. Calmly she voiced, "What I am saying, Phil, to you, Adkins and Jonesy is that this is a chance for me to release these demons that haunt me. If I can help catch this maniac, how could any of you deny me that?"

Phil shook his head slowly and said, "How can I get it into your head that you would be in real danger. "God, if anything were to ever happen to you, Allie. I don't know what I'd do. A police woman on the other hand is trained how to handle these situations and herself in times of emergency."

Allison sensed that she was talking to a stone wall and he was not going to see things her way. Not wanting to argue the matter further, she gave him a stern look and said, "Fine, we'll see who makes the first date, me or the police woman."

Adkins interrupted the back and forth sparring between Allison and Hall. "Hall, do you have a better idea or suggestion?"

"Sir, I think it's a good plan, but not with Allison as the bait."

Jones nodded in agreement. "I tend to agree with you Sergeant. But if I know the tenacity of this woman, when she says she will, with or without us, we'd better listen. If she does this on her own, the only protection she will have is the fact that she knows he's coming. With us in the plan, we can take steps to make sure she isn't harmed."

Phil reluctantly agreed to the plan but insisted that he be in charge of the stakeout details. He followed his commanding officers orders to secure a house owned by the city which had been used in other sting operations. Allison was given the go ahead to begin her calls. She kept track of the time spent on the telephone for the department to reimburse her. The sting was set. The details of the operation were in the hands of not only Hall and Allison, but in the hands of the fates as well.

* * *

Allison knew from her two prior experiences with the nine hundred secrets line that everyone who participated had a pseudo name. With the help and the imagination of Phil she decided upon the handle of Nochturna. Allison began her calling campaign as Hall monitored and recorded the conversations. He wrote down the names used by the talkers on the line. Phil would shake his head and roll his eyeballs at some of the names. Domatra, Ophelia, Black Widow and Miss Morbia forced him to repress an urge to laugh.

During her third call to the line, she sat cross-legged on the sofa. The desk phone rested on the cushions of the sofa. Phil used the portable telephone to ensure that he had mobility to change tapes and do whatever else was needed to be done while she talked. Nochturna was in good spirits and had been accepted by the group.

A knock at the front door to Allison's apartment averted Phil's attention long enough for him to open the door to find Robert Kayhill on the threshold. Without a word, Phil motioned for Robert to come into the apartment. Robert peered at Hall with suspicion showing in his eyes. Hearing Allison's voice Robert moved into the living room and listened to what his daughter was saying on the telephone. His eyes widened with surprise and he blurted out, "Allison Diane Kayhill." Phil quickly moved around Robert and made a shushing gesture with his fingers to his lips.

Allison swiveled her head quickly to meet the gaze of her father. "Well, gang, I gotta go. The old parental sperm donor just darkened my door. Check ya'll later gang!" Allison hung up the phone and took in a deep breath and then let out an even deeper exhale. "Dad," said Allison. "What are you doing here?"

"I came by to see if you are alright. I couldn't reach you at your office, all they would say is that you're on some special assignment."

Phil stepped forward. "Mr. Kayhill, let me explain."

Robert gave Hall a glare and replied, "I don't want to hear your explanations. I want to hear my daughter's."

"Phil honey, why don't you go on back to head quarters? Let me and my dad talk for a while."

Phil's objections were futile once Allison said, "Please Phil, please. Let me talk to my dad alone. And don't worry, I'll be fine."

Hall allowed his eyes to dart quickly between Allison and Robert. He then walked into the kitchen and pulled his jacket off the back of the barstool. "All right, Allie. I'll be in my office until 4:00 this afternoon. Then I'll be back to pick you up for dinner." Before leaving he brushed a kiss against her cheek.

Robert listened for the door to close as Allison fidgeted. "Now, what's going on here?" questioned Robert.

"I'm helping Phil's department with an investigation that's all."

Robert narrowed his eyes, "No that's not all. Why do they need your help? Who were you talking to in that disgusting manner?"

"It's an underground type of a deal, Dad. One of those nine hundred chat lines. I'm helping to set a sting, and maybe catch a killer."

Robert stumbled backwards. "You're what? What is this crap? Are you telling me that you're going to be the bait?"

Allison stiffened her body posture. "Yes that's what I'm telling you. I won't be in any danger."

Robert pointed a shaking index finger at Allison. "Now, you listen to me little one!"

Allison bristled as she had never done before. She approached her father with a stern and strong voice and said, "No dad. You listen to me! You have no say in what I do. You can't control my life any longer."

Robert's face turned a bright vermillion. He turned and headed for the door. As he turned the doorknob he said, "We'll see Missy! We'll see." The next thing she heard was the slamming of the door. She shook from head to toe and sat down on the sofa to re-gain her composure.

* * *

Sometime later Phil Hall watched as Robert Kayhill pushed his way through the swinging doors leading to the homicide department. He walked briskly into Jones's office without benefit of an announcement. "Jones," he shouted, "I want to talk to you and I want to talk to you right now!"

Lt. Jones nodded and motioned for Robert to sit down in his companion chair. He stood up and swung the door closed. Phil acted like he was working on paperwork but his mind was really dwelling upon the conversation which was going on in the Lieutenant's office. He heard muffled shouting and saw red faces through the windows of the room. All at once Robert settled back down into the chair and appeared to be listening. Then slowly he stood and looked in the direction of Phil Hall and he left Jones's office.

Robert's face seemed ashen and his body language slumped as he pushed through the outgoing door. Phil caught him in the hallway. "Mr. Kayhill," said Phil. "I know you're upset about this and believe me, Allison is very head strong. She insists upon doing this."

Robert stared flatly into the face of Hall as Phil said, "I didn't want her to do this either. I'm totally in your court with this."

Kayhill said, "Why Hall, what's her motivation behind this idiocy?"

"Mr. Kayhill, do you remember a friend of Allison's named DeeCee?" Robert nodded his head in affirmation and said," You bet I do. And you know, I wish she were here right now. I bet DeeCee could talk Allison out of this madness."

"Robert, Mr. Kayhill I mean. DeeCee is dead."

A look of shock and denial crossed Robert's face. "No, oh my God that poor kid. I'd never heard about her death from anyone. What happened to her?"

Hall drew in a deep breath and said, "I'm going to have to betray a confidence here, but it is truly for the better good of someone we both love, Allison. I think she hasn't talked to you about this and I really am sort of at a loss as to how to begin."

"Just come out with it man," replied Robert.

"Allison is driven to catch the man that killed DeeCee. And we think that the same slayer killed DeeCee as the woman killed here a couple weeks ago, JoAnn Campo."

The two men walked out of the building together as they discussed Allison's history with DeeCee. Phil imparted the Denise Haver story to Robert.

* * *

Allison continued with her calls to nine hundred secrets. Many of the male participants referred to themselves as Rebeck,

Say-Tan, Warlock, Hell's Disciple, Master Agony and Count Cruel joined the line regularly. Count Cruel and the almost monotone voice which belonged to him, held the interest of both Allison and Phil. Occasionally others would join in on the line. Their familiarity instantly understood by the reaction of the dark gathering. The accepted members were always greeted boisterously. Phil would place an asterisk next to the name that seemed to evoke the highest greetings. Satanica would assert herself from time to time as well as a man with a strong but melodious voice. His line name was Prince Odious.

During her respites from the line she and Phil would discuss the names and strange practices of the people she was working to familiarize herself with. After the fifth call they agreed. One particular member of the line seemed to be unlike his counterparts he seemed to have a flair for the pain/pleasuring penchant and discussed with relish his collection of torture devices. He called himself Master Slasher. Slasher seemed to especially revere his knives and talked about the time he took to be certain they were sharp.

Allison and Phil agreed that he seemed to be a highly likely candidate and targeted Master Slasher for the date. Slasher's smug self-confident attitudes as they reflected on the line seemed to fit the personality profile of an individual that would take pride in the deaths of women. Also of interest was the reaction of the group whenever he joined the line. Master Slasher was obviously well known and had participated for quite some time.

Her task was to begin to align herself with Slasher in order to portray lusts in common. The process of gaining entry would tax not only Allison's patience but imagination as well. She knew she'd have to call many times and involve herself with the accepted crowd long before she would be able to open the door to arrange a date with her target. At times, her guise shocked Phil. Her role-playing and frank discussions and fabricated interest in sado/masochistic philosophies totally unnerved him. She seemed to have an uncanny ability to blend into this secretive society.

*   *   *

Several addresses were given to Hall in order for him to select the proper friendly house. After viewing each residence, he chose an upper income dwelling that had been seized as part of a drug raid. The large home was soon to be put on the auction block to pay for the prosecution of its owner.

The rambling two-story brick home was large enough to be in keeping with the image Nochturna had portrayed during her calls. The ornate interior of the home benefited the police in their attempts to hide wires and microphones. The furnishings remained inside the house which was another plus. Phil made certain that all preparations at the friendly house were in ready condition. Wiring of the home was a complex operation. When completed, Allison was shown through the house several times. "She needed to become familiar with not only the lay out, but the location of the listening devices as well. Allison liked the contemporary nature of the décor. The house felt comfortable to her.

The officials on the case worked out a visual signal of trouble in case one of the listening devices failed. Everyone decided the signal would be to close the vertical blinds covering the large bay window in the formal living room. Sound tests were conducted to ensure the transmissions were clear and audible. Everything was prepared for the entry of Master Slasher. Allison's excitement was equal to Phil's nervousness regarding her safety.

Phil and Allison had completed another walk though if the safe house. He tried once again to talk her out of following through with the plan. He finally gave up his campaign. Feeling frustrated and anxious, he backed the unmarked Van down the driveway of the safe house. He was only paying half attention. Suddenly they heard the squealing of tires and a blasting of an air horn. Phil slammed on the brakes to avoid running into a tan Chevy Suburban. He wheeled around to see the Suburban skidding sideways in the street. A long whip antenna reeled in wide arcs.

The driver leaned forwards on the steering wheel when the vehicle finally came to a full stop. He appeared to be trying to collect himself after the near collision.

"Shit," exclaimed Hall. He leapt out of the van and ran over to the Suburban. He needed to make sure the driver was alright. He noted the personalized license plates which read, PCH TRE. The driver was shaken but not harmed. He accepted Hall's apology. Phil asked the driver what his personalized license plates stood for. The driver smiled and said, "My C.B. handle is Peach Tree."

As the driver of the Suburban drove away, Hall only half noticed the small mock license plate behind the driver's head. The Plate read "BOOTS".

Now that the friendly house was set, all that remained was for Allison to succeed at making a date with their target, Master Slasher.

CHAPTER 19
Hannibal The Slayer

After two weeks of role paying as Nochturna, Allison finally struck pay dirt. She succeeded in making a date with Master Slasher. The date was set for the following Friday as six p.m. Her nerves were on edge and the tormenting dreams she had gone through had grown even more compelling. DeeCee's chilling stare combined with JoAnn Campo's and applied pressure to the fear she was already experiencing. The incessant ringing telephone and sinister laughter echoed into her waking hours. Phil's concern for her grew as Allison awoke drenched in perspiration night after restless night. Finally the day of the date had arrived.

*   *   *

Sergeant Carter was under a lot of pressure to make an arrest in the Sherri Connelly murder case. His only suspect was determined by biological evidence not to be the killer. Kreger's semen analysis and DNA didn't mach samples found outside of the wound on Connelly's abdomen. Kreger's handprints were found in the house but only in the rooms he had admitted to being in. There were none inside the bedroom. Hand writing analysis proved Kreger had not written the hideous message on the wall. He had no traces of Sherri Connelly's blood on him and no change of clothing. These facts had long since eliminated Kreger as a murder suspect.

Regardless, Kreger was interviewed again and again. Carter's entire reason for continually questioning Marshall Kreger was that he was positive Kreger was withholding evidence. Carter was sure that he hadn't gotten the entire story from Kreger.

Years of police work and service to the detective squad provided Carter with a strong sense called blue sense provided him with strong instincts about people. Carter knew that Kreger was holding something back. He felt strongly the name of Hannibal had something to do with the case. Kreger had not been forthcoming about his reasons for the nickname Hannibal the slayer.

Carter opened the file and examined the piece of notebook paper found in the doorway to the death chamber of Sherri Connelly. He put in a call to Marshall Kreger and set an appointment for yet another interview.

*　　*　　*

Weeks had gone by since Marshall Kreger had read about the connection of the Oakland and Chicago murders. His intentions of going to the police had never been fulfilled. He was sure the police would have read the same story and would not be bothering him any further.

The pseudo identity of Hannibal the Slayer was no longer a faction of his personality. Kreger had tried very hard to put the memory of Lady Cassandra far behind him. He was confident he could prove his whereabouts during the time of at least one of the other murders. The fact that he had never been to either Illinois or to California would, in his opinion, effectively eliminated him as a suspect. Marshall was surprised when he received the message on his answering machine from Detective Carter.

Kreger dug through his stack of newspapers attempting to find the Sunday Arizona Republic which contained the article written by a woman by the name of Allison Dean. His frustration mounted as he could not find that particular day's edition. He surmised that he had recycled the paper. Kreger couldn't remember the exact date he had read the article but had a general idea of when it was published. He kept the appointment with Detective Carter, armed only with indignation.

*   *   *

The expression on Carter's face belied his determination to get to the truth. His patience with Kreger was at an end. He feigned confusion as Kreger asked him why he was being called in once again.

"I've answered every question you guys have asked. Why the hell are you hounding me?"

Detective Carter had noted in previous interviews, Kreger's adverse emotional response when being referred to as Hannibal. The pseudonym became a tool to assist Carter in obtaining the information he wanted. "Quite simply Hannibal, you're the only link we have to the killing of Sherri Connelly. We need to put this case to bed."

"Why the fuck then, don't you contact the other guys'," demanded Kreger.

"What other guys?"

"The guys, you know police officers," Kreger dropped his head into his hands and spewed words laced of anger and frustration. Suddenly his head shot up as Kreger glared into Carter's determined eyes. "The cops! The one's working on the murders in California and Illinois."

Carter didn't want to appear uninformed to Kreger. He leaned forward and said, "Why don't you tell me about the other killings."

Kreger shook his head in apparent frustration. "I don't know anything about them except for what I read in that article a few weeks ago."

"What are you talking about?"

Kreger slapped his forehead with his palm and hissed, "You jerks missed it!"

Carter stared at Kreger coolly, "Enlighten me then why don't you?"

"A story in the Republic a few weeks ago. About a murder in Oakland being linked to another in Chicago."

"Yeah so what?"

"It sounded just like the Connelly murder that's what!"

Kreger exploded, "Man I tell ya! You guys oughta get your act together!"

Carter, feeling perplexed gathered his files and said, "I'll check it out. But in the meantime Hannibal, I want you to wait right here."

"Shit," spewed Kreger as he flopped into the chair. "How about a cup of coffee or something, or is that too much to ask?"

Detective Carter left the interview room and returned to his desk. He called the Arizona republic and got in touch with the city desk. He found that there was such an article printed and arranged for the test to be faxed to his office. Minutes later the transmission was complete. Carter read the article and found astounding similarities between the cited cases in Oakland, Chicago and his own case in Benson, Arizona.

He called Oakland Homicide department to talk to the investigator of record on their murder case, Sergeant Phillip Hall. Claire Lang intercepted the call for Hall who was out in the field. Carter asked if Claire was Hall's secretary. He laughed as Claire explained to him, that the only time she referred to herself as a secretary was during Secretaries Week. And that was only to get the goodies. Other than that particular week, she was known as an administrative assistant.

Carter was given the dates of the murders that had been linked. Claire promised to fax him the copies of the bulletins that had been sent out to the other fourteen reporting agencies. Carter knew where Kreger was at the time that JoAnn Campo was murdered. He had tracked him down to ask him some questions about the Connelly slaying. Kreger had been in the middle of a two day conference in Phoenix the very same date and approximated time of Campo's death. Still the chafing suspicions that Kreger had not been totally honest grated on him, He decided once he had the transmission in hand to push the reluctant Kreger to the breaking point to find out what he was hiding.

*   *   *

Marshall Kreger paced the floor in the tiny interview room waiting for the return of Carter. The door opened and a woman handed him a cup of coffee. She set a large chrome thermos on the table and said, "There's more in the pot if you want it."

Kreger demanded, "Where in the hell is Carter?"

Before she closed the door, she glared at him and said, "He asked me to tell you he'll he a few minutes. You're to chill as he put it."

*   *   *

Detective Carter waited for the fax transmission from Oakland that Claire promised she'd send. He sat next to the plain paper fax machine, virtually willing it to ring. Carter didn't worry about the length of time Kreger was alone in the tiny room. From a purely psychological viewpoint, this stratagem was extremely effective. Typically the longer detainees stewed and fretted the more cooperative they would be at the interviewers return. Carter felt in the pit of his stomach the information from Oakland would give some valuable clues.

He wanted to know what the names of Hannibal and Lady Cassandra really stood for.

*   *   *

The friendly house was prepared. All testing of the wires were positive and set to go. Officer McAllister drove Allison to the house on twenty-second street. Allison was scheduled to be there several hours early. She had given the telephone number to Master Slasher to call in case he would be late. She needed to appear to live in this house.

Phil had been ordered to finish the last of his reports on the recently captured Sunday Torch. The torch would be in court first thing Monday morning. Normally Phil would have spent the weekend preparing the paper work. His plans unraveled when the district attorney demanded to have the information over the weekend in order to solidify his prosecution tactics. Phil would join the stakeout about an hour before the suspect was due to arrive. McAllister accompanied Allison into the house and performed the final microphone test. All was in place and ready for Master Slasher to arrive for his engagement with Nochturna.

*   *   *

More than two thousand miles away, Captain Burton Sanders joined Sergeant Kidd for another interview with Sharon Glass. Her condition had improved substantially enough for them to re-interview her about her assault. The call from Allison describing the conversation on the nine hundred line dogged him. When they arrived at Sharon's bedside a minister looked at them coldly. Sanders asked if she felt strong enough to answer their questions. Sharon nodded and thanked the minister for spending time with her.

Sanders began, "You most likely don't remember me. I was here a week or so after you were attacked. Do you recall?"

Sharon seemed to study Sanders for a while and then said, "I'm sorry, I don't."

"That's okay. "I'll start at the beginning. I'm Captain Sanders. I'm in charge of the Homicide Department for the Chicago Police Department."

Sharon narrowed her eyes, "Homicide?" Why is someone from homicide interested in me?" She smiled and said, "Don't tell me that I'm really dead and I didn't know it."

Sanders rewarded her joke with a laugh as he pulled up a chair and sat beside her. "We think there's a possibility that the man who did this to you is responsible for other crimes."

"He killed someone?"

"We believe so Ms. Glass. You're the lucky one. You lived through the attack. Fifteen other women weren't as fortunate as you."

Tears began to roll down her cheeks. "Ms Glass, are you all right?"

She nodded and said, "I just realized how close I came to having my prayers come true."

Sanders looked closely at Sharon. He felt more than saw the pain in her eyes. He spoke to her in a voice laden with mystification, "Why on earth would you want to die"

"I don't anymore. I feel very different now. I have had time to think and consider. And my minister helped me to understand, I'm far removed from the person that was brought in by ambulance a few short weeks ago."

Sanders pulled a tissue from the box next to the bed and gently dried her surging tears. He found himself wishing he didn't have to ask his questions now. But wishing and reality were very different things. "Sharon, can you describe our attacker? Did you have a date with him? Did you meet this guy through a nine hundred talk line?"

The questions came so fast that Sharon couldn't answer them as quickly as he seemed to need the answers. She raised her fingers on her cast-laden hands. "Yes, I can describe him. No, he wasn't the one I had the date with. He was an imposter. The name he told me was Prince Odious. Yes, I had talked with my date through the nine hundred line. I think Prince Odious must have been listening in on the line. My Date was with Maxmillian." Sharon took a deep breath.

"Sharon, what was the number?"

"It's the secrets line. 900-732-7387."

Sanders's excitement made his heart pound. He thought of Allison and with that thought, his dread became pervasive. He turned to Kidd and said, "Get the sketch artist back here now. I've got to get in touch with Oakland right away."

He took one last look at Sharon Glass. He would have hugged her had he been able to find any place on her that wasn't bruised or in a cast. "Thank you Sharon. You have no idea how much help you've been for us and this case."

As he was leaving, Sharon called out to him. "Captain Sanders, will you pray for me?"

Sanders turned and looked into the eyes of Sharon Glass. "Nothing would give me more pleasure, young lady. You get better now, you hear me?"

"God Bless you Captain," were her words as he rushed out of her room and from Cook County Hospital.

*   *   *

Carter decided to call Oakland back and push them to send the information right away. But before he finished dialing the number, the fax line rang. Oakland was transmitting. He read the copy as it scrolled from the machine. He finished reading the material during his jaunt back to the interview room where Marshall Kreger cooled his heels.

Carter stepped back into the cubicle, his patience with Kreger at an end. Marshall Kreger tipped the coffee urn emptying the last of its contents into his styrofoam cup.

Kreger spat, "It's about friggin' time, Carter!"

Carter dropped any pretense of patience with Kreger. He fired upon him the moment he sat down. "You're holding back information, Kreger and I want to know what it is!"

Kreger squirmed in his seat and avoided eye contact with Carter.

Carter pounded the desk with his fists. "I'm telling you Kreger, we know you didn't kill Sherri Connelly. We've known that for some time now."

Carter watched as Kreger went ballistic. "Then why in the fuck don't you just leave me alone?" Why do you keep hounding me?"

"Because you're not telling us the whole story! You're holding back information that we think will help us nail this son of a bitch, that's why! I want to know what you were doing at her house. I want to know about your association with Sherri Connelly!"

Carter leaned toward the face of Kreger and formed the most menacing expression he could. "I want to know now!"

Kreger simply stared at his feet and said nothing.

Carter decided to play the last of his cards. He slammed his fist on the table. "You're under arrest, Kreger."

As the police officer began to repeat the Miranda rights. Kreger stood and shouted, "Under arrest! What the fuck for? You assholes got nothin' on me."

Carter spat back at him, "Nothing but obstruction of justice."

"You pricks can't hold me for that!"

"For a while I sure as hell can. And I tell you something jerk off, if you don't cooperate now, I'll tattoo one of my investigators to your ass. You won't be able to take a shit without us knowing how much toilet paper you use. By God, you'll wish you'd bought stock in Charmin."

Marshall Kreger seemed to finally be shaken by the venom in Carter's voice. He dropped his head and said under his breath, "She wasn't a pen pal."

"What was that?" Carter leaned forward to listen more closely.

"Kreger lifted his head and blurted loudly, "She wasn't a pen pal."

Carter began taking notes. "Okay it's about time. Where did you meet her?"

Kreger hesitated and Carter increased the pressure. "I'm waiting Hannibal!"

"Alright, alright, what the fuck," said Kreger. "We met through a telephone talk line. But I never met her in person. It was one of those sex talk groups."

Carter narrowed his eyes and furrowed his brow, "A sex talk line?"

"Yeah, shit man, you know what I mean."

"What's the number," demanded Carter."

Kreger sullenly replied, "Nine hundred secrets."

Carter looked at him and then at the dial pad of the telephone.

"900-732-7387," said Kreger sullenly. "We started talking on that line. You know how it is. Everyone has a secret name so no one knows who you really are. My name was Hannibal the Slayer. Her name was Lady Cassandra. Christ man, I didn't even know her real name until I read about her murder in the paper."

"Why didn't you come clean with this before now?"

"Look Carter, I haven't called the line since that day. I didn't tell you because I was sure you'd think I was some sort of pervert. If you found out about the nine hundred number, you would have thought that for sure."

Carter shook his head and said, "You're damn right I would have. But, better be thought a bit on the strange side than be thought of as possibly a murderer."

Kreger picked at his fingernails for a moment. Marshall raised his head and with all of the sincerity he could invoke said, "Carter, I may be strange but I tell you it takes someone a hell of a lot more than strange to do the things that fucker did to Cassandra."

"What else haven't you told me?"

"Me and Lady Cassandra, Sherri Connelly, I mean, made a date over the telephone line. She gave me the directions and told me when to show up, but when I got there well, well you know what I found."

"So what you're telling me is that someone else showed up earlier and did her. Is that it?"

"That's what I'm telling you." Kreger leaned forward and shouted into Carter's face." I told you about the red sports car. What the hell have you guys done about that?"

"How do you know it was a sports car?"

"Because, of the sound of the engine. You know as it was driving off. Only a sports car sounds like a sports car."

"Is there anything else?"

"That's everything."

"Okay Kreger you're free to go."

Kreger walked to the door. As he reached for the knob, Carter said, "Kreger if you're holding anything else back and I find out about it." Carter picked up his pen and tapped it soundly upon the note pad." Well I guess you know what will happen, am I making myself clear?"

"Clear," said Kreger as he left the offices of the police department.

Carter filled out a fax transmission sheet to be sent to Oakland. He needed to let them know that the killer is not the person who makes the date. The killer is another person who shows up early. Carter's instincts told him the information would be important.

CHAPTER 20
Caught

Before leaving for the fifth time, Officer McAllister made certain the bay window blinds were open and operational. Their visual signal as well as the electronic listening devices checked out fully operational. Each time that he knocked at the door, Allison's nerves frayed even more. He checked his watch and said, "How are you doing, Ms. Dean?"

"I have the worst case of heebie-jeebies I've ever had."

McAllister tried to reassure and comfort Allison's obvious anxieties. "Well, just try to relax. We're less than three minutes away and your date isn't due for another few hours."

"Has Phil arrived yet?"

"Not yet," replied McAllister. "But he did call and say that he'd be here within an hour. Said he was finishing up the case files for the Sunday Torch."

"Oh, that's right, the torch case goes to trial on Monday. I'll try to mellow out. But I would feel better if I knew Phil was here. You'll let me know when he arrives. Right?"

McAllister patted her on the shoulder and said, "Sure I will, the very moment he arrives. Try not to worry."

Allison gave the departing officer a grateful nod as she accompanied him to the door. "Thank you, I appreciate all that you've done. But now you're sure you're finished in here this time?"

"I'm sure. Sorry for all the interruptions, Ms. Dean. We just need to make sure everything is right."

McAllister walked through the entry as she closed and locked the door behind him. He returned to the vehicle where Paul Chaney, his partner waited. "Shit man, I'm starved. I didn't have time for lunch today."

"Me neither," agreed Chaney.

McAllister tapped his fingers on the steering wheel. "You know, I think there's a burger place just a couple blocks away."

"Yeah I saw it when we drove over here," replied Chaney.

McAllister checked his watch again. He reached over and picked up his pack set and called out for the team working the listening post.

"Baker 1 to Charlie 3."

Charlie 3 responded, "Baker 1, go. Yeah Mack, what do you need?"

"Listen man, we have plenty of time till our actor shows up. Chaney and I are going 10-7. We'll go over and grab a burger. We'll 10-8 in about oh, ten to fifteen minutes. You guys want anything?"

"Negative Baker 1, we'll keep our ears on. Charlie 1 out."

"10-4 Baker 1, out and 10-7."

*   *   *

Allison paced from room to room as she sipped on her cola. Her head ached from tension. She rifled through her purse looking for her stash of aspirin. Her search grew frantic as she had a difficult time locating the small metal box. Finally she resorted to dumping her purse out and spreading the contents over the table. She realized the packet had been in the place she had always kept it. She clenched her teeth in frustration over her growing anxiety.

Allison gulped down four aspirin with healthy swallow of soda. She was annoyed and more than a little surprised that she was so tense and frightened. The capture of this killer had been the single event that would free her from the eyes of the ghosts haunting her dreams. She left her belongings lying on the table and tried to settle herself.

She began chattering to the walls knowing the police could hear every word. Soon the ramblings irritated even her. "Okay," said Allison, "I'm going to try to rest, get it guys?" She looked around the rooms toward the myriad of listening devices. "Tell McAllister that I'm putting out the do not disturb sign." She laughed in a tight giggle as she laid across the sofa in the darkened living room. She silently tried to relieve the pain in her head. All was in readiness for the entrance of Nochturna's date.

* * *

Phil bunched the completed reports regarding the Sunday Torch into a stack. He hastily grabbed at his coat and promptly dropped it to the floor. He picked up the coat once again and headed for Claire's desk. She wasn't anywhere to be seen. He placed the hand written notes on her desk to be typed. In a few rapid strides he reached the swinging doors. Claire called to him just as he passed through. She chased him down the corridor.

"Phil, stop! I have some messages here for you," shouted Claire.

He waved his arms above his head, "Not now Claire, I've got to get to Allison and the stake out on 22nd street."

"Phillip Andrew Hall," she yelled. "Stop now! You have to look at these."

Phil dropped his arms to his side and whirled around to see Claire's alarmed expression. It was a terrified look. It was a look that he had never seen on her faced before. He looked at his watch and said, "What is it?"

She handed him the reports from Sandy which detailed his interview with Sharon Glass. The second fax was yet another report from an officer Carter with the Benson Arizona police department.

*   *   *

Two blocks from the friendly house, the man with the handle of Peach Tree began to transmit from his Citizens Band Radio. There was very little activity from his local cronies on the airwaves. But Peach Tree was not to be daunted. He reached over his equipment and flipped the switch on the power booster known in the jargon as 'boots'. The booting illegally augmented the power of the transmitter over five times that of a normal C.B. He was able to immediately pick up on long-range conversations on the invisible highway. His signal was powerful enough to override and obliterate almost everyone's signal in the area, including the low band frequency of the friendly house's electronics. The ears of the friendly house were deaf as Peach tree said, "Breaker, breaker."

* * *

Allison lay quietly on the sofa, rubbing her throbbing temples. Her fingertips rotated in gentle circles first clockwise and then counter. Relaxing was not easy for her. Finally the pain in her temples began to fade. She grimaced with exasperation, as there was yet another knock at the door. "McAllister," she said out loud. She swallowed an exasperated gulp of air and went to the door once again. She opened the door with a jerk and said, "What now?"

Before her, stood an incredibly good-looking blond haired man. In his right hand he clutched a black sports travel bag. His eyes were the most piercing green color she had ever seen. The whites of is eyes showed no trace of veining. They gleamed brightly even in the shadows of the verandah. A prominent jaw line combined with strong cheekbones offered clean facial lines. His features were enhanced by the straight back way he combed his blond wavy hair. His full lips curled up at the edges exposing a brilliant and well-kept smile. The dimples on his cheeks provided an aura of youth. His voice was strong, confident and penetrating.

"Hi there Nochturna, I'm Master Slasher."

* * *

Phil's eye bulged as he read the communications from Benson and Chicago. He realized in moments that Master Slasher was not the killer. The real killer was an imposter who shows up early. The last line in the fax from Sanders in Chicago told him the killer's pseudo name was Prince Odious. A name he recognized from monitoring the line with Allison.

Hall dashed down the corridor, shouting orders, "Claire, get down to dispatch right now. Let the guys on 22nd street know that our guy shows up early. Tell them to be on their toes and I'm on my way."

Sergeant Hall slid into his unmarked car. He hastily placed his blue flashing light on the roof and sped from the garage. "Fuck," he screamed to the heavens, "Right Church, wrong pew."

*   *   *

Allison stood for a moment frozen to the floor. The eyes of DeeCee and JoAnn seemed to materialize in her mind. Their imagined voices talked to her. He's here, help us to rest." These thoughts resolved her to follow through. Confident the electronic equipment was in working order Allison collected herself and invited Master Slasher into the house. She closed the door behind him and watched as he eyed the surroundings.

He was enormous. She guessed his height to be well over six foot six. His weight a very well muscled two hundred and thirty pounds. She didn't wonder why no woman stood a chance against him.

Master Slasher was impeccably dressed from the tip of his glasslike polished leather shoes to his white button down long sleeved shirt. The khaki sweater tied around his massive shoulders matched exactly with his pleated slacks. Allison briefly mused to herself as she compared her jeans and sweatshirt to his obviously expensive ensemble.

Her visitor turned and set down his black nylon bag. Allison could almost feel the invasion as he stared deeply into her eyes. Allison steeled herself and walked by him. She opened the glass paneled French doors leading into the formal living room and the hidden microphones. He stepped through the opening in five stealthy steps. She turned her back on Master Slasher and began to pull the doors closed. In a flash her visitor grabbed a huge handful of Allison's hair in one hand and covered her mouth with the other. His one hand could almost cover her entire face. He jerked her backward pinning her against his chest. Her hands instantly flew to his as Allison pulled at his huge fingers in an attempt to pry them loose. A deep chill coursed through her body as he whispered a light laugh into the ear of Nochturna. Allison tried to break his grip as he breathed the words, "time to play."

The telephone began to ring. Allison tried kicking out at the telephone in an attempt to upset the receiver. Master Slasher immediately pulled her away from striking distance of the incessantly ringing telephone. She screamed more in panic than pain but very little sound escaped through his fingers. He pulled her tight to his chest and moved the hand that had been covering her mouth. He wrapped his fingers around her throat.

"What the hell are you doing?" squeaked Allison.

He squeezed her throat gently with his free hand. In an unruffled and almost detached voice he said, "Are you having fun yet?"

* * *

Phil was racing to 22nd street. He tried to contact the officers on stakeout through the radio without success. Claire checked in with him as he turned the corner to the freeway onramp. "Hall, I can't raise the men on 22nd. Something is blocking our signal in that area. I think we have an illegal C.B. working in the vicinity."

Phil shouted, "God damn it to hell!" He prayed he'd be in time.

Claire's communication continued, "Hall, I tried to call the friendly house via land line, but no one answered."

Phillip Hall pressed the gas pedal of the already speeding car to the floorboard. Steering with one hand and issuing orders through the hand set in the other. He yelled, "Triangulate that son of a bitch! Call out all other units that can hear! Get them to the scene. Keep trying to get through to Allison!"

Every muscle in his body strained when he said, "I'm at least fifteen minutes out."

The officers in the sound van heard nothing but dead air and an occasional slight buzz coming from the speakers. McAllister munched on a French fry. Hearing a slight buzzing he leaned forward and placed his ear close to the speaker. He very faintly heard the words, "Breaker, breaker." He tried without success to contact the other units that were in hiding.

* * *

Allison's panic and fear helped her with a burst of strength enough to twist way from her attacker. She tore herself free, leaving a chunk of long hair entwined in his fingers.

Allison screamed, "Help, someone help me." She spied her cell phone that was lying mixed in with the contents of her purse which she'd dumped earlier. The moment she looked at it, her line of sight was followed by the intruder. He side stepped over to the table, picked up the phone and threw it against a wall, smashing it to pieces.

Allison circled the living room trying to keep a step ahead of Master Slasher. He matched step for step with her. He kept his eyes riveted upon her, his prey, as a lion selects its next meal. As the landline telephone came into his reach he jerked the cord out of the wall. His green eyes showed no sign of his savage intentions. His unadulterated peacefulness was unnerving to Allison.

Exhibiting not so much as an inkling of urgency he said, "There's no one to help you."

Allison tried to gather herself. She knew that any second the police would burst in. "Listen, Master Slasher, I'm not into the rough stuff. No matter what you may have thought from our conversations on the secrets line."

Her opponent spread his arms and his frame to what seemed to be an incredible size. He then dropped his gaze upon Allison once more. He quietly and coolly said, "I'm not Master Slasher." A cruel grin crossed his lips. His eyes seemed as hollow as a shark, as lifeless as DeeCee's and JoAnn's. He introduced himself, "I'm Prince Odious."

Allison stammered, "Prince, Prince Odious?" the name was familiar. A mix of confusion traveled through her mind. As she continued to circle the room with each step she wondered if Prince Odious was the killer that she'd hoped to trap. "Prince Odious," said Allison, "I'm a friend of Vixen. You do know Vixen, don't you?"

An even smile traced his lips. "I remember them all."

Seemingly to possess the speed and agility of a huge cat, Prince Odious darted forward and grabbed at her arm. She wriggled away from him and made a life or death dash for the bay window. Her life depended upon reaching the visual signal. But before she could get to the alcove, he caught her. He wrapped his strong hands around her small throat and began to press against her airway. Allison kicked wildly at his groin and held on to his hands trying to free her throat. Tears surged from her eyes from the pressure being placed against her airway. Prince Odious was incredibly strong. Try as she might she couldn't break his grip. He held her taut till Allison would begin to gray out. Then he would loosen his grip and permit once again his playmate to draw in life sustaining air.

He released her throat and began running his hands down her body. He squeezed and grabbed at her breasts and crotch. Allison punched, kicked, bit and scratched at her assailant's body. He lifted her off the floor by her neck and brought her to face to meet his own. He drew his tongue across her tear soaked cheeks. Once again he savored the spice of his victims fear.

Allison retaliated by jamming her knee into his groin. Every ounce of strength she could muster seemed to have little Impact. Prince Odious grimaced and bent slightly. But his grip upon her did not fail. He seemed to be possessed by a demon, an evil spirit feeling nothing but the demand for satisfaction of his own selfish desires. In a few short moments he seemed to recoup from the ache in his genitals. Prince Odious chuckled and shook his head as if to indicate that her struggles were merely a nuisance.

Once again he lifted Allison off the floor by her hair. When she was suspended for a few seconds he gingerly tossed her on the sofa. He flung himself on top of her. Straddling her flailing body, Prince Odious tore her blouse open. He bent and began to bite her breasts. Allison slapped at his face and body with as much power as she could. His reaction was to pin her arms with his knees. She fought with her legs from that point. Her screams for help were met with blinding flashes of pain as he slapped his open hand across her face. Still, she persisted in her wild struggle. Suddenly the legs on the sofa gave way. The two were pitched onto the floor. Allison scrambled on her hands and knees trying to get to the front door. Just as she reached the knob, Prince Odious jerked her to her feet. He wrapped his forearm around her neck. Allison grabbed at the material on his shirt and tore away part of the sleeve. An oval red birthmark upon to his arm came into view. Allison struggled to keep her wits about her and couldn't figure out where Phil and the other stake out officers were. She looked up to see a fist heading toward her face. Darkness slammed upon her from a crushing blow of his right fist thundered down upon her jaw. The devastating blow he had levied upon her sent her crashing into a wall. She lay sprawled out on the floor of the entry hall, unconscious.

* * *

Now was his time to prepare the setting for his amusement. Prince Odious looked down at Nochturna as she lay crumpled on the entryway floor. He casually reached over her and picked up his black bag, filled with the tools of his amusement. He walked to the rear of the house looking for a bedroom in which to play out his thrilling game of conquest. He found no room on the lower level that met his fancy. He decided to drag his captive to the upper level. Zachary returned to the entry hall. He set the black sports bag on the floor next to the stairs. He reached down and picked up Nochturna and tossed her over his shoulder in a fireman's carry. Even as dead weight he handled her easily.

Allison's awareness slowly returned. She felt the bumping of her stomach against something round and firm. She heard a humming sound combined with a sharp ringing in her ears. A warm trickling sensation traveled from her ear down her face. Before she had the strength to open her eyes she felt herself being tossed onto soft flat surface. Allison fought to bring herself to consciousness. She felt as if she were pulling herself out of a very deep well. Searing pain accompanied her opening eyes. She tried to move and focus at the same time. Her right arm was partially suspended and held immobile. She at last was able to focus on her attacker, Prince Odious as he began to tie her other wrist to the headboard of a large bed. Once again but clearly this time she saw the red oval mark on his right forearm. Kathy's words rang in her ears between the pulsing of pain. She had said, "I used to play the love button game with Zatch." And before he could secure her completely she said to him in a soft, unthreatening voice, "Zatch."

The calm in her voice startled him. His head snapped up and he looked right into Allison's face. "Zachary," she repeated. "I'm Kathy's friend. She told me how she used to play the love button game. "Where's your love button Zachary?"

Prince Odious's eyes seemed to glaze over as if he were trying very hard to access a memory of a former and gentler time. He slowly looked down and turned up the belly of his arm and revisited the only kindness he'd known in entire life. He started at the round strawberry mark on his skin.

"Zachary, Kathy told me how awful your mother treated you. Allison used the time of confusion to gently slide to a sitting position. "I'm not Adelle, my name is Allison. I don't think you really want to hurt me." Allison slowly freed her right arm and scooted to the far side of the bed. He sat quietly looking at the birthmark. He shook his head as if to drive away the mix of memories and emotions that were pushing through to his mind. His blank face and dead eyes showed that a battle of major proportions was taking place in the mind of Zachary Pendrake. As Allison turned and stood up from the bed, she saw her reflection in the mirror. The left side of her face was swollen and massively bruised. A dried stream of blood crossed from her ear to just beside her mouth. Her sweatshirt had been sliced up the front exposing her breasts.

Zachary sat in the bedside chair, staring off into nothingness. Allison gathered the cut edges of her sweatshirt and quietly headed for the door. Before she could make her escape, he was upon her. His face was contorted with rage. It's not that easy, cunt," he spat. He pulled Allison's face close to his. Gone was the cold emotionless person. Now there was only a huge man filled with fury. His voice was filled with hate as he said, "Just look at what you have done to me!" Allison screamed with every ounce of her strength and once again darkness enveloped her.

* * *

Zachary threw Nochturna on the bed once more. He took one look at her sprawled body and smiled once again, his calm grin. He walked down the stairs to retrieve his bag. As he reached his tote and began to go back upstairs, he heard the sound of screeching tires. Prince Odious bolted through the living room to the bay window in order to see what was happening. From his vantage point he could see a dozen or more uniformed police officers darting from one source of cover to the next. Weapons in hand, the police were surrounding the house. Suddenly he heard the sound of the back door being crashed in. Prince Odious sprinted from the living room toward the entry hall and stairwell. Rounding the corner he was met by the pointed barrels of six police officer's guns.

One officer circled him and ordered him to drop his satchel. He dropped it on the floor spilling part of its contents. A set of handcuffs and a sheathed eight-inch hunting knife bounced with a thud into the hardwood floor. Prince Odious complied with the order for him to kick the bag away. As the bag finally came to a rest on its side, a single tube of red lipstick and an eyeliner pencil rolled out onto the floor. Police officers spread out throughout the house with orders to find Allison.

Prince Odious stood motionless and indifferent. One of the men dressed in street clothing grabbed at Zachary. "Where is she, you son of a bitch," he demanded. It took the combined efforts of three officers to pull the frantic man away. Suddenly an officers' head popped around the corner of the stair landing, "Hall, up here! She's hurt."

"Oh God Allie," said Phillip Hall as he climbed the stairs taking them two and three at a time, "someone get an ambulance right now."

Prince Odious known by few left living was now in the hands of the police. Zachary Payne Pendrake was caught.

CHAPTER 21
Justice

Zachary Payne Pendrake refused to answer the hammering questions of the police. He used his telephone rights to contact Karl Jacobs. He complained bitterly about how awful it was being placed in a cell with common criminals. Karl Jacobs contacted Hastings, Kilmer and Brock.

Phil Hall plowed through the massive stack of leads and found the information given by Kathy St. John-Cocheran and added it to the gargantuan file. He knew he needed to work fast in order to beat the legal arsenal of the Pendrake Industries. Arrest bulletins were faxed to all of the reporting agencies in different states working on their cases. The notification that a suspect was in custody generated private celebrations in seventeen cities, all of which reported crimes with the same pattern of actions.

Upon receipt of the bulletin, Sandy faxed to Oakland a copy of the Terry Marsh assault report. The date of the assault coincided with the assault on Sharon Glass. The report substantiated that Zachary Pendrake definitely had the opportunity to commit the crime. He was also able to get copies of the car rental agreement that Pendrake had signed at the airfield. Bits and pieces of the evidence held in limbo by the different states were now flooding onto the offices of Detective Hall and the Oakland P.D.

Sergeant Carter also faxed copies of a car rental contract. The vehicle listed was a deluxe model, red Corvette. Once again the date and time was a matching link in the death of Sherri Connelly. The last piece of damning evidence was the fact that the mileage registered on the vehicle was exactly the amount of the miles between the airport and the home of Ms. Connelly.

The F.B.I. contacted the Federal Aviation Administration and received full copies of registered flight plans for Zachary's private jet. Each trip listed, paralleled a date and location of a reported murder. Each trip correlated with a murder commited and followed the same method of operation. And the paper trail linked directly to Zachary Pendrake.

Zachary's hand and fingerprints matched the crime scenes. His blood type and semen analysis proved to be a 99.9% certainty that he was the donor. The sperm also yielded D.N.A. profiles that matched him to the same degree of certainty. He was undeniably responsible for the violent and horrendous deaths of seventeen women across the United States. Across the nation law enforcements agencies interviewed individuals relation, a major note comparing was happening for their cases. Oakland finally won their bid to subpoena the nine hundred line customer records. Their case was tight.

* * *

Karl Jacobs put through a call to the Governor of California with the ultimate intent of pressuring Oakland to release Zachary. Jacobs recounted to the various elected officials the sizable amount of contributions which had been made on their behalf. The Governor contacted the Attorney General and demanded he obtain the release of young Pendrake. In a matter of two hours the Attorney General for the State of California flew in from Sacramento. He met with the Mayor and the city District Attorney as they reviewed the evidence against Pendrake.

The Attorney General placed a call to the Governor who waited anxiously for the news. The Pendrakes were making threats against his political future. The dialogue culminated by the Attorney General telling the Governor that there was absolutely, no way the police had made a mistake. The final impact was made when the Governor was told, "I've been advised of the evidence against the Pendrake heir held by the various departments. With everything in consideration I must advise you sir that if you have this guy released and the public finds out, you could kiss your career goodbye. And that is with Pendrake money or no Pendrake money."

The Governor confirmed, "You're absolutely certain about this?"

"Yes sir, I will fax to you right away a comprehensive listing of the evidence against the young Pendrake. Once you see this documentation you decide for yourself. But I'm confident we will be in agreement."

Upon arrival of the documentation sent to him, the Governor read the material.

He shook his head slowly, obviously saddened and feeling the hard recesses between that proverbial rock and hard place. He put in a call to Karl Jacobs.

*   *   *

Jacobs hung up the phone, having a clearer picture of the untenable predicament Norman Pendrake's baby boy had brought down upon them. Jacobs thundered, "That son of a bitch! God damn it to hell. This little prick has really screwed things up."

Jacobs bellowed for Prentiss.

Moments later Prentiss stood in front of Karl and watched as he swung his arms wildly clearing his desk of the paperwork and accessories. Prentiss knew better than to interrupt a tirade of Karl Jacobs. He simply stood by until his superior finished venting his anger. Karl's energy wasn't what it used to be and the aging executive soon slumped into his massive desk chair. Exhausting a heavy breath his anger seemed, to rise again as Jacobs detailed the turmoil.

"We've got to find a way to keep this under wraps. If Satto would find out about this, we would lose his rice futures and the billion dollar deal will be a bust!" Jacobs rapped his fingertips solidly on his desk top. "We can't afford to make a mistake right now. Not one misstep do you hear me, Prentiss? If Satto finds out I am not just telling you that he'd take a walk on us, I can even tell you how fast."

Jacobs whirled around in his chair and once again looked into the eyes of Norman Pendrake's portrait. He pointed at the picture and said, "It wasn't only the whore of a mother that's a problem! You're spawn is just about to ruin a deal that this corporation and I have worked on for over two years. The fucking little bastard!"

Prentiss saw his opportunity when Jacobs sat quietly. "Karl," Prentiss began, "I seem to recall something in Zachary's file. Didn't he sign a certain codicil after his father died? It was something having to do with insanity? If I remember correctly, that might be an angle for us."

Karl's mind began to clear and race backward in time. He now recalled the negotiation between the attorneys Lanchester had hired for Zachary and Pendrake Industries. Karl Jacobs's eyes brightened. "Get me that file now, and get Kilmer on the phone," demanded Jacobs.

After reading the codicil Jacobs smiled and said, "You're right Prentiss. This is our way out of this. This codicil and a few dollars sprinkled in the laps of the powers that be and we will close the door on this episode and do it quietly. I know how we will approach the state hierarchy. Get me the Governor right away."

Prentiss waiting for the connection to go through and said, "How are you going to handle the publicity?"

Jacobs simply smiled and said, "Money talks Prentiss, money talks."

*   *   *

Jacobs offered the officials of the State a deal. Major contributions would be made to a multitude of politicians and sent to their favorite charities. Karl knew that the money would land in the accounts of each of the politicians, but the expense was worth the gain. Substantial contributions would be made to each campaign for re-election of the co-operating officials. Pendrake Industries would save the state the considerable expenses it would take, to prosecute Zachary Pendrake.

The trade off would be that there was to be no publicity regarding Zachary. The corporation would exercise the insanity clause of their agreement with young Pendrake and would make certain that he'd never walk free again. All charges would be dropped and his name would not appear on any police file.

* * *

Allison awoke to the harsh lights of her hospital room. Her eyesight was as blurry as the voices she thought she heard. She felt the touch of a warm hand against her chilled fingertips. She trembled with cold and drifted in and out of consciousness. She opened her eyes ever so slowly at first. Then she began blinking rapidly to clear the haze. Allison began to scream and thrash wildly, until reassuring hands braced her and said, "It's all over Allison, you're safe and in the hospital. Your family is here waiting to see you. You're alright, Ms. Dean." Her senses began to kick in and she realized that yes she was in the care of doctors and that all was well. The scent of roses wafted up to her senses ad Allison rejoined the world.

Four days had passed sine Prince Odious had assaulted her. She at last was able to focus upon the warm eyes of Phil. He gently called her name. She suddenly remembered being in the house and said, "Did we get him?"

"Honey, yes, he's ours, hush now rest. Everything is going to be fine."

"I had a dream sweetheart, DeeCee's eyes."

Phil's attempts to comfort her were joined by her mother and father. "Hush honey, try to rest," Janet said as she softly caressed the cheek of her daughter.

"No, let me finish before I forget the dream. Phil, her eyes looked at me. They were all blue and not the blue lined black holes I have seen in my dreams. Not the empty eyes I remember." Allison's eyes began to flutter and close. "Phil, they seemed to smile just before they vanished." Allison had tapped her short burst of strength as she drifted off into a quiet slumber.

*　　*　　*

Harry Satto arrived at the San Francisco Hilton ready for his dinner date with his friend Allison Dean and her young intended. During the flight into the city he thought of his first interview with the spunky girl with the light red hair. He had begun to think of her as a member of his extended family. He looked forward to meeting the man she wanted to marry.

Harry checked his watch as the doorman held open the limousine door. He was fifteen minutes late for his appointment. Satto was surprised to find that Allison was not yet at the restaurant. He dialed her cell phone number and her home number and received no answer on either. When the machine answered the call he assumed she was on her way. He waited and consoled his disappointment with a black Russian. When another half hour had passed he called the Tribune and learned what had happened to Allison. He left for San Francisco Memorial immediately.

* * *

The next time Allison's eyes opened she felt much stronger. She was able to see the masses of floral tributes that surrounded her bed. Her mother was asleep in the chair next to the bed. The same way that she was the day Allison had to have her tonsils removed. She looked up to see the door slowly open, her eyes widened when she saw the smiling face of Harry Satto. He walked into the room with an armful of roses.

"Harry," squealed Allison.

Her voice awoke her mother. Janet stood up and touched her daughter's forehead. "How are you feeling honey?"

Introductions were being made when Phil walked into the room with Robert at his side. Phil carefully kissed Allison on the cheek and said "Hello loved one."

Harry Satto beamed a toothy grin and said. "Well, young man you must be this Phil I have heard so much about. Don't you think it's sort of rude to stand up a dinner date?"

Phil looked at Allison with an expression of complete confusion.

Her eyes opened wide. "Phil, what day is this?"

Satto asked, "Who's going to tell me the whole story here? The paper would only say that you were here."

Phil and Allison told the story of Zachary Payne Pendrake and the horror Allison had been through. "Can you imagine Harry? Someone with the advantages of Zachary Pendrake becoming such a monster?"

Harry smiled, but Allison could tell that there was much more behind his eyes than he was saying. He said, "Allie, money doesn't ensure a happy life."

Allison said, "Yes but."

Harry held up a hand to hush her. He said, "You know, my father was a very wise man. He made me a gift of his philosophies. I would like to tell you what he told me many years ago and what he would say to you right now, He would tell you that we are all cast upon this earth with the ability to grasp our own successes. Unfortunately there are those whose grasp becomes a strangle hold on life." He went on to say, "In cases like that of this Pendrake fellow, where a person lives in bitterness, they have no other face to show to the world. Their fame quickly relents to infamy."

Robert stepped forward and asked, "Any more dreams, Ms Dean?"

She looked deeply into the worn face of her father. "Dad, you called me Dean!"

He responded by shrugging his shoulders and saying, "That's who you are, you're Allison Dean and you're my daughter, one in the same and yet different. Then he smiled and cocked his head to the right. "You are your own person. Isn't that what you've been trying to pound into both our heads? He leaned forward and met her gaze. "I get it now."

Phil interrupted gently, "And the dreams?"

She smiled and took Phil's hand. "No dreams now, they're all gone. I think both DeeCee and JoAnn are finally at rest."

Harry kissed Allison on the forehead. "As soon as you two are married, the honeymoon is on me. But as for me, my business that I had here has been canceled and I need to get back to my work and my offices and take care of a few things. But the next time I'm here, we still have our dinner date. Is that a deal?"

Harry Satto left for the airport with his rice futures intact.

*   *   *

Two massive orderlies guided Zachary Payne Pendrake down a sterile white, feature-less corridor. It was far from the splendor that he was used to. His shackles clanked as he was forced for the first time in his life to walk to the pace of another man's command. The tiny steps required by his leg irons and chains humiliated him as they compelled him to shuffle his feet. His rage was unequaled.

Strong as he was the young Pendrake knew he couldn't vanquish the white-jacketed bodyguards who directed him. Nor could he liberate himself from the chains that bound him. The sentinels walked slightly behind and beside their new inmate. They felt assured of their authority. Silently the prisoner and his guardians moved toward Zachary's cell.

Zachary watched as a nurse pushing a woman in a wheelchair strolled closer and closer. The wheel chair's passenger stared off into space with lifeless gray eyes. Just as the patient in the wheelchair drew near, Zachary pushed away from his guards. He grabbed the catatonic woman by her throat. He tried to strangle her with the chains that bound him.

The two guards wrestled him away from the hapless woman. His overseers pushed Zachary to the floor. A doctor ran to aid the struggling attendants. Zachary was injected with a tranquilizer. While he was pinned to the floor the nurse and her charge were able to get away from the melee.

Nurse Tere Case raced down the corridor pushing the wheelchair. She rounded the corner and stopped to check upon the welfare of her patient. "I'm so sorry Amanda. Let me see if that bad man hurt you." Amanda Reynolds didn't acknowledge the attack.

The orderlies pulled Zachary down the stark white corridor his head hanging in a narcotic induced stupor. Upon reaching his cell, they laid him on his side and removed the restraints. Before they locked the door to his cell the larger of the two men said, "We don't permit that kind of behavior here at Avery Center and Retreat Mr. Killingworth."

The end

Made in the USA
Coppell, TX
15 April 2021